THE MOON IS MY WITNESS

Alexandra Connor was born in Oldham and still has strong connections with Lancashire. Apart from being a writer she is also a presenter on television and radio.

'Saga lovers will want to curl up and enjoy *The Moon is My Witness*. A good read!'
BETTY BURTON

ALEXANDRA CONNOR

The Moon is My Witness

HarperCollins*Publishers*

HarperCollins*Publishers*
77–85 Fulham Palace Road,
Hammersmith, London W6 8JB

A Paperback Original 1997
3 5 7 9 8 6 4

A catalogue record for this book is
available from the British Library

ISBN 0 00 649841 8

Set in Sabon by
Rowland Phototypesetting Ltd,
Bury St Edmunds, Suffolk

Printed and bound in Great Britain by
Caledonian International Book Manufacturing Ltd, Glasgow

This book is dedicated to
my father, Jack Connor,
who taught me strength.

Prologue

1903

Hurriedly he ran through the park gates and then stood, panting, on Queen's Road, the weak dawn light coming fitfully over the horizon. Factory chimneys jutted their chins belligerently up to the sky, the first smokes coming heavy and yellowed, the terraces tiny beneath. But the houses weren't tiny here. Here they were five-storeyed, windows lofty, crowned with stained glass, the doors imposing: carved and closed, oak.

Queen's Road . . . He ran the words over his tongue and then began to walk again, pushing his hands into his pockets and sniffing in the cold. The smell of coal was everywhere – even here – damp and acrid at the back of the tongue, little dashes of soot marking the brave front gardens. Queen's Road, Rich Man's Row, the place where the successful came to prove what they had achieved. Like old man Cotter and Dandry Fairclough – mill and pit men, whose wives wore clothes from Deansgate, Manchester, and whose children never went close to the council school on Dacre Street.

He had left a note. Thought about it for a long time, then wrote it once, and then again, readdressing it to his mother. His father would never be able to understand why he had left; neither would his mother. But she would defend him: he's gone, just like he said he would . . . His father would bluster, infuriated: but he's only fourteen, for God's sake! Yes, she'd say. Fourteen going on forty . . .

Sighing, John Crossworth stopped walking and turned at the head of Queen's Road. The Oldham park looked back at him balefully in the shrouded Northern dawn. Do you know where you're going, John? Do you know what you're going to? . . . He shivered, suddenly anxious, then turned to look at the bank of houses rearing up beside him.

I will come back, he promised himself; and when I do I will buy a house here . . . A few streets away he could hear the mill girls starting off for work, their voices travelling loud on the cold, still air . . . I will come back when I have proved myself . . . Their voices lifted him, curls of laughter marching in time to the clacking of their clogs . . .

Back home, very soon, his mother would be rising. She would find the note and then reluctantly wake his father. Together they would look for their son, and then, after a while, they would look intermittently, and in the end, stop looking . . . John jumped, suddenly startled. A gaslamp had gone on in a basement window, a maid making an early breakfast, her figure a featureless shadow against the drawn blind.

For one scintillating instant John wanted to turn back, make for home, slide into bed, taking the note off the kitchen table before anyone saw it. Stay safe, stay loved . . . But he couldn't. Even though it was cold – even though he had never been further than Manchester – something urged him on.

Slowly he began to walk again, his head down, but when the first milky rays of the Northern sun rose over Queen's Road, he looked up. The houses were suddenly transformed, gilded, tall-turreted, for an instant surreally beautiful, the light turning the Oldham street into Avalon.

He would carry that image in his mind and heart until the day he returned.

Without looking back he walked on.

Chapter One

Nine years later, Oldham

She was watching him, without his knowing. Watching as he washed, towelled himself, and then pulled on his underwear. His back was unmarked, his hair damp from the bath, his eyes shaded in the semidark. The blind was still down at the window; a dark heavy blind making the room mahogany. Silently, Sarah leaned against the door frame and stared at her husband. She could see every vertebra of his spine as he bent forwards to pull on his socks, the ribbing of his bones as even as the teeth on a bicycle chain. Stretching, he stood up, and she ducked back hurriedly, continuing to watch him through the crack in the door.

John Crossworth had come back to Oldham with his wife, his success assured. Or was it? she wondered, watching as he buttoned his shirt and then turned up the collar around his face. She was filled with the urgent longing she had for him; the longing she *always* had for him. Familiarity did not breed contempt, it bred something bordering on obsession.

He was unrecognizable from the fourteen-year-old boy who had left Oldham nine years before; there was no hesitancy any longer, and the wary look of childhood had given way to hard self-possession. She scrutinized his features one by one, as though checking that they were unchanged from the previous night. High cheekbones, deep-set grey eyes, a wide, but narrow-lipped mouth. Stern, some might think it: but she knew better.

John pulled on his jacket, and then slid his pocket watch

into his waistcoat and fixed the gold chain across his middle. Then, and only then, did he pause and stare at himself in the mirror, his expression unreadable. Sarah's heart jerked into an unsteady rhythm. What was he thinking? Was he wondering if he had made a mistake in marrying her? He had run away to earn his place in the world, to be successful, to come back to his home in triumph. But with whom had he expected to return?

Not her, surely ... It hadn't seemed so terrible when they were elsewhere. People didn't know him in Liverpool, or Birmingham, and there her accent was unimportant. But now John Crossworth had come home and brought his wife with him.

And she was a Jewess.

Tensing, Sarah glanced down at her hands, her skin olive against the dark grey silk of her dress. She attracted attention everywhere, with her dark coiled hair, her fine Roman nose; taller than average, handsome, exotic, and very, very composed.

Emotionally, they had been perfectly matched – she with no family except a silent, eccentric father, John with an estranged family whom he never saw. When they had begun to talk they automatically trusted each other – two outsiders, two loners – and gradually, cautiously, John had told her about his past.

'You should have been in touch with your parents,' she'd chastised him gently, 'you should have sent word that you were all right.'

He had looked at her, bewildered, having never considered that his family might worry for his safety.

'I can fend for myself.'

'You know that – and so do I,' Sarah had countered. 'But imagine how your mother felt all these years, never knowing what happened to you.'

She gave him a conscience, a thoughtfulness which he had never possessed before. He was a good man, honest, but he was driven, and at times blindly insensitive.

'Listen, Sarah, there's no point contacting them now. When I go home, I want to go home a success,' he had explained, momentarily flustered. 'I want to show them what I've become. I want to be in a position to help them, to do things for them.' He'd turned away from her, then laid his hand on her lap, the fingers closed together. 'The morning I left home I stood looking at Queen's Road for a long time . . .' She had heard the story before, but didn't interrupt him. Queen's Road was his mistress, the ephemeral vision he worshipped, the goddess at whose altar he laid his achievements. '. . . It looked so beautiful . . . I *had* to leave home, Sarah,' he had said firmly. 'I had to go – just as one day I have to return. It's the way it's supposed to be. You leave, and then you return to close the circle: from the beginning to the end of life. As the moon is my witness, I have to go back.'

That conversation had taken place years earlier, when the idea of returning was a long way in the future. But now they were really back. The day had finally come, John Crossworth was home. The town was going to judge him – and the wife he brought with him.

Panicked, she wanted suddenly to run away and found no comfort in her husband's expressionless face as he stared into the mirror. Was he hesitating because he was ashamed of her? Was he nervous of the hostile reception she might provoke? Oh God, what was he thinking? she thought blindly.

And whilst she wondered, John Crossworth stared in the mirror. What he saw was *beyond* the reflection, the dream of a lonely child many, many years before. What would his family say to him when he saw them? Would they be changed? As changed as he was? And – he paused, almost ashamed of the thought – would they be proud of him?

Light catching the watch chain drew John's glance downwards, his fingers straying pleasurably over the gold. It had been his first prized possession. He had struggled to earn the money and put down a few shillings – or whatever he could afford – monthly, until the day he walked into the jeweller's and left with the watch and chain in his hand. Six months later, he added a small seal to it, with his initials – JC – intertwined. A man of importance, bound to inherit the world.

But the world had many inheritors and some were suspect, unscrupulous, grubbing for any chance to undermine their rivals. Cold-eyed and honourable, the young John Crossworth came in quiet and stayed the course, earning a solid reputation as he slowly began to buy property, then a small cotton mill off Ash Lane, outside Shipley in Yorkshire. He was known as a just employer. Not gregarious, but fair. After eighteen months he sold on his first mill, bought some more terraced houses, and then became part owner of a small covered market, selling cotton goods. For one to have made so much money so young was a triumph, but for one to have made it honourably was remarkable.

It had meant long hours, cold days, colder nights. It had meant gruelling periods at the market, working the stall himself, and later, interviewing the many people who came looking for homes to rent. John Crossworth was fair, but careful. He took on tenants who were in need, but those whom he himself respected. The families might be poor, but his tenants were always responsible. At first there was little money, and what there was, was saved, every pound kept, invested, turned into another pound. John Crossworth, the saying went, never spent a shilling if a penny would do. Not that he was mean. Just careful. After all, he had a future to look out for.

The work was grinding, unending, the rents collected by John himself, although a bout of pneumonia laid him out for weeks after he had collapsed at one of the market stalls. Sarah had been with him at the time, and although they weren't yet married she had been the one to continue collecting his rents whilst he recovered.

Had he known, he would never have allowed it; but he

was in no fit state to put forward any objections. So Sarah, tall, unusual and charming, went round the back streets and collected for him. Incredibly, she had little trouble and on the few occasions she met with resistance, was more than able to cope. But although she could be formidable with adults, the children loved the lofty creature who came trailing the longing scent of gardenia into their streets.

When John recovered and found out what Sarah had done he'd offered to split the rental money with her.

Blushing furiously with indignation, she'd turned on him. 'I don't want money! I didn't do it for that.'

He was abashed, unsure of himself. 'But I wanted to say thank you.'

Snatching up her hat, Sarah was flinty with anger. 'Well, you've said thank you – so let's hear no more about the matter,' she replied coldly, moving away.

But he hadn't been prepared to let it rest, and stretched his arm across the door to prevent her leaving.

'Sarah, what is it? What did I say?'

She had been only inches away from him, her scent making him light-headed. Her skin, he'd realized, was uniformly olive, the dark brows framing the sloe-shaped eyes, a strand of her hair caught in one of her garnet earrings.

'Here, your hair's all caught up . . .' he said softly, reaching to unfasten it, his fingers brushing against her cheek as he did so.

She'd felt the touch and closed her eyes, John untying the hair and then – without thinking – he had leaned forward and kissed her, his skin burning for an instant against hers.

The memory still thrilled him as he continued to look into the mirror, his face impassive. The secret of success, he thought wryly, is to never let anyone know what you're thinking . . . His eyes fixed on the glass, then his gaze flicked over his figure, carefully, from head to toe, taking in the tailored and expensive clothes with some satisfaction. I did it, he thought to himself, then immediately changed the words – *we did it*.

He had made enquiries about the coal pit the night before, and would finalize the deal at the Star Inn tomorrow. A new mine, a new business, and God knows the men in Oldham needed work. It was to be a fine homecoming... John pursed his lips. Hard times come and hard times stay, he thought bitterly, then rallied, remembering that this was his victory day. He was back, he was home.

Home to Oldham and Queen's Road – he said the last two words to himself and felt the hairs prickle on his arms and at the base of his neck.

Then he saw her, reflected in the mirror behind him, unreal for an instant in the dim light. Frowning, he lifted the blind and the light came in, illuminating his wife's face as he put out his hand to her and smiled.

'Sarah...'

She took his hand warily; this was the most important morning of her husband's life.

'...will you walk with me?'

She nodded, unable to speak.

'Will you always walk with me, my love?'

'Wherever you go,' she said at last. 'Wherever you go.'

Chapter Two

They knew they were coming. Word was out. John Crossworth, who had run away from home when he was a kid; John Crossworth who had bought the old mine outside Oldham; John Crossworth who had houses, and money; that same John Crossworth who had now come home with his wife.

They walked up Union Street together, then passed the Town Hall and the library, then turned towards the park – Alexandra Park, leading to Queen's Road. Out of the corner of his eye John noticed several people turning to stare as he passed, but he never looked in their direction, his hand firmly holding Sarah's. He could sense the measure of her anxiety in every step. Yet when he glanced at her, her face was as still as a millpond.

She had suggested that he warn his family that they were coming, but John wanted to do it his way. But you don't know what you'll find, she had replied. They're my family, what have I got to be afraid of? he had queried mystified. I didn't say you had anything to be afraid of, Sarah replied calmly, but people change, and remember that they're older now. A surprise might not be good for them.

Fazed, John lapsed into silence, but for all his apparent ease, when they finally made that walk into town he was as nervous as she was. He had left so long ago and sent no word. Would they be pleased to see him – his father, his mother, his sister? How was she? How *old* was she now?

John stared ahead; the road was flanked with trees, some of the few green trees in Oldham. His eyes lingered on the high terrace and he felt suddenly groggy, so strong was its impact.

He had walked back into his old dream: the image he had last seen as he left Oldham as a child; the image he had carried as another man might have carried a beloved's picture – that same image was now in front of him. And it was no smaller. It hadn't faded, reduced, or disappointed him. It was waiting for him, unchanged.

'Is this the place?' Sarah asked, glancing at her husband.

He nodded. No words came.

Curiously she followed his gaze. The houses were grand, imposing, rising unexpectedly out of the cotton mill town. And opposite this select and silent island the park stood back and took a bow ... A sudden fleck of rain fell on her cheek and she brushed it away.

'It's raining.'

'It's wonderful,' was all he said.

She had never had a fierce affection for any place; had been too long the nomad, a foreigner, moving from city to city in an alien country. It was difficult for her to understand the emotion her husband was now feeling, and she thought, on looking round, that the houses were impossibly grand. Another thought followed on immediately: whilst they might accept John Crossworth on Queen's Road, would they accept her?

The rain splattered heavily on her face, her spirits faltering. She had not realized how high the town was above sea level, cold, stark and bleak as they crossed the Market Place for a hackney coach, waiting outside the Old Post Office Hotel. The fare – written up on a slate board – was 9d a mile, every additional third of a mile an extra 3d. The horses were impatient, stamping their hooves in the cold, vapour coming from their nostrils. Under Sarah's feet the cobbles were slicked with rain, John pointing out West Street and telling her that it once housed a building which had been used as the village prison. The dungeon, he called it, glancing over her head towards the Red Lion.

His excitement was obvious, and as he helped her into a carriage he kept talking, unusually loquacious. He was obviously captivated by the place, although to Sarah the town seemed oppressively dark: dank buildings, soot-covered streets; terraces, row after grinding row. Washing was hung out of upper windows, children sat on doorsteps, a woman pushed an old pram along, full of coal.

'Look,' he said excitedly as they rode along the High Street, 'look at that.'

She followed his gaze. At the entrance to Hilton's Arcade a clock chimed, the time measured out in doughty notes, the life-sized figures of King Richard, Friar Tuck and Robin Hood coming out to take a bow in the sooty air.

'Wonderful, isn't it?'

She smiled distantly.

He hadn't noticed that the people they had passed had stared at his wife curiously. But Sarah had seen their interest and her courage teetered, sudden and unexpected tears prickling behind her eyes.

'Twelve o'clock,' John said, checking his watch beside her.

Her hands tensed on her lap as she fought panic.

'God,' John went on, 'it's so good to be home.'

Home . . . the word echoed in her ears. It was his home, but hers? No. A woman glanced up at the carriage as they passed and Sarah automatically raised her hand to her face. She was out of place, she realized, and horribly unsure, almost frightened.

'I've dreamed of this moment for years. My town, my family . . .'

Glancing down, Sarah bit her lip hard. They wouldn't like her. She knew that now. John's family would look at her as these other people did, and whilst they would cheer the Prodigal's return they would resent her. Anxiety left her breathless, her arm tensing under her husband's touch.

He turned, alerted.

'What is it?'

'Nothing,' she said simply, aching inside.

Let's go, John, let's go. Go back to Birmingham, Yorkshire. Go abroad, go anywhere – but not here.

He squeezed her arm tenderly. 'Look again, Sarah,' he said, almost awe-struck, unable to keep away from the place, 'Queen's Road.'

The carriage drew to a halt, John paying the driver and helping Sarah down. The horses' hooves echoed hollowly on the cobbles as they moved off. Slowly she glanced up, but felt nothing of her husband's excitement. Indeed, the houses on Queen's Road seemed almost malevolent to her, over-large, judgemental, imperious. This isn't the place for you, someone whispered to her. Go away. Leave John here, he's earned it, but you, no. Not you. Not you.

'I'm going to buy a house here, Sarah,' he said quietly, pride like a warmth in his belly, 'and here we're going to live.'

Taking in a breath to steady herself, Sarah looked away.

He was suddenly concerned, and turned to her. 'What is it?'

'Nothing.'

'You look ... Sarah, what *is* it?' He was bemused, curious.

'Nothing, John. Really, I'm fine,' she answered, rain falling solemnly onto the brim of her hat.

He stared at her anxiously, his head uncovered, hair falsely darkened. Her diffidence baffled, almost hurt him. She seemed – he thought incredulously – to be close to tears.

'Sarah, please don't worry,' he began, misunderstanding the reason for her unease. 'Everything will be all right. My family are bound to like you.'

Her face was wet with rain as she looked at him.

'John?'

'Yes?'

Her next words shocked both of them. 'If I asked you to come away with me now – would you?'

He smiled: thought she was joking. 'What did you say?'

'Would you come away with me, if I asked you to?' she repeated, taking his hand. It was cold, chilled against hers. 'Would you come away with me now?'

'Sarah, I'm bringing you home –'

'This isn't my home, it's yours!' she snapped, uncharacteristically sharp, the rain puddling coldly against her cheeks.

Stunned, he stared at her, his coat darkening on the shoulders, lamps going on in the grand houses behind them, his wife's face dimming as the light faded and a faux night began.

'This is your home too,' he answered at last.

The words dangled dangerously in the sooty air. Sarah knew the importance of the answer she was about to give. Her reply would determine the future, *their* future. Behind them her husband's dream stood waiting to be claimed: between them stood her own terror of disappointing and ultimately losing him. But what was the choice? If I take him away I might keep him for a while, she thought blindly, but he would always come back here. And if I *do* take him away, he might grow to hate me and then I would lose him for ever.

The moment counted out its breath, the rain falling steadily on the immobile couple on the rainy Oldham road, and then Sarah spoke again.

'I love you.'

'I love you too,' John answered, frowning.

What was my life before you? And what would it be after you? she wondered, knowing the answer already.

Without you there is nothing. *Nothing* . . . So I'll follow you, John, whenever and wherever you go.

Howard Crossworth knew they were coming. He sat by the window of his terraced house and waited. He wondered what he would say. Whether he would welcome his son and what words he would use if he did. Uncomfortable in his seat, he shifted position and then leaned forward to look down Brompton Street. No one there. An image of John as a fourteen-year-old boy came back to him with pungent clarity. A withdrawn, almost sullen child, immersed in his own thoughts. A clever boy, they said at school, but one who would never concentrate for long. Not a dreamer exactly, just old for his years, always staring out of the window at the world beyond. Ready to be off.

Howard grimaced, moved position again. The room was damp, the fire out. He could have made it welcoming, but he didn't want his son to think he had gone to any trouble. Instead he wanted him to think he had taken his father by surprise – only the surprise was going to be his.

Hettie Crossworth didn't even pause, just snatched up her coat and began to run down the road towards the park. She knew only too well where her brother would be; staring at the houses he had stared at so often in his childhood. Soon out of breath she crossed the street and paused under the row of lamps before running on, her feet making clicking sounds on the pavement. John was home! Her brother – her beloved elder brother – was home.

She saw his outline as she turned in through the park gates. Knew him at once although he had been a boy when he left; knew the same posture, the outline of shoulder and hair. She had longed for his return, for the conversations they would have; the stories shared – and then she saw the woman standing next to him . . . Her steps slowed at once, her breathing fast as she studied the tall figure with its fashionable clothes, the wide-brimmed hat casting a shadow over her profile. But not obscuring it.

Hearing the footsteps behind her Sarah turned, Hettie pausing a little way away. For an instant both women regarded each other, Hettie eager to dislike the stranger, Sarah's expression wary, unsure.

'Hettie! Hettie!' John shouted, breaking the impasse, his sister running the last few yards to him. He caught hold of her eagerly, warmly, kissing her on the cheek as Sarah hung back, amazed by the open show of affection.

'This is my sister,' John said eagerly, holding Hettie at arm's length. 'God, I would have known you anywhere.'

'You too,' she replied, glancing over to Sarah.

He picked up the cue immediately.

'This is my wife,' he said, his tone admiring. 'This is Sarah.'

Hettie's pert face was unreadable. 'Dad heard you were coming.'

'I said this was my wife,' John said sternly. 'Say hello.'

Her mouth was sullen, unwelcoming as she turned to the newcomer. 'Hello.'

'I'm so pleased to meet you, Hettie,' Sarah replied pleasantly. But her voice sounded horribly Jewish to her; it grated on her ears just as she was sure it grated on theirs; and she fell silent again.

Hettie had noticed the voice, but that wasn't what had sparked her jealousy. It was the sheer presence of the woman. Her darkness, her tallness, her thunderous beauty. It would have been hard for her beloved brother to come home with any wife, but this one! It was too much. Much too much.

Envy made her spiteful: 'You're not English –'

'Hettie!'

'It's all right, John,' Sarah replied patiently, used to such comments. 'No, I'm not English,' she admitted to the slight girl standing proprietorially next to her husband. 'I'm Jewish.'

'But we don't have any Jews in Oldham,' Hettie replied slyly, 'apart from old man Moses – and he's crazy.'

There was a hideous moment of silence, the two women sizing each other up, John staring disbelievingly at his sister.

'I never thought,' he said finally, cold with fury, 'that I would live to say it, Hettie, but I'm ashamed of you.'

Flushing, she rounded on him. 'Why? I wasn't the one

to run away! I didn't go away without saying goodbye – and stay away. You didn't care about us. Any of us! You didn't even care when . . .' she trailed off.

'When *what*?'

'Nothing.'

John took her arm. 'When what?'

Sullenly she shook him off. 'Nothing. Nothing!'

The air was chill with animosity, the high terrace watchful behind the three of them. Shocked and disappointed, John stood between the two women and then turned away, walking back towards the park gates. For an instant the women hesitated, then Sarah moved, Hettie following. He said nothing as they walked down Park Road, merely took his wife's hand as they crossed into Brompton Street.

Her arms folded, Hettie followed. She had gone too far and she knew it. Knew also that it would be difficult to make amends. It always had been, even when John had been a boy. Cruelty incensed him, and she had, she realized, been bitterly cruel. Anxiously she stared at the back of her brother's head, ignoring Sarah. She had waited for years for this day, longed for it . . . He'll come back, she had told their father and mother. You wait, John'll come back. He should write, the idle bugger! their father had replied. Too bloody busy getting on and making money. Well, he needn't think he can just sidle up here and make amends when it suits him . . . Their mother had tried to placate him. You know what John's like, Peggy had said, the boy always had a wanderlust . . . But even as she said it, she was fighting against her own feelings; against the longing she had for her first-born. Was her child – was John – safe? Was he well? Was he *alive*?

At night she had watched for him in Brompton Street. When her husband was asleep she had gone to the window and looked out, picturing him. He was only a child, Peggy thought, too young to be out in the world alone . . . Night sounds made her restless, sleep elusive. Where are you, John? Where are you? . . . Outside, the sound of the nightsoil men reverberated in the quiet, and later in the year, when it was foggy, she sat staring into the sulphurous mists and wondered whether her son was alive or dead.

At first, every movement challenged her, because every sound of footsteps might be his. I'm back, Mum, back . . . But they never paused outside the house, and after a while she realized that her son would not be coming home until he had made his fortune. Memories were as strong as pain. I don't like to see you struggling, he'd said, older than any fourteen-year-old, quick to take on the responsibility. I'll make money and I'll come back and buy you a big house . . . Well, she'd held him when he said it, and teased him and told him that there were things more important than big houses. But he was adamant, determined that his love was going to be proved when he bought her a house. No more taking in washing, no more cooking for the old bachelor, Dr Martin, he – *her son* – would make it all right.

Of course Peggy knew how much her husband resented such talk. But she couldn't stop it – and in a way she didn't want to. John's father was, if not idle, unambitious. Envious of success, but unwilling – or unable, she was never sure which – to achieve it for himself. Instead he became bitter, seeing in his son all the promise he could never understand or match.

So after John left Howard spoke little of his son, even resented any mention from his daughter or his wife. But years after her son left, Peggy Crossworth was still waiting for the one step she recognized.

Well, time went on and the house on Brompton Street became too much for them. The rent too high. Where's your bloody marvellous son now? her husband asked her. Not so quick to get you out of trouble now, is he? All that fancy talk – fancy bloody talk was all it was! . . . He grumbled endlessly – off work, angry about the lodger, Hettie moving out to live with her aunt to ease the family finances. Bloody lodgers, he went on, watching his wife taking in more washing, and working now not only for Dr Martin, but for Dr Lyall as well.

'There's no point going on about it. Someone has to do it,' Peggy told Hettie bluntly. 'We need the money and who else will bring it in if I don't?'

Despair slunk into place between them.

'Maybe if I tried to contact him . . .' Hettie offered tentatively.

They both knew who she meant.

'No, leave him be.'

'But, Mum, if John knew how you were struggling –'

'He might be struggling himself!' Peggy replied shortly, folding Dr Lyall's single bed sheets and setting them aside to iron later. Overhead the lodger's feet sounded emptily on the lino floor.

'It's not my house any more, not really,' Peggy confided dully. 'I never thought it would come to this. Really, I didn't.' Her voice faltered, her hands moving fitfully over the bed linen.

'Mum, please let me try to find John –'

Turning, Peggy stared at her daughter. 'Let him be! If he'd done well, he'd have come home already. I know my son. He must be on his uppers to stay away . . .' Her fingers slid over the white sheets, the corded veins raised on the back of her hands. Old at fifty. Aged with disappointment. 'I'm glad you're happy living with your aunt.'

'I miss home.'

'I wish your brother did,' Peggy replied sadly, sitting down in front of the fire.

A quick wind started down the chimney and made the coals flame hotly for an instant. An unemployed husband, a daughter given over to her sister, laundry piled up in bales, and a lodger to help meet the rent . . . It paid to be tired, Peggy thought. Being tired meant you had no time to think, and that was good, because otherwise you saw how terrible things really were.

'Let me help you, Mum.'

24

'No, love, leave me to it,' Peggy replied distantly. 'The doctors'll only moan if I don't do their ironing. You know how it is.'

'I miss John,' Hettie said suddenly, sitting beside her mother.

'D'you think of him?'

She nodded, both of them looking into the fire. 'Every day.'

'Look!' Peggy said suddenly, almost cheerfully. 'I can see Africa!' Her index finger pointed towards the flames. 'Oh, do look, Hettie. Can you see it?'

Leaning forwards, her daughter stared at the fire shapes in the hot grate.

'Yes! Yes! I can see it.'

The firelight was playing over Peggy's features, flattering her back into youth.

'D'you think John's there?'

'Where? In Africa?'

Her mother nodded eagerly.

'Chasing tigers?'

'Shooting them!'

'Is he rich, d'you think?' Hettie asked her mother, both of them still staring, transfixed, into the fire as though they could read the future there.

'Oh yes, he's very rich,' Peggy replied firmly. 'And everyone thinks well of him.'

'Does he have a big house?'

'Huge.'

'And servants?'

Peggy nodded enthusiastically. 'Dozens; to clean his boots; lay his table; wash his clothes . . .' She stopped, the flames dying as the coal shifted, the pattern of Africa suddenly gone, the reality of Dr Lyall's thin sheets lying unwelcoming on the table behind her.

Laboriously Peggy rose to her feet and then, slowly and purposefully, she began to iron.

* * *

He hadn't expected the nerves, but now that John was standing outside his parents' house on Brompton Street he was cold with anxiety. The door was the same in size, but needed painting, the knocker long gone, and the windows were blanked out by nets in need of washing. He frowned. It was unlike his mother to neglect a detail like that; she had always been so house-proud in the past.

Hesitating, he turned to look at Sarah, then tried to catch Hettie's glance, but she had moved aside a little and was waving flirtatiously to a young boy on the other side of the street. The house – John realized – looked sourly poor. But he had come home in good time. He would move his parents out of this place and settle them somewhere outside the coal lung of the town, somewhere where the air was sweet and high, somewhere where his mother could have that garden she had talked about for years.

After all, he had the money now. He could give her a better way of living, a kindness she had never known before. He thought of his father then. There had never been any understanding between them; they had been too disparate, but it didn't seem to matter now. He would help his father too – despite their differences – because in helping him he would help his mother. An unexpected guilt nudged him suddenly. Maybe he should have been in touch over the years; maybe he *should* have written to his mother. But he hadn't wanted to; he had waited instead until he had proved himself and could return in triumph. Then she could be proud of him – say, look, this is my John. See what he's done, and see how he's come back for me. Just as he always said he would . . .

'How do I look?' he asked Sarah suddenly, bashfully.

She stared at him, amused. 'You look very handsome. The son any mother would be proud to have.'

He nodded, then frowned. 'It's nine years since I left here . . . maybe I should have sent word that I was coming.'

'John, go on. Just knock at the door,' Sarah encouraged him.

He paused, then turning, reached up and struck the wood twice. The sound echoed in the space behind and made an empty, dismal echo. He felt, for an instant, afraid.

'Try again,' Sarah urged him, aware that by this time they were being watched by several neighbours on Brompton Street. 'Knock louder.'

He did.

'I HEARD YOU! HANG ON! HANG ON!' a voice bellowed as the door was wrenched open and an old man stood on the step, blinking blindly into the daylight.

'Father?' John said simply.

'Well, you got that right,' Howard Crossworth replied curtly. 'I suppose that's something.'

Embarrassed, Sarah stared at the bowed figure in the doorway. He was leaning on a stick, his collar undone, the front of his shirt and trousers stained. Even from where she stood, he smelled of old pipe smoke and liniment.

John was pale with anxiety. 'Father, I've come home –'

'I can see that.'

Sarah could feel the eyes boring into them; could sense the people hanging around to watch the outcome of the encounter. Dear God, she thought desperately, why doesn't he let his son in?

'Father, I want to talk to you –'

'Bit late, isn't it?' Howard replied sharply, enjoying his moment of attention. People were listening to him now; what he said would be repeated round tables and in the pub that night. He was the centre of attention – for once.

Distraught, John tried to move past his father, but the old man blocked his way.

'Hey, I'll have none of that! This is my house, whatever you might think!'

John's voice was low with distress, his hands trembling. 'Please let me in. I have to see my mother.'

'Then you're in the wrong place,' Howard replied brusquely. 'She's not here.'

'She's out?'

'In a way.'

John frowned, bewildered. 'Then can I wait for her inside?' he turned to his wife. 'Can *we* wait for her inside?'

'Only if you've got plenty of time to waste,' Howard replied, enjoying his revenge on the boy who had shamed him years earlier, the upstart kid who had run off to make his fortune and show up his father's limitations. But now it was Howard's turn; now *he* was going to bring his son to his knees and see how *he* liked it.

'Just tell me where my mother is,' John said coldly, 'and we'll go to her.'

He would remember the moment for ever. His father smiled at him and for an instant he nearly returned the gesture – until he realized the malice which lay beneath.

'Father, *please* . . . where is my mother?'

'Leesfield. Leesfield Cemetery,' Howard Crossworth replied, turning and starting to close the door. 'She died a year ago.'

Chapter Three

He was an old bugger, they all agreed on that. So maybe
John Crossworth did leave home, but he came back to
share his triumph, didn't he? It wasn't his fault that his
mother had died in the meantime. Besides, John had loved
his mother; his father had no right treating him as though
Peggy's death were his fault . . . But John could have stayed
in touch, some said . . . Why? He was coming home, others
answered. He had made a success and was returning to
Oldham to share it. It was his way, they continued, he was
proud, like all young ambitious men. Surely, the important
thing was that he had come home in the end to share his
fortune?

But that fortune meant little now. John's mother was
dead. The reason for his striving was gone – and Sarah
understood instinctively. Her husband might dream
of owning a house on Queen's Road, but that dream
had been tempered by the belief that he would also
be rich enough to rescue his mother. A child's dream,
of course, but then he *had* been a child. And, like
all children, he had expected that everything would
remain the same; that all would be as it had been when
he left. He had never thought that the one person he
had respected, and worked for, would not live to see his
triumph.

Shame-faced, Hettie had watched her father break the
news. She had winced when he did it: felt cruel for not
warning her brother. But it was too late now – now that
he turned away and, shaken, reached automatically for his
wife's hand. The rain had started up again, darkly sombre,
the street suddenly emptying of people. They had come to

watch the show and now felt shamed by what they had seen.

'John, come away,' Sarah said softly, seeing Howard close the door on his son. Her hat was stained with rain, her face shadowed. 'Please, sweetheart, come away.'

He moved towards her, silent, white-faced, and as Sarah turned she caught – for a moment – Hettie's glance.

The girl was standing motionless, waiting. For *what*? Sarah wondered. To gloat?

'I . . . I meant to write . . .' Hettie began, hands deep in the pockets of her cheap coat. 'I just . . . well, I didn't know where you were . . .' She trailed off, the rain was falling on her too, making her cold, her teeth chattering. 'I didn't think Dad would act like that.'

Without answering, Sarah looked at her, then glanced back to John. He was still staring at the house, and the door which had been closed to him.

'I never meant . . .' Hettie continued, tears beginning, miserable under the bad daylight. '. . . Sorry . . . sorry . . .'

So this was the triumphant homecoming, was it? Was this what her husband had worked so hard for? Sarah's own anxiety had gone, all that mattered was the unutterable distress she could feel emanating from the two people in front of her.

Sighing, she put out her hand. 'Hettie?'

The girl hesitated, then took it, Sarah automatically drawing Hettie towards her. For a moment the three of them stood together under the rain, all Sarah's uncertainty dissolving in those brief moments, her protective instinct aroused as fiercely as her anger.

'Well, I'd like to know where 'e got 'is money from,' Nick Miller, a wiry Irishman whose parents had come to Oldham in the Famine, said in the Star Inn a day or so later. ''E weren't exactly from a rich family.'

'He earned it,' the landlord replied wearily. He had had this conversation several times already: John Crossworth's return and subsequent buying of the mine having become the favoured item of gossip amongst his customers. 'Crossworth worked bloody hard for his success.'

'How the 'ell d'you know?' Nick Miller replied waspishly. 'You 'is bank manager, or summat?'

'I just know –'

'Well, I know more,' Miller said smartly. 'Anyway, I were talking to a bloke who works with Dandry Fairclough –'

'Hah!' the landlord snorted.

'I said *worked* with Fairclough, I didn't say 'e were a friend of 'is . . .'

'Good job.'

'. . . and this bloke said that Crossworth thinks 'e can take on old man Cotter and Fairclough. Said that was why 'e'd come back.'

'Who? Crossworth?'

'No, the bloody King!' Miller snapped. 'Who else but Crossworth?'

Stung, the landlord moved away and started to polish the bar top, Miller's eyes following his every move. 'D'you know about 'is wife?'

'I've heard.'

'She's foreign,' Miller said cautiously. 'Jewish.'

Bristling, the landlord's tone hardened. He didn't like bigots – of any kind.

'So?'

'Well, I've 'eard that Crossworth – how old is 'e, anyway?'

'Why? What's that got to do with it?'

Suddenly the man standing next to Miller turned, grinning broadly; 'Because it's 'ard seeing a man do well at fifty, but to see 'im doing well at twenty-odd is bloody 'eartbreaking!'

'I didn't see you there, George,' the landlord said cheerfully, pulling him a pint. 'So you've heard all about Crossworth too then?'

Nodding, George Lyman leaned onto the bar. 'And I say good luck to 'im. I need a job myself and if 'e's really opening up the old mine again then I'll be first in line.'

'Rumour says it's not safe,' Miller said sourly. 'I 'eard that were why it were closed in't first place.'

George turned to the thin Irishman, his tone brusque: 'You 'eard wrong – and if I were you I wouldn't go believing what blokes who work for Dandry Fairclough 'ave to say.' He downed half of his pint before speaking again. 'Fairclough's got a rival now – and so 'as old man Cotter. And not before time. They'd do well to watch their backs.'

'Nah!' Miller blustered unconvincingly. 'Crossworth's only a boy –'

'So was David when 'e went up against Goliath,' George Lyman replied calmly, 'and we all know what 'appened there.'

The question was, should he sell or not?

Undecided, the old man looked at John Crossworth and wondered how he could afford to buy a house on Queen's Road. He had called on him the previous night; apparently having just returned to his home town. He had asked him outright if it was true that he was thinking of selling his house. Well, the old man had been amazed, the question coming from such a young man. But he'd said he was thinking about it, and then he'd made a few enquiries the following morning and found out about the terraced houses John Crossworth had bought and rented out in Yorkshire, then about the market stalls, and finally about the mine – but a house on Queen's Road? That was another matter. Quite another matter indeed.

The old man tapped his front teeth with his fingernail. He'd like to give the youngster a break, but would he fit in? It was so important to fit in with all the professional people who lived there ... But then again, he had decided to leave and Crossworth had the money ready – in cash. So why should he worry about the neighbours now? Besides,

Crossworth looked respectable enough, and even if his wife was – well, *different* – they seemed a quiet couple. Not exactly the sort who usually bought a house on Queen's Road, but times were changing, so who was he to judge?

'I can pay you as soon as you like,' John said calmly.

'We've been very happy here,' the old man went on, wasted in a dark suit, reluctantly civil. 'We've made good friends here.' He tapped his front tooth again thoughtfully. 'People are *so* sociable . . .' he let the implication hang out to dry.

John ignored it. Wanted the house; wanted to own the bricks and mortar for which he had left home. Even if it was too late for his mother to see it. 'I like the house very much.'

'Yes . . . we always liked it . . .'

Slowly Sarah smiled at the old man. 'You've made it very beautiful.'

He swelled under the compliment. 'Well, as I say, we always liked it.'

'We would look after it too,' she went on soothingly, 'keep it as nicely as you have.' Her gaze went round the room longingly, John watching her.

Only he knew she was pretending, that the house meant little to her. It wasn't *her* dream, after all, it was the one she had taken on, along with him. His thoughts went back to the day of their return to Oldham and the shift in their relationship that rainy afternoon.

When she comforted both him and his sister she manacled his heart for ever. They didn't need to talk about the humiliation he was feeling, or the vast white grief which winded him when he was told his mother was dead. She understood; and she also understood that there were no words up to the job – John had lost more than his mother, he had lost his way. It would take a long time for him to recover.

'Could you be happy here?' John asked her, looking round.

She nodded, as though it mattered. 'Yes, I could be happy here.'

Together they looked at the old man. Challenged him.

'Well . . . I suppose . . .' he paused, then flicked away his misgivings as he thought of the money. 'Well . . . I hope you'll both be very happy here.'

But it wasn't just going to be the two of them.

As they walked down to the park gates moments later, John was quiet, Sarah watchful. She had expected triumph and had therefore interpreted his reserve as sadness.

'Your mother would have been proud of you.'

He nodded absent-mindedly.

'John, what is it?'

'I was wondering if you'd mind if Hettie came to live with us . . .'

She said nothing.

'I don't want her around my father, and she's too cramped living with our aunt. We'd have plenty of room in the new house.'

'If that's what you want, John.'

He glanced over to her questioningly. 'No, it's what *you* want, Sarah. I haven't said anything to Hettie, and if you don't like the idea, I won't mention it.'

In silence she walked a few paces on. A man passed and tipped his hat. Someone who knew John, not her.

'Don't you like Hettie?'

'I hardly know her,' Sarah countered.

'She's my sister.'

'Is that what this is all about?' she asked quietly.

'All what?'

'Taking Hettie in. Is it really because she's your sister, or because you feel you let your mother down and want to compensate for that?'

He looked at her, his eyes hard. Be careful, Sarah willed herself, don't anger him.

'Is *that* what you think?' he asked coldly.

'I don't know, John. I want you to tell me.'

'You think I'm taking on my sister to make up for failing my mother?'

'You *didn't* fail your mother,' she replied evenly, 'you just think you did.'

'She died –'

'I know.'

'– before I had time to make everything all right for her.' He caught his breath, stared back towards the row of houses on Queen's Road. 'Jesus, Sarah, I wish I'd never seen this place!'

She winced at his distress.

'I fell in love with a row of houses. *Houses!*' he said disbelievingly. 'I thought I'd got it all mapped out. I was so arrogant, so thoughtless. You see, I just thought I'd go away, make a fortune, come back and change everyone's lives and they'd be grateful. But they weren't, Sarah, and I was too late!'

'Ssshh, you're upset.'

'We should go away!' he said suddenly, turning to her, his expression intense. 'Get out of here. Never come back. It's unlucky here. We should go.'

Anxiously she touched his forehead: 'John, we'll do whatever you want. Whatever you feel is right.'

'No one can live in a dream, Sarah!' he said distractedly.

'No one is asking you to.'

But he wasn't listening; his composure had gone and he was – she realized incredulously – frightened.

'I carried this place in my mind every minute of every day.' His voice was thick with disappointment. 'I knew each window of each house. Each roof. I could walk the rooms in my sleep. I saw my mother in those rooms with me. Saw her there as clearly as I see you now. I never thought that she would die before I could achieve it. *I never thought of that!*'

She caught hold of his hand hurriedly, felt his nails burn into her palm.

'I was so arrogant!' he repeated. 'I should have written to her! Told her things were going well, told her it was all coming right and that I'd be back for her. I could have kept her going, kept her spirits up.' His eyes were desolate, throat acid with remorse. 'I could have kept her alive –'

'No one keeps anyone alive,' Sarah said firmly, turning his head to look at her. 'No one keeps *anyone* alive. D'you hear me? It's up to God, not you.'

'But I should have done more –'

'You did what you believed to be right,' she replied emphatically. 'Most people go through their whole lives without being able to say that.'

Slowly his head bowed. 'Shall we stay here?' he asked, his tone deadly. 'Or shall we go?'

'John, don't ask me that,' she replied. 'I can't make that decision for you.'

'Then just tell me – is it lucky for us here, or not?'

She stared at the top of his bent head. This wasn't John Crossworth, always controlled, unemotional, cool. Who *was* this distressed stranger who was asking her about life and loss and luck? A part of her husband had surfaced at a time of intense pain, a portion of him which was hidden to outsiders and exposed only to her. The shadow of the child who left home to walk alone.

'What are you afraid of, John?' she asked at last.

He met her eyes.

'That if we stay here I'll lose you, and then there would be *nothing*. Nothing at all.'

'Then we stay here,' she replied calmly, looking ahead, 'because I'll never leave you. *Never.*'

Chapter Four

'If you ask me, he'll only last a year,' Dandry Fairclough said dismissively to his accountant, shifting his overdressed bulk on the high-backed leather chair in his office. 'John Crossworth's a bloody kid, with about as much idea of how to run a business as a eunuch has of running a brothel.'

'He's bought the old mine –'

'I heard!' Fairclough snapped impatiently. 'Old news, Forecourt. I don't pay you for that. I want to know what's going on *now*.'

'I don't have any more information, sir.'

'Then find out some!' Fairclough barked, nibbling at the side of his thumbnail, his heavy-jowled face sour. 'I want to know every move that bastard makes. What he says, to whom. What he buys. Everything – even when he goes to the bloody lavatory. And how often. You got that?'

'Well, there's a rumour that Crossworth's buying a house on Queen's Road –'

'Queen's Road!' Fairclough snapped, sitting bolt upright. 'Bloody upstart!'

Forecourt didn't like to mention the fact that Dandry Fairclough's father had been a fairground barker.

'It's only a rumour –'

'AT TWENTY-THREE YEARS OLD!' Fairclough bellowed. 'How the hell's he doing it?'

'He buys well –'

'I don't need a lesson from you about business, Forecourt!' Fairclough retorted. 'I was just thinking aloud.' Bitterly, he slumped into silence, Forecourt watching him and secretly rejoicing.

About time! he would say to his wife later. About time

that he was going to be given a run for his money. He and old man Cotter had had a stranglehold on everything that went on in Oldham for years. Sure enough, Cotter wasn't the man he used to be, but he was still as cunning as a hungry wolf and Dandry Fairclough – for all his fat posturing – was a dangerously ambitious man. Forecourt thought of the brief glimpse he had caught of John Crossworth and smiled to himself. Crossworth looked older than his years because he never smiled, but he had a quietness about him which was soothing, and word was out that he was an honourable man.

An honourable man ... Forecourt glanced at Dandry Fairclough and mentally willed John Crossworth on. For an instant the hatred of his employer was so intense that he imagined Crossworth in Fairclough's chair and was surprised by the feeling of pleasure the thought gave him.

John hired Sammy Upton, having been tipped off that he was a steady worker with a large family to support. At one o'clock that same day Upton came in, hair newly washed, shiny suit pressed, the cuffs of his shirt sleeves turned back to hide the fraying. Diffidently he stood in front of John, his expression defensive as John informed him that he was putting him in charge of the rent collections of his newly acquired properties and offering him a bonus if he got them in on time.

'But no heavy-handed tactics,' John said firmly. 'Be persistent, but no threats.'

'Sometimes that's all people understand.'

'If you can't do it my way, then work for someone else,' John said, rising to his feet.

'I can do it your way,' Upton replied quickly, eager to keep the job as he followed his new boss to the door.

Pausing, John looked across the yard to the pithead, overshadowed by the vast, unmoving, mine wheel.

'The men were asking me in the pub when you're going to be opening up the pit again.'

John stared at the iron wheel. 'When I'm sure it's safe,' he replied without looking round. 'But you can tell them that – if all's well – I'll be looking to hire on next week.'

'There's many who'll be glad to hear that,' Upton replied sincerely. 'Work's needed round here.'

'I know.'

'Men don't feel right when they're not working,' Upton continued, talking for all the unemployed he knew, 'and some of the bosses around here aren't popular – even if you're desperate.'

John was still staring across the yard. 'Like who?'

'Old man Cotter and Dandry Fairclough.'

'I thought Cotter was ill.'

'He was, but he's back on his feet again,' Upton replied, staring at the back of his boss's head and trying to read his thoughts. 'Mean old devil.'

'What about Dandry Fairclough?'

'Bought the Monkey's Paw pub last month. That's three pubs in Oldham – and the mill. Made a pile, he has. And got himself a bad name along the way.' Upton paused. 'He works his employees hard and never pays the going rate . . .'

John nodded, but still didn't turn round.

'. . . and there's talk that Fairclough's daughter and Cotter's grandson might be getting engaged soon. Sort of unite the two families and keep all the money safe.' His voice was quick with bitterness. 'They need stopping.'

John's voice was impassive: 'People marry who they want.'

'I don't mean that,' Upton countered, 'I mean that Cotter and Fairclough need stopping.' He paused, uncertain of how far he could go. 'People are glad you've come back, Mr Crossworth. People need someone on their side.' He paused. The words filtered over to John and then, when he didn't reply, Upton left.

* * *

Sarah realized that she had to be very careful in the way she furnished the new house. Nothing too unusual, nothing to alarm any of her new neighbours; nothing to set her too much apart from the norm. Otherwise people would talk ... Not that she minded for herself; people had always talked about her and her father, but she *did* mind about John, and how gossip of any kind would affect him.

Which is why, in a way, she was glad that Hettie had come to live with them. Temperamental, quick-tongued Hettie, sullen and affectionate by turns, desperate to let everyone know that she was living on Queen's Road. She was allowed to be a little brash because Hettie was young and because she was, after all, one of them. A Northerner. An Oldham girl. She might have come from a poor family, from an unemployed father and a mother who took in washing, but she was born in the town. And that made her acceptable – even on Queen's Road.

Smiling to herself, Sarah looked at the new furniture she had bought. Antiques, paintings, silver – creating an instant past for two nomads. She stared at the portrait of an unknown woman which John had bought recently – knowing that Hettie would hint to strangers that she was an ancestor – and wondered who the woman was.

'We have to have a piano!' Hettie said suddenly, walking in and breaking into her sister-in-law's thoughts.

'Why?' Sarah asked, raising her eyebrows. 'No one plays.'

'But *everyone* has a piano,' Hettie replied guilelessly. 'You should ask John for one.'

'Why don't you, if it matters to you so much?'

'Because he listens to me, but he only *hears* you,' Hettie responded, slumping heavily into an armchair.

Not as foolish as you make out, are you, Hettie? Sarah thought to herself.

'All right, I'll ask him. But I can't promise anything,' she said evenly. 'How's your room?'

Hettie grimaced: 'Not as nice as the one opposite.'

'So take that one –'

'But mine has a view over the park!' Hettie replied impatiently, as though Sarah should already have guessed. 'The other one looks out over the main road.'

You lived all your life on Brompton Street, Sarah thought incredulously, and now in only a few weeks, you're a snob.

'In that case, keep the one you have.'

'Of course,' Hettie said peevishly, 'yours is the best. Yours and John's.'

The remark went unchallenged, Hettie glancing round pettishly, eager to pick a fight.

'So where *is* my brother?'

'At work.'

She grimaced extravagantly. 'I don't know how you stand it! He's *always* at work. I want to marry someone who'll stay home with me. A man who'll never want to leave me.'

'Then prepare yourself for a lean time, Hettie,' Sarah replied crisply. 'Because the only reason we can live in a house like this is because John works all the hours God sends.'

'D'you think He does?'

Baffled, Sarah stared at the girl. '*Who* does *what*?'

'God – d'you really think He sends the hours?' she asked archly. 'Or does *your* God work a different way?'

'What are you talking about, Hettie?'

Her eyes widened. 'About you being a Jew – does it make a difference?' The words swung with malice.

'I didn't know you were interested in religion,' Sarah replied after a moment.

'I'm not really,' Hettie retorted, glancing over her shoulder again. 'I was just wondering. Showing an interest. You know, being sisterly.'

Her words tingled between them. Sarah's voice was expressionless when she answered, 'Jews believe in the same God as you do. But we don't believe in Jesus Christ.'

'I suppose that makes you a heathen then,' Hettie replied calmly.

The room was suddenly oppressive, the girl assuming some form of spiritual superiority. All her life Sarah had experienced such moments, but this time – in *her* house, under *her* roof – she was not about to let herself be undermined.

'Hettie, don't goad me –'

'I wasn't!' she wailed piteously.

'We can – we *should* – be friends,' Sarah went on, her voice controlled. 'We should live together happily here. And we will – unless you spoil it. I'll never mention this again, Hettie, but listen to me now and remember what I say. *Never* – by word, or thought, or even a look – try to undermine me. Or you'll live to regret it.'

Old man Cotter wasn't having any of it. He had been told repeatedly by his doctor that he wasn't fit to go out, but he'd still made the trip to his niece's wedding, and was now suffering for it. Blood in his handkerchief, chest like a fire grate.

'Bastard doctor!' he roared, white-haired, white-faced, red about the nostrils. A huge white stoat's head surrounded by an astrakhan collar. 'I pay that man good money and I'm *still* sick.'

'You're sick because you don't listen to advice,' Dandry Fairclough replied patronizingly, squeezing into the carriage seat next to Cotter's.

'You want to lose some poundage, Dandry!' Cotter replied sourly. 'I'm sick of riding home with your arse on my lap.'

'And you could do with putting some weight *on*,' Fairclough responded, piqued by the reference to his size. 'Anyway, I've been dieting.'

'Then take the bloody lead weights out of your pockets, and give the horses a chance,' Cotter replied, staring gloomily out of the carriage window, a handkerchief pressed to his lips.

He didn't like Fairclough, never had. But he was useful, and that was all that mattered really. Out of the corner of his eye, Cotter stared at his companion's tight, flashy, dark green jacket. The man had no style, no *breeding*. He looked, Cotter thought slyly, like an over-stuffed olive.

'I saw that bugger Crossworth today –'

Cotter coughed vigorously.

'– smug as you like, walking up Queen's Road as though he owned the bloody place.'

'He soon might, he already owns a house there,' Cotter said sharply, gazing out of the window as the Oldham mill chimneys came into sight. 'And he's just bought that old mine.'

'Which I had my eye on.'

'So why didn't you get there before him?' Cotter queried, dabbing at his raw nostrils.

'He beat me to it.'

'Bad business,' Cotter said disappointedly. 'I was hoping either you or I might get that place. Keep it in the family, so to speak.' He laughed shortly. 'How's your daughter?'

The implication was obvious.

'Blossoming,' Fairclough replied eagerly. 'How's your grandson?'

'Looking to settle down,' Cotter replied, sinking his stoat's head further into his fur collar. 'I was hoping those two could come to an understanding, Dandry. Get married. It would be a neat little solution for both our families, and keep the money safe. After all, you know how I've always admired your business sense.'

Suddenly queasy, Fairclough realized the implication prickling under old man Cotter's words. He was under threat. Crossworth had undermined him when he bought the mill, made him look a loser ... It had all been so easy before – he and Cotter combining interests, Fairclough's daughter set to marry Cotter's grandson.

'I hear he's married.'

Fairclough was preoccupied, sweaty with angst. 'Who?'

'Crossworth.'

'Oh yes, he's married,' Fairclough said with some relief.

'But his sister isn't.'

Fairclough could feel old man Cotter's thigh pressed against his in the limited space of the carriage. It felt cold, as though he were sitting next to a corpse.

'But she's just a girl!'

'Twenty next,' Cotter replied.

He'd been making enquiries! Fairclough thought incredulously. The old bugger had been sniffing round already, giving himself options, trying to weigh up which was the best bet – the Faircloughs or the Crossworths. As though his flaming whey-faced, wall-eyed grandson was a catch for any girl . . .

'Crossworth's got no breeding!'

Cotter turned, giving Fairclough a cadaver's dead-eyed look.

'You didn't exactly come from the aristocracy yourself, Dandry,' he said, his voice betraying no hint of a Northern accent.

Smarting, Fairclough glanced away. Cotter had come from a long line of landowners and was unimpeachable in that respect. His home was a Victorian mansion, his education supplied by private tutors, his wife a Yorkshire heiress. Fairclough's twitched with unease; *his* mother and father had been fairground workers, and as for an education – *what* bloody education? He'd ducked and dived and thieved his way to the top. His wife was no better either. Moneyed, but common. Common as muck.

'But Crossworth's only a lad –' Fairclough spluttered finally.

'You keep saying that,' Cotter replied, 'but it's not Crossworth's age I'm worried about. I never liked competition, and I don't want some upstart bothering me now.' He wheezed impressively. 'Not at my age.'

Oh God, here he goes again – playing the dying old man card, Fairclough thought cynically. The same card he'd been playing for the last ten years.

'I want some peace, Dandry,' Cotter said, staring at the mill chimneys as they came closer, 'and so should you. You're not as young as you were.'

'I'm only forty-nine –'

'Lying bugger!' Cotter said, giving another snatched bark of laughter. 'You're nearer sixty than fifty.'

Feeling more than a little dissatisfied by the way the conversation was going, Fairclough gingerly moved his bulk and peeled off his gloves. His hands – as he had expected – were damp with sweat.

'We have to stop Crossworth.'

Fairclough was sullen. 'How?'

'Put pressure on him.'

'Word's out that Crossworth's going to be offering bigger wages than us.'

Cotter turned his pink-rimmed eyes towards the horizon. 'Aagh! Flash in the pan. He'll never keep that up.'

'Besides, the pit's old, well-mined,' Fairclough said hopefully. 'It might not be worth reopening.'

'If that's true, then why did you want to buy it?' Cotter queried, his tone icy.

An uneasy silence fell over the two men.

'It's not my fault,' Fairclough said at last, surly at the thought of all his plans being unexpectedly scuppered. 'How was I to know what Crossworth was up to? To look at him, you'd never think he'd amount to anything. He never comes out with more than two words at a time.'

'If only the same could be said for you,' Cotter said with feeling as they entered the mill gates. 'If only the same could be said for you.'

Sammy Upton soon became more than a rent collector; he became John's ears and eyes. As he went about Oldham he heard all the gossip, mutterings in pubs and on street corners – and all of it he reported back to his employer, keeping him fully aware of the opposition he faced. Not that John worried; there was high unemployment and the men employed by Fairclough and Cotter were paid minimal wages which circumstances forced them to accept. John's aim in raising their wages was not a bid for popularity, but for a reliable workforce. He wanted not love, but loyalty.

And he got it. Within days of his reopening the mine, it was giving work to a hundred men and bringing in more coal than anyone had anticipated. Soon afterwards John bought another terrace in Little Lever nearby and a tobacconist's in the centre of Oldham. He had, everyone agreed, a god's luck with business.

'Money makes money,' John explained to Sarah over breakfast one morning. They had employed two maids, one of which Hettie referred to as her 'personal maid' even though the girl undertook a variety of duties in the house and was no more attached to Hettie than to anyone else. 'With what I get for the rents I can afford to buy on.'

'Why don't you buy a dress shop?' Hettie asked suddenly, smoothing down the front of her expensive morning dress.

'I don't need a dress shop,' John replied patiently.

'But it would be so nice. Better than a pit any day. Even Father agreed with me on that . . .' she trailed off, suddenly shamefaced.

John's expression was unreadable. 'I'm not looking for my father's approval –'

'I didn't say you were!' Hettie blustered nervously. 'I just bumped into him and told him about it.'

'You don't have to explain,' John replied evenly. 'If you want to see him, then do so. He's your father, after all.'

'*Our* father.'

John laid down his knife and fork. 'Hettie, don't try and make me feel guilty. I don't want to see him, or talk about him any more.'

'But –'

46

It was Sarah's turn to intervene: 'Hettie, let it rest,' she said firmly. 'I don't want any ill feeling here.'

'But it's different for you,' Hettie said woefully. 'He's not your father.'

'My father is dead,' Sarah countered, 'and I think you would be best advised not to interfere.'

'I *never* feel at home here!' Hettie snapped, getting to her feet and throwing down her napkin. 'You never wanted me here, you never made me feel welcome.' Her face was pinched with self-pity. It gave her a sudden resemblance to her father.

'Oh Hettie –'

'Don't "oh Hettie" me!' she snapped at Sarah. 'You never liked me.'

'Perhaps she has good reason, the way you behave,' John said icily. 'I don't know why you can't –'

He didn't have time to finish before Hettie ran out, banging the door behind her.

It took several seconds before John spoke again: 'It was a mistake having her come to live with us.'

'Give her time,' Sarah said soothingly. 'She'll settle down in time.'

But he was exasperated. 'Nothing has gone right since I came back,' he said bitterly. 'My mother's death, my father . . . and now Hettie. Nothing's the way I thought it would be.'

'You expected so much. You built it up in your head for so long.'

'If I didn't have you it would be unbearable,' he said simply. 'Strange, isn't it? You carry a dream with you for years without realizing what it will cost you. Without ever knowing what you have to sacrifice for it. And in the end you have to wonder if it was worth it. I feel a terrible emptiness inside, Sarah. God forgive me, but I do.'

'But what if you'd stayed in Oldham?' she countered. 'What would have happened then? You'd have had little education, probably an apprenticeship to some tradesman.

47

Not your own boss, but at the beck and call of someone else's whim.' She moved over to him and stroked his hair. 'You could never have stood for that. You know you couldn't.'

'But if I'd stayed home my mother would still be alive.'

'You don't know that. You have to stop blaming yourself and let life go on.'

'I want to, but I can't,' he said blankly. 'It's as though something is missing and nothing I say or do can bring it back to make up the loss.'

'Nothing?' Sarah asked gently. 'What about a child?'

He looked at her for a slow, paced moment, his eyes questioning.

'Is it true?'

She nodded, taking his hand and resting it against her stomach.

'February.'

Without speaking, he rested his head against her shoulder and felt, for one glorious moment, a promise of peace.

Chapter Five

'I 'ave to say that I never thought Sarah Crossworth would settle down. Not 'ere,' George Lyman's wife said to her neighbour. 'Looked too posh for words when she arrived, and . . .' she mouthed the next word. *Foreign.*

'Goes to show,' her companion replied, 'that you can never tell with people. Mind you, I wouldn't have that girl in my 'ouse.'

' 'Ettie Crossworth?'

She nodded. 'Nothing but trouble. I saw 'er fooling around with some boys the other night. Out far too late on 'er own. Laughing and showing off and worse. They can't control her.' She glanced round. 'It's a shame, John Crossworth's a good man. Quiet like, but sound.'

'George says the same. A fair boss. A bit curt sometimes, but fair.'

'But that sister of 'is is no good. If I was Sarah Crossworth I'd 'ave sent 'er packing long before this.'

Mollie Lyman was all ears. 'I wonder 'ow she'll take the news of the baby, then.'

'*What* news of the baby?'

Luminous with triumph, Mollie went on eagerly, 'You didn't know? Why, Sarah Crossworth's pregnant. Baby due in February.' She smiled wryly. 'I bet that'll knock our 'Ettie's nose right out of joint.'

Well, she hadn't expected it, had she? I mean, who would? Sarah pregnant. Pregnant! She had even been talking about making the room next to hers a nursery. So how was she supposed to get some sleep with a baby crying all night? It wasn't fair, when she'd just got comfortable. And it was no good talking to John about it; he was besotted with his wife – even more so since she got pregnant.

She looked so smug too. Married and living in a big house, with money and now a baby on the way . . . Hettie smouldered with envy. It was deliberate, of course. It was Sarah's way of making her feel her place. She had never wanted her in the house and now she was trying to make her leave.

'You should see her, Dad,' she told Howard sullenly. 'All puffed up with her own importance.'

'I never liked the look of her,' he replied meanly. 'Too dark-skinned to be trusted.'

'John adores her.'

'More fool him.'

'Thinks she can do no wrong.'

Gripping his stick firmly, Howard heaved himself to his feet. The room was damp, as was the rest of the house, the curtain over the back window permanently drawn. Beside the unlit fire the day's newspaper lay folded at the racing pages.

'He's making so much money,' Hettie went on, driven by jealousy to make mischief. 'John should help you out.'

'I don't want his help!' Howard barked. 'I can look after myself.'

Undeterred, Hettie's tone was silky: 'He never even brings you some ciggies – not even now that he owns a tobacconist's. Mean, I call that.' She stood up and kissed her father briefly on the cheek. 'I'll come and see you soon, Dad. Keep you posted.'

'There's nothing about those two I want to hear!' he called after her, secretly longing for the next injection of bile. 'There's no good'll come of them. You mark my words.'

'I want to continue the checks on the mine every month.'

'Every month?' Graham Cox, the foreman, replied

incredulously. 'There's no one round 'ere who does checks every month. Every six month more like.'

John was implacable. 'I said every month, and that's what I meant. The Albany mine should have been checked more regularly – if they had, they would have avoided that fall.'

Nodding, the foreman glanced over to the pit wheel. 'I'll see it's done. I suppose it pays to be careful – though I 'ave to say I've never been in a fall myself.'

'I have,' John said quietly.

Surprised, Graham glanced over to his employer. 'Where were that?'

'Yorkshire.'

'Yorkshire?' He repeated the word carefully, not knowing how far he could go with his questions. John Crossworth was not a man to condone familiarity at any time. 'Were it bad?'

'Three dead.'

Graham whistled between his teeth.

'You own that mine too, Mr Crossworth?'

'No,' John replied evenly. 'I worked it.' His eyes turned on the foreman. 'I was a miner for two years. That's how I learned about pits and the running of them. That's where I learned about safety – or the lack of it.' He held the man's gaze. 'I would never ask anyone who works for me to do anything, or go anywhere, that I wouldn't myself.'

It was all over the Star Inn that night: John Crossworth had been a miner. They had a boss who really knew what he was doing; a boss who was one of them.

'I wouldn't go that far,' George Lyman said drily. ''E's not exactly chatty.'

Ted Morris stared at him bleakly. 'You don't want chat in a boss, you want action.' He stared into his pint, one of the older miners, going down for his thirtieth year in the pits. 'And Crossworth's looking after us all right. More than that fat bastard Fairclough ever did.'

'I 'eard 'e were struggling to find men.'

'On the wages he's offering, he's lucky if he'll find any now that Crossworth's hiring.'

Thoughtfully, George stared towards the door. It opened briefly, the smoggy air entering for a quick look round before being excluded again.

'Crossworth can't 'ire every man in Oldham though, can 'e?'

'At the rate he's going he might soon be able to do just that,' Ted replied, wiping his mouth with the back of his hand. 'I bet that sour bugger Cotter's wetting his pants.'

Overhearing their conversation, Sammy Upton leaned over towards them. 'Word is that Cotter's thinking of changing his tack. Instead of a match with Dandry Fairclough's daughter, he's wondering if his grandson might get lucky with Hettie Crossworth.'

'Well, if 'e doesn't, 'e'll be the only lad in Oldham who 'asn't!' George replied, laughing, then staring hard at Sammy. 'You *are* joking, aren't you?'

Soberly, he shook his head. 'As God's my judge, that's the rumour.'

'Hettie Crossworth and Cotter's grandson – what a match,' Ted said despairingly. 'Although I can see that girl'd jump at it. She'd love Cotter's money, all right, and I don't suppose old Howard Crossworth would be against it either. He'd do anything to spite his son.'

'Question is, how would John Crossworth take to the idea?'

George Lyman smiled to himself. 'Oh, 'e's not stupid. 'E's probably expecting something like this; 'e's already waiting for either Fairclough or Cotter to make a move.'

'I put my money on Cotter to be the first in,' Ted said evenly. 'Fairclough's not got the upper hand at the moment and he knows it. He thought that he and Cotter were running mates, but now a new dog's come into the race and he's got competition. It's Cotter who has the grandson who's looking to get wed, so it's Cotter with all the cards.'

Sammy Upton stared at the ageing miner; 'So – what d'you reckon'll happen?'

Grimly, Ted smiled. 'I'd bet a round on Cotter trying to hitch his wagon to the rising star.'

George frowned. 'Crossworth?'

He nodded. 'Watch him. I bet he'll try and get pally with Crossworth; try and get him as a running mate –'

'Never!' Sammy said loyally. 'Not the boss.'

'I'm saying Cotter'll try,' Ted replied drily. 'I'm not saying he'll succeed.'

Wheezing into his astrakhan collar, old man Cotter sat inside John's office, waiting. He was aware that he was being watched, and several times caught a pair of eyes fixed on him through the window. Outside he could hear the sound of voices and twice turned to the door, expecting John to enter. But the voices receded and after ten minutes Cotter was about to leave when Hettie suddenly walked in.

'Oh, sorry,' she said, flustered. 'I was looking for my brother.'

'You're not the only one,' Cotter replied, smiling grimly. 'I've been waiting a while myself.'

Quickly Hettie noted the expensive clothes, the silver-topped walking cane – and then remembered the carriage waiting outside.

'Can I help, Mr . . . ?'

'Cotter.'

Cotter.

'Mr Cotter,' she repeated, savouring the name like a good meal. Cotter – rich as Croesus, owner of half of Oldham, if what she'd heard was true. Certainly owner of Marstone Hall on the hill outside the town. Cotter, with his money – and his unmarried grandson.

Her tone was placatory when she spoke again. 'I'm so sorry for the wait. I'm sure my brother will be along soon. I'm Hettie Crossworth.'

Cotter surveyed the girl as though he were assessing a building. Pretty, but not too pretty; dainty, but not too dainty for children. And quick, he could see it in her eyes. An opportunist – he'd put money on it. In fact, he might end up doing just that.

'So you're Hettie?'

She basked at what she took to be a compliment. 'You know about me?'

Everyone knows about you, Cotter wanted to reply, but checked himself.

'I heard you were a pretty girl – and they didn't lie.'

Her vanity licked its lips at the words.

'So what are you doing here?'

Hettie gave him the benefit of her most guileless smile. 'I just popped in to see if my brother wanted anything.' She had, in fact, been about to complain to John about Sarah.

'That's a good sister,' Cotter said, equally insincerely. 'I hope Mr Crossworth appreciates you.' Instinctively sensing some unspoken grievance, he pressed his chance. 'I was about to invite your brother – and his wife – to dinner.'

'Dinner!' Hettie said excitedly, then fell into a sulk. 'I don't suppose they'll accept, they never go anywhere. Now if it was me, I'd go.'

The suggestion tingled between them for an instant, but before Cotter could respond John walked in.

'Mr Cotter,' he said, his voice expressionless. 'Forgive me, but I didn't think we had an appointment.'

'We didn't –'

'He wants to invite you to dinner!' Hettie said, beside herself with excitement and eager to forge a friendship between the two men. After all, Cotter didn't seem so bad – even though she had heard John criticize him many times. He was just an old man. What harm could an old man do? Besides, he was a rich old man with an unmarried grandson . . .

'Hettie, please leave us to talk,' John said coldly.

'But –'

'Please, leave us to talk,' John repeated.

Sullenly, she moved over to old man Cotter and put out her hand. 'It was nice to meet you.'

'It was charming to meet you too,' he responded, holding her hand an instant longer than was necessary. 'And if I can persuade your brother to visit me, I would like you to come along.'

Her face flushed with eagerness. 'Oh, how lovely –'

'Hettie, I'll see you at home later,' John said quickly, nudging his sister towards the door and closing it after her.

Silently, he then moved back to his desk and glanced at the papers laid on the top, ignoring Cotter. Aware of the snub, the old man coughed hoarsely and then tapped his stick on the floor.

'Mr Crossworth . . .'

John looked up.

'. . . I came here today to welcome you – as a newcomer – to the town.'

'I was born here,' John said evenly.

'Well, perhaps not as a newcomer,' Cotter backtracked, 'but as someone who has returned to Oldham triumphant.' His stoat's head jerked forwards suddenly. 'You have done very well for yourself, young man.'

John said nothing.

'I always admire business acumen. I have it, my father had it, and his father before him. They say it's clogs to clogs in three generations, but not with the Cotters. We made money and we held on to it.' He nodded to himself, an amenable old buffer, except for the cold eyes. 'You could be a big man in this town. There's others who think they're important, but their stars are fading, whilst yours is in the ascendant.' He tapped his cane vigorously on the floor, smiling thinly. 'I would like to be a friend to you, Mr Crossworth. I could help you with contacts. I know people.'

In silence, John listened, his face betraying nothing of

the disgust he was feeling. Old man Cotter had laid off his grandfather, he remembered – not that Cotter would. He thought of the time his grandfather had come home and the way his grandmother had taken the news. They went to church to pray for help. But it never came. All that came were the bills and then the bailiffs and then the poorhouse, their son named as a poor child of the parish and put out to be apprenticed at nine.

Myriad cruelties kept the Cotter name on many people's lips. No overtime, no sick leave, a mill girl who lost an arm when caught by her hair in one of his unguarded machines. She lost her job, then her mother lost hers when she complained. Marstone Hall had been built on a multitude of such injustices and neglects, and an unstoppable, insatiable, greed.

'I know all the people I need to know, Mr Cotter,' John said at last.

'But you're not part of the social life of the town,' Cotter replied. 'Some of us are lucky that way. Bred to it . . .' He let the implication soak through, playing on any feelings of inferiority John might have. Digging for the weaknesses which would make him pliable. 'Others before you have relied on good friends to help them up in the world.'

'I have no interest in socializing,' John said steadily.

'Ah, *you* might not have, but your wife won't feel the same. The ladies – God bless them – all love a chance to dress up and chatter.'

'My wife is indisposed at present.'

Cotter's eyes flickered like two candles in a dark room. 'A happy event expected? What wonderful news. My wife must call on her.'

'My wife takes no visitors.'

Cotter's expression hardened. 'Maybe after the birth?'

'I doubt it.'

'Then perhaps,' Cotter said slowly, 'you might like to come to dinner with your sister? I'm sure Miss Crossworth would enjoy the occasion.'

Abruptly, John stood up. 'Mr Cotter, if you would excuse me, I have work to do. I appreciate your invitation, but I'm afraid we have to decline.'

Laboriously, Cotter rose to his feet. He was, John noticed, unexpectedly tall.

'I think you're making a mistake.'

'No,' John replied evenly. 'To accept would be the mistake.'

It was inexcusable! Hettie railed inwardly. The old man was just trying to be nice, and there was her brother turning down an invitation on her behalf. John had no right! She had her own life to lead, after all. She didn't have to obey him in everything. For an hour she brooded furiously, then tackled John after dinner that evening.

John was incredulous. 'Don't you realize that Cotter was responsible for our father being declared a poor child of the parish?'

'But he might be trying to make amends!'

'God!' her brother snapped angrily. 'Are you *really* that stupid? Cotter doesn't even remember what he did to our family, let alone care enough to make amends for it.'

He lowered his voice: above Sarah was sleeping. They had been told that she was expecting twins and was easily exhausted by any exertion or emotional turmoil. Not that Hettie cared about that; in fact, she had been even more difficult of late.

Exasperated, John stared at his sister.

'Just tell me – why do you want to go to dinner with the likes of Cotter?'

Her expression hardened. 'I don't see why I should be part of an old grudge –'

'But Cotter caused our family immeasurable harm.'

'It was in the past!' she challenged him.

'And that makes it all right?'

The door opened behind them, Sarah walking in.

'I heard raised voices,' she said quietly. 'What's the matter?'

'Nothing, darling,' John answered soothingly, moving over to her. 'Nothing important.'

'Mr Cotter invited us to dinner,' Hettie said, defying her brother's warning look, 'and John refused to go. He said you wouldn't want to – and he said I wouldn't either.'

'He was right,' Sarah said simply, sitting down and laying her hands across her stomach. She was tired, the skin under her eyes frail, transparent. 'You know what a bad name Cotter has in this town. Associating with him would do us no good.'

'But we don't associate with anyone!' Hettie shouted angrily. 'We don't go out –'

'You go out all the time,' John countered.

'Not with anyone important.'

'So old man Cotter seems important to you, does he?' John asked incredulously. 'Think, Hettie, think. What good would it do for us to be seen with that man? He treats his workers badly, he's greedy and immoral, and he's hated. I want to challenge his type, not join them.'

'You just know you wouldn't fit it!' Hettie retorted, beside herself. 'You're too bull-headed, and your wife's foreign –'

'Get out of this room!' John said furiously. 'Get out now before I say something I regret.'

'Oh, I'll get out!' Hettie said, hurrying to the door. 'You want to stop me getting on because you're jealous. Your way might be right for you, John, but it doesn't have to be right for me. I have my own life to lead.'

'Then lead it,' John replied coldly. 'But if you go to that dinner at Cotter's don't expect to come back here.'

Startled, Sarah glanced up at her husband. 'John . . .'

'I mean what I say. If Hettie goes to that man's house I want no more to do with her.'

Her expression defiant, Hettie faced both of them.

'It's my life.'

'Which you must live your own way,' John said gravely, 'but whilst you are under my roof you must abide by my rules. You are my sister, Hettie, and I care for you, but I cannot condone this.' Generously, he extended his hand to her. 'Think carefully, Hettie. What you decide to do now may well have consequences far beyond anything you can imagine.'

Chapter Six

It didn't take long for the news to circulate. Hettie Crossworth had been thrown out of the Queen's Road house, her brother having taken a stand with her. There were two versions of events: Hettie had been thrown out because her brother no longer wanted her there – especially now that the babies were due; and the second, that Hettie Crossworth had been causing trouble. The second was the one which was believed.

Ted Morris's wife, Iva, in height as small as a child, put it succinctly: 'She were trouble from the first. Never trust anyone with a top lip fuller than the bottom.' She leaned towards George Lyman's wife, Mollie. 'Threw in her lot with Cotter, I heard.'

'Never!'

Iva nodded, brick wall behind her, the clank of an outside bucket toilet echoing in the cold.

'She did. And after what that Cotter did to her grandfather.' Iva rubbed her chin. 'Thinks she's a cut above the rest, she does. Forgets the past, thinking she'll feather her own nest now. I'm not the only one to guess she's got her eye on that wall-eyed grandson of Cotter's.' She stared over towards some washing, hanging stiff in the cold. 'She hates Sarah Crossworth too. Not that that's unexpected. Mrs Crossworth's too much of a lady for that little tart.'

'Someone said that 'Ettie always called 'er "the Jewess" when she talked about 'er.'

Iva rolled her eyes. 'That woman took her in when no one else would have done – just because her husband asked her to. Hettie wasn't anything to her, she could easily have

60

said no. But that girl was never grateful, put on airs and graces from the start. All hat, no knickers.'

Mollie Lyman was keen to contribute: 'The 'ousemaid was telling someone that 'Ettie was always causing arguments, even when she knew it would upset Mrs Crossworth in 'er condition.'

'She probably did it *because* she knew it'd upset her,' Iva replied bitterly. 'Too much like her father, that one. Not a bit like Peggy.' She stared at the suspended washing. 'Sad, her dying like that, before John got home. She didn't even know she were ill; no one did. Not that Howard cared much – nasty old bugger.'

'John's a lot like Peggy, isn't 'e?' Mollie said suddenly. 'I can remember 'ow she used to wait for that boy coming back. We'd be talking and she'd suddenly stop and crane forwards to get a look at someone. Then she'd shrug and smile half-heartedly. "I thought it was John," she'd say.'

'If she were still alive I wonder what she'd think of all these ructions?'

Mollie considered the question carefully. 'She'd be proud of John and she'd love that beautiful wife of 'is. She'd be wanting for the babies being born and she wouldn't half tell that 'Ettie what's what. She'd 'ave told John not to take any notice of 'is father too . . .' She trailed off, unusually wistful. 'It would have all been so different if she'd lived, wouldn't it?'

'Who knows?' Iva said soberly. 'Who knows if any of us ever make that much of a difference.'

The one thing which was important – the only thing which was important – was that she stay calm. It didn't help if she got agitated, the doctor had told her. Slowly Sarah breathed in, then exhaled, then breathed in again. Breathe, inhale, exhale. Her father, Silent Samuel, never used to talk much. Hence his nickname. But when he did speak it was for a good reason. He liked to walk in the wind . . . Sarah smiled, the memory was soothing. The only time he ever left her was when he went wind walking. He said he could see pictures when it was windy and feel ghosts pushing past him.

Some people thought he was simple-minded. Odd. Strange. Mind you, many people thought that anyone foreign was strange. But he wasn't odd, just contained. Quiet in himself, set away from the clamour. He used to wear the skullcap: never even got angry when kids used to try and snatch it from his head. Knew every word of the Torah, kept one at home. At every home they ever had. And they had plenty. Liverpool, London, Birmingham. It was in Birmingham that she first met John. John Crossworth, whom her father took to, just like that. Strange, because he seldom took to anyone. But he liked John, watched him, listened to him, showed an interest. At first, Sarah was worried, anxious that he would see the stranger as someone coming to steal his daughter away from him. But it was never like that. He saw John as a continuation, the person to whom he wanted to hand over his daughter. She didn't know that then; just as she didn't know how ill her father was. It only made sense later, after he died.

Turning over, Sarah thought back to the years she had spent with him travelling, moving from place to place, looking for work ... What do you do, Mr Levenson? ... I'm a jewel cutter. A diamond cutter in particular, he'd reply ... We don't need jewel cutters ... Then what do you need? I can do anything. Just tell me what you need, and I'll do it.

He took on numerous jobs to feed them, Sarah looking after the home and him, laughing when he mimed for her. Because he *did* talk – only it was with his hands and his body: didn't seem to get on too well with words. But *miming*, in that he was eloquent. He'd mimed a dog scratching itself once, as though it had fleas, and she had laughed so hard she'd fallen off the chair and banged her head on the table.

Suddenly Sarah caught her breath, winded, missing her dead father. He had died away from home, the message coming to her in the rented flat in Birmingham where she was waiting for his return. Sorry, they said, your father's gone . . . Gone where? she had asked, baffled, knowing he would never leave her. He's dead, miss. Sorry, sorry . . .

Now, come on, be steady, she told herself, just breathe . . . John had looked after her then, married her, taken on her father's role and finally brought her to Oldham. She had never thought she would settle in the town, had been so anxious, yet gradually the people had taken to her, and after John's stand with Cotter, and Hettie's departure, their attitude had definitely warmed to her. They approved of what she and John had done.

Only the morning after Hettie left Martha Bennett came to see her. Well, actually she came to see John, but he had left by then and Sarah invited her in. The woman was anxious at first, in awe of the house and the beauty sitting opposite, then gradually, peg by peg, she nailed up a series of events and hung a story on them. Her husband was too old to work in the mine, and her last son too young. They were finding it hard. You know the kind of thing, she'd said, then checked herself. How could this woman know what she was talking about? But Sarah nodded, and well, Martha said later, she sort of made you feel like she might know *just* what you were talking about.

'We can't get by any longer and the rent's due . . .'

Sarah looked at the woman carefully. 'Where do you live?'

'Gladstone Street.'

Sarah's tone was steady. 'My husband owns the houses on Gladstone Street.'

'I'm not asking for charity –'

Soothingly, Sarah put up her hands to silence the woman. They had had one landlord in Birmingham who had thrown her and her father out one night. It was winter, ice on the street, the neighbours watching as they left just after midnight. Samuel hadn't said anything; and she had walked behind him for over a mile in the freezing cold until finally they had come to the synagogue. An old rabbi, long-coated, with forelocks, had answered the door and let them in. His rooms at the back of the synagogue were damp, a fire long since burned out. At the window he had a menorah, and he let them stay for three days until Samuel found work again.

'I don't like asking for help,' Martha said, on the defensive immediately.

'No one does,' Sarah replied. 'I'll talk to my husband when he comes home.'

'But we should pay the rent tonight. Sammy Upton's due to collect.'

'Tell Sammy to come and talk to me.'

Martha stared at Sarah helplessly. 'I don't want to cause trouble.'

'There'll be no trouble,' she replied. 'Just tell Sammy to call here and I'll sort something out for you.'

'It doesn't seem fair,' Martha said anxiously, 'to worry you in your condition.'

'You're not worrying me. I would have been more worried if you hadn't come and told me about your problems and I'd found out afterwards,' Sarah replied honestly. 'My husband's a fair man. He'll help you.'

'But what about Sammy Upton?' Martha said, struggling to explain. 'It's like this, Mrs Crossworth. I don't want people knowing ... you know, that we can't pay ... and I don't want to face Mr Upton and have to argue the toss with him.' She leaned forward. 'Oh, I know you said send him round to you. But you know what people are like, they talk, and well ...'

Without speaking, Sarah rose to her feet and left the room. Moments later she returned and handed Martha some money.

'Give Sammy Upton this, and then we'll sort it out

privately later,' Sarah said evenly. 'There's no reason why anyone else should know about our arrangement.'

'I can't thank you enough, Mrs Crossworth,' Martha said, eyes lowered, wrong-footed by the unexpected kindness. 'I'll pay you back, I promise. Just as soon as I can, I'll pay you back.'

Thinking of the incident, Sarah stirred in her seat. The pregnancy was draining her, making her weary only hours after she awoke. Slowly, she forced herself to breathe regularly, staring at the clock over the mantelpiece and hearing the sounds of a milk cart passing down Park Road. In a moment there would be a knock at the back door and the maid would answer, swopping gossip with the milk boy. Gradually, Sarah felt her eyes closing, sleep crowding her consciousness out. If she just closed her eyes for a moment, she would feel rested . . .

Then suddenly she imagined John there, taking out his gold watch and tapping the glass face. Behind him, somewhere, St Mark's clock chimed the hour and he listened, head tilted to one side . . . Sarah's hands slid over her stomach . . . He was talking, or was he? Saying something about Queen's Road and about how he wanted to live there one day . . . Suddenly they were in the High Street, passing the site once known as Cock House Ford, then moving on to the Co-operative Society Fountain, the water falling sweet in the sunshine. John was walking next to her with his head down. It was summer, streets hot with people, a dog scratching itself at a corner and moments later a delivery boy rode past on his bicycle and whistled a tune from a music-hall song.

Then, in her dream, John suddenly took her hand and lifted it to his face, resting it against his cheek, his skin as hot as the sunlight.

Whilst Sarah dreamed, John was at the mine, watching the next shift going down in the pit lift. Slowly the mechanism lowered the men, a few stragglers left at the gate, hoping that some men had fallen sick and there was a job going begging. Beside John, Graham Cox blew on his hands to warm them. It was one forty in the afternoon, a wind coming fast over the Pennines, Oldham darkening rapidly with the menace of rain.

'Cold, innit?'

John nodded, although he was bare-headed and wearing only a suit.

'I heard your missus is about due. Twins, they say.'

'That's right, Graham,' John replied distantly, watching the pit wheel turning. 'You had that checked again for me?'

'Like you said, every month.'

Glancing upwards, John took in the darkening sky. 'I don't like the look of that. We've had more than enough rain lately. It makes me worry about the water down below.'

The foreman followed his employer's gaze upwards. Across the dank sky a few clouds – black as crow's feathers – blew in from the hills.

'Levels were fine when they were checked,' he said firmly, impressed by his boss's concern. No one else cared about his men as much as Crossworth. 'Nowt to worry about there.'

Frowning, John glanced over to the men standing patiently at the pit gates. 'Nothing for them?'

'Nothing today.'

'I don't like to see men out of work,' John replied evenly. 'Are you sure we've nothing?'

Graham shook his head. 'We 'ad a full turnout today. No one ill. Men like to work at this pit, Mr Crossworth. They'll not give up their spot easily.'

They'll not give up their spot easily . . . John remembered similar words being spoken to him when he was a miner. Only eighteen, jostled and chivvied by the other men, teased about his reserve. The Orphan, they called him, because he would never talk about his family, or where he had come from. Give it to the Orphan, they'd say, looks like the lad could use a good meal. But for all they teased him, they also watched out for him, and when John went looking for lodgings, one of the miners took him in.

'My wife can't cook too good, but the house is clean, and it'll be cheap, lad.'

He was diffident, defensive, all his belongings in a roll on his back.

'I'll pay the going rate.'

The miner had laughed loudly. 'Aye, you will that,' he'd assured. 'There's no one can afford to do favours round 'ere.'

But they did, of course, charging John the minimum rent and feeding him as well as their own children. He slept on a straw mattress under the stairs, his knees slightly bent because of the lack of space, his head against the wall. In summer it was stifling, in winter chilling, but it was out of the weather and it meant that John could save. And dream ... Quiet and industrious, in his spare time he took on odd jobs around the house, and ran errands for the widow Carthage down the street. He could decorate too, and clean, and within months almost anything that anyone wanted doing, John did.

And all the time he saved, dreaming in that space under the stairs about a bed which was so big he could stretch out his legs and never even reach the bottom. Day after day, as John laboured up on roofs, or down in the pit, he focused on his aim – Queen's Road. Then one day he was sitting on the end of the gable of someone's house, staring across to the horizon as though mesmerized, until a passing miner called up to him.

'Aye, John! What the 'ell you looking at?'

'My future,' John had answered quietly.

'Your WHAT?'

'MY FUTURE!' he had shouted back unexpectedly, rising to his feet and beginning work again.

Oh, he was an odd one, all right. Everyone agreed on

that. But there was nothing bad about him, nothing wicked. Just different. Then one day John Crossworth just upped and left, taking another step towards his future, waiting on that horizon for him.

'Mr Crossworth?'

John's attention snapped back to the present as he turned to his foreman.

'Sorry, what did you say?'

'It's raining,' Graham replied. 'You'll get soaked.'

Smiling, John nodded and then hurried in, the winter sky low and angry above him.

Below ground. A third of a mile below. The pit, dark, confined, the turn of the pit wheel an echo from above. Water dripping, steel rails laid out to push the stacked carts along, a row of candles making light. Almost like a church. Almost.

'. . . it's from the music 'all,' George Lyman said, lifting up his pick and beginning to whistle again.

Ted frowned. 'It's no tune that any bugger could put a name to. You never could whistle.'

'I can whistle good as anyone,' George retorted brusquely, shovelling coal into one of the pulley carts and then stretching up. The space was six feet in height, a comfortable place to work where a man could stand up. But before long they would have to move on, tunnelling further along, the space narrow, constricting, headroom limited.

'I 'eard 'bout Martha Bennett.'

Ted paused, glanced over his shoulder. The shadows of the men were distorted, lumbering silhouettes in the candlelight.

'*What* about Martha Bennett?'

' 'Bout Mrs Crossworth 'elping 'er out.' George frowned. 'My missus told me that she wanted to keep it quiet.'

'Who? Mrs Crossworth?'

'Nah, Martha!'

'Keep *what* quiet?'

George sighed expansively. ''Bout Mrs Crossworth lending 'er money to pay the rent.'

'She never!'

George nodded. 'She did. Just so Martha wouldn't 'ave to tell Sammy Upton she 'adn't got it.'

'It'd have cut no ice with Upton. He's used to hearing people can't pay.'

'That's why Mrs Crossworth lent 'er the money.'

'I hope she can afford to lose it.'

'Nah, Ted, that's not fair. Martha's paid 'er back today,' George countered. 'She was full of it, the missus, all 'bout what a lady Mrs Crossworth was –'

'Until the next time,' Ted added slyly.

'Martha never asked for 'elp before,' George snapped. 'You're a sour bugger, and no mistake.'

'I'm just wondering what her husband would make of it,' Ted replied phlegmatically.

'Crossworth adores 'is wife, you know that as well as anyone.'

'Which is why Martha were clever enough to go and see Mrs Crossworth instead of him,' Ted retorted, turning round suddenly. 'What's that?'

'What?'

Both men listened.

'Nothing,' Ted said finally. 'I just thought I heard something.'

George was still thinking about their previous conversation. 'You always think the worst of people.'

'Eh?' Ted snapped.

'You – you always think the worst,' George repeated, lifting his pick and slamming it into the coalface.

'Well, I were right 'bout Hettie Crossworth.'

'We were *all* right 'bout 'Ettie Crossworth,' George replied drily, thinking about the recent gossip. 'Fancy 'er going off to dinner at the Cotters on 'er own. My missus said it were a disgrace.'

'I saw her walking with Cotter's grandson only yesterday,' Ted replied, leaning against the coalface and coughing hoarsely. His skin was sheened with coal dust and sweat, his ageing arms sinewy.

'It won't do 'er a bit of good,' George replied flatly. 'Cotter were only interested in 'Ettie if 'e could get pally with 'er brother. Without Crossworth, she doesn't stand a chance of nailing the grandson.'

'Not that she won't try,' Ted responded cynically. 'She were clinging to him like a lifebelt when I saw them.'

'Man overboard!' George said, laughing. 'I don't fancy that lad's chances if 'Ettie Crossworth's got 'er claws into 'im.'

Sarah woke to find John watching her. Smiling, she turned on her side and stretched out her hand. He took it, and then lay down on the bed next to her, moulding his body against hers. The day had folded, evening coming in cold and unwelcome. In the grate a fire burned, curtains drawn against the town outside.

'How are you, my love?'

'Tired, but otherwise fine.'

'No problems?'

'No problems,' she replied, smiling. 'But I don't think it will be too long now.'

'The doctor said a fortnight.'

She rubbed her head against the crook of his arm. 'I don't think they'll wait that long.'

Sighing, John slid off his shoes and pulled the counterpane over both of them. The semi-darkness was soothing, the warmth making him unusually relaxed.

'I love you.'

'I'm glad,' she answered, smiling again as she drew in the scent of him and slid her hand down his back. Please, she prayed silently, don't let anything disturb us for a while; no calls, no sudden demands which will call him away. Just let me have him for a little while . . .

The fire flickered in the grate, making ghostly shadows on the wall. John's breathing was low and regular. She thought, for a moment, that he was sleeping.

'We did it, didn't we?'

'What, darling?'

His breath was moist against her neck. 'We made the dream come true. You and I. Just the two of us.'

'Yes, we made it come true.'

'And nothing will spoil it,' John said firmly.

'No, darling, nothing will spoil it.'

Outside the window the wind started up, the park trees sabre-rattling their branches against the cold.

'I would die without you,' he said simply.

Her hand pressed against his back. 'Why did you say that?'

'Because it's the truth,' he answered.

Slowly she stroked his back and then his arm, his hand sliding across her stomach and resting there. Curled against each other they listened to the evening's slow descent, the night dark as a warrior coming out to fight.

Chapter Seven

It was a bitter night, cold even for February, the winds coming down from the Pennines and slicing into the Oldham streets. Down by the pithead, the lamps hissed and spluttered in the gale, the men going down for the night shift. Slowly the pit wheel was turned, the lift lowered: air rank, the damp smell of coal making the men cough as the cage shuddered to a halt underground.

No one was talking. Not that the miners did talk that much at night. Especially when it was this cold. Walking along the tunnels towards the coalface, they felt the air pinching at their cracked nostrils, a slow dripping of water echoing a long way off. After walking almost a quarter of a mile, they reached the coalface, George Lyman dropping his bag and billycan and rubbing his hands together briskly.

'Bloody 'ell, it gets flaming colder.'

Beside him, Ted Morris grunted, pulled out some candles and lit them, watching as they spluttered fitfully into life.

'Our lad's starting down pit next week,' George offered, putting his pick over his shoulder and ducking as he moved towards the coalface. 'It's no bloody life for 'im, but what else is there?'

'If he wanted to better himself, he could go in the church,' Ted said sourly.

'Like 'ell!' George snapped. 'Can you see my lad in church?'

'What's wrong with it?' Ted replied, ducking and following George to the coalface. 'I mean, tell me honestly – if you had your time again, would you go down the pit?'

'No,' George agreed, 'but I wouldn't be a bleeding priest either.'

Ted jerked his head away, coughed hoarsely. 'How old is your lad?'

'Fourteen.'

'Seems like only yesterday he were a nipper.'

'They grow up,' George replied sadly.

'Aye, that they do.'

They arranged the candles to give the maximum light, then George whistled down the tunnel to where the other men were waiting, fifty or so feet away.

'Where's bird?'

A long way away, a voice answered him. 'With us. Get your own bloody bird.'

'It were my bird!' George snapped, aggrieved. 'I got that bloody canary myself off t'market.'

'Well, now we've got it!' came back the answer. 'It's singing too.'

George looked at Ted and rolled his eyes. 'It's supposed to let on if there's gas down here, not do a bloody music-'all turn.' Spitting on both hands he then lifted his pick and swung it over his head.

The sound slammed dully underground.

Above ground, the wind was increasing in violence, two chimneys on Forshaw Street toppled, a cart which had been carrying coal almost turning over at the corner, the horse panicked by the flapping of a loosened tarpaulin. At around midnight it began to rain again, the water flinging itself against the windows, the cobbles slicked, greasy with the downpour.

Inside the terraces, rugs were hurriedly pushed against the bottoms of the doors, the wooden entrances of the outside toilets rattling, Martha Bennett's cat coming in with half its tail missing.

'Bloody rats!' she said angrily, cleaning off the blood, the animal swearing warningly at her. 'Rats always come out in force when it's this windy. It's a bad night all round.'

No one argued with her, the moon hurriedly rising,

clouds pushed away impatiently as the wind continued to quicken. Almost blown off their feet, the few remaining pedestrians hurried into the terraced streets and slammed their doors, the vast pit wheel and the wooden shaft over the pit mouth a bleak shadow, buffeted mercilessly. The moon was evil that night, its cold light striking the stacked banks of coal; the sad puddles; and the brick hut tucked against the wall beyond, whilst below the men continued to work, a sense of foreboding creeping along the tunnels to join them.

At one in the morning underground, the candles were suddenly blown out, George swearing and fumbling to relight them, Ted leaning exhausted against the wall. His face was gaunt as he coughed and then spat blood into his handkerchief.

Anxiously George lifted a candle and looked into his face. 'You want to see doctor about that.'

'And get laid off?' Ted countered, sliding down the wall and drawing his knees up to his chin, his head bowed.

The coal was blinking around them, in patches shiny as jet, a trickle of water running down the centre of the tunnel, the faraway sounds of the other men disembodied, remote, the noise of the pit ponies' hoofs scuffing eerily in the distance.

Silently George poured his tea and offered some to Ted.

Ted's expression was blank. 'I don't like it.'

'Liar! You love tea.'

'Not the sodding tea!' Ted replied, coughing again. 'It's this place. Listen . . .' He cocked his head to one side. 'Quiet, isn't it?'

'What did you expect down 'ere, a band?'

Unmoved, Ted looked at his companion. The cold was intense, the coal dust worked into the skin of his cheeks and the pores of his nose.

'Ever been in a fall, George?'

He sipped the tea. 'Nah. Why?'

'I were. Once . . .' Ted's gaze moved down the tunnel as though he were looking for something. 'There were a feeling about the place before it happened. It were quiet like.'

The words settled round them, the candlelight flickering in the quick draughts, making the shadows of the seated men vast, Gothic against the low coal arch of the ceiling.

'After it happened, I told our Iva not to worry. "Lightning never strikes twice," I said.'

Affected by Ted's unease, George shifted around uncomfortably.

'You're a cheerful bugger, and no mistake.'

'Once you've heard it, you never forget it,' Ted went on, ignoring him. 'It's like the mine knows what's going to happen before you do.'

'Bloody 'ell!' George snapped. 'Stop your dooming and glooming, we've got work to do.'

His face grim, Ted reached out and clasped his companion's arm. 'There's going to be a fall, George.' His skin crawled with fear. '. . . I know it.' Wide-eyed, Ted stared down the tunnel, listening, then hurriedly struggled to his feet, ducking his head automatically under the low roof. 'Come on, let's get out of here!'

Angrily George tried to wrench his arm free. Ted had obviously cracked up; he was panicking, George thought. A miner got that way sometimes – and Ted had been poorly for weeks.

'Calm down, lad, and let's get on with our work.'

'There's going to be a fall,' Ted repeated, staring into George's face.

It was his calmness which finally convinced George, and for an instant he was tempted to drop his pick and run down the tunnel, making for the mine shaft and the exit. It would take a while to get there – they were a long way underground, almost a quarter of a mile along the tunnel – and even if they ran they might not make it in time.

God! he thought suddenly. What was he thinking of? He was getting as windy as old Ted.

Impatiently, he shrugged off the miner's grip. 'Leave off! Let's get on with it. We've work to do.'

'George, listen to me!' Ted implored him. 'I tell you –'

In mid-sentence he stopped, a sudden rumble silencing him. It seemed to come from a long way away, almost miles, gathering volume like thunder. Transfixed, the two men stood immobilized, both turning in the direction of the sound. Then there was a sudden violent exclamation of noise – cries, names called, the ponies whinnying – all within a fragment of an instant before the roof of the tunnel fell inwards, coal landing heavy on the backs of the men and snuffing out the candles.

Every one.

Restless, Sarah turned over in bed and reached out, trailing her hand down her husband's arm. The wind had kept her awake, that and her pregnancy, the swollen weight of belly dragging on her, even lying down. Out on the landing she could hear the clock ticking, and then the slow sonorous sounding of the chimes. One thirty in the morning, and all's well.

Or was it? Sarah wondered, staring upwards, the wind lashing against the windows, the moonlight sliding meanly through a gap in the curtains. Idly her hands rested on her stomach. So little time left, she had been told, maybe a fortnight, maybe less. And twins. She smiled at the thought. Two babies.

'How do you know?' she had asked the doctor.

'Two heartbeats,' he had replied simply.

Two heartbeats. Two hearts. Two people ... Again, Sarah smiled to herself. Would it be a boy and girl, or two girls, or two boys? Oh Lord, what did it matter what sex they were? Her hand slid down her husband's side and came to rest against his thigh; John sighed, breathed in deeply, then lapsed back into sleep. Two sons would be wonderful, Sarah thought, two boys to inherit their father's ambitions. Would they be like him? Same high cheekbones, same grey eyes? Same look?

The wind snatched at the window, battering a branch against the pane, the black shape unsettling in the semi-dark. Unsettled, Sarah shivered. She had never liked the wind since childhood, since that long lonely stretch of years when she and her father had been together. When it was windy he was animated and went out to walk. He liked the wind, liked to feel it on his skin. But Sarah didn't like it because it meant that her father left her. Wherever they were, at whatever time, he left her.

The branch slashed at the window again, jerking Sarah into complete wakefulness. There was something wrong, she realized, and it wasn't just her fear of the weather. She touched her stomach gingerly, stroking the babies back to sleep, and then finally, exhausted, she closed her eyes and slept.

'Jesus!' George shouted. 'Dear God, 'elp me!' He was scrambling desperately under the fall of coal, pushing it away from him, the darkness damp and silent around him. 'Ted! TED!'

Silence.

Panicked, he kept scratching at the coal, seeing nothing in the dense blackness, his fingernails ripped and bleeding.

'TED!' he shouted again, then paused, feeling something soft and yielding.

His eyes were wide open, but there was no light, no sound. Urgently his hands moved over the softness trying to recognize what he felt. It was Ted's arm, his fingers splayed open.

Unmoving.

Startled, George dug frantically at the fallen coal, finally pulling the miner out and moving the coal away from Ted's face, then feeling for a pulse at his neck.

77

There was nothing. Only something warm and wet against his fingers. Blood. Ted's blood.

Slumping back on his haunches, George moaned once and then stared blankly into the darkness. It was absolute. Without a prick of light. No illumination. No sound. He was almost a quarter of a mile underground; earth and houses pressing down on top of him, the air already rank.

From the loss of sound and sight he could have been buried alive. George stared ahead blindly, realization coming fierce and brutal. He *was* buried alive.

She thought at first that it was the clock ticking in her dream, and then, disorientated, Sarah roused herself and saw her husband hurriedly pulling open the window to answer someone's knocking. The wind lashed into the room immediately, the rain mottling the curtains as John leaned out and looked down into the street below.

His hair was flapping wildly around his head, his eyes screwed up against the onslaught as he shouted: 'I CAN'T HEAR YOU!'

'THERE'S BEEN A FALL AT THE PIT!' the man called up, Sarah hearing the words and struggling to her feet to join her husband at the window.

'HOW BAD?' John called down.

'THEY GOT MOST OF THE MEN OUT – BUT THERE ARE TWO STILL TRAPPED DOWN THERE. GEORGE LYMAN AND TED MORRIS.'

John tensed.

'I'M COMING OVER!' he shouted, then felt Sarah's hand on his arm.

'John –'

He turned to her, shook his head, then shouted to the waiting man below, 'TELL THEM I'M COMING.' Closing the window, he reached for his clothes. 'I have to go.'

'I know,' she said reluctantly, passing him his shoes. 'But don't go down the pit. Please.'

'Sarah, I can't promise you anything.'

'I'm pregnant, John, and I couldn't survive if anything happened to you.'

'And I couldn't live with myself if I didn't do everything to help those men,' he replied, touching her cheek. 'I know the mine, Sarah. I know it as well as the miners do. I won't take any risks, believe me.'

She leaned her head into his hand, rubbing her cheek against his palm.

'The miners might not be trapped any more. The others might already have got them out.'

'Maybe, maybe not. I'll know when I get to the pit,' he replied, pulling on his coat and standing up. 'If they have been brought out, I'll be back soon.' He smiled distantly. 'Put something warm on, Sarah. You'll catch cold.'

'I'm coming with you.'

'No –'

'John, I'm coming with you.'

He put one hand over her mouth and then laid his other hand on her stomach. Under his fingers he could feel a timorous movement and closed his eyes, deeply moved.

'Sarah, stay here and stay safe,' he said at last. 'I've told you, I'll come back.'

'But –'

'No buts,' he commanded her. 'I've told you, I'll come back.'

The pit wheel was a huge black circle in the darkness, the paraffin lamps spluttering in the wind, the pit mouth gaping with a yellow sulphurous light as John made his way over to it and looked down. There was a group of men already standing around the pithead and all fell silent when they saw him, a snaggle of women standing a little way away from the miners. Waiting.

John glanced round, then signalled for the foreman, Graham Cox. 'What happened?'

The man's eyes were running with the cold, two white stripes marking the blackened face.

'We were just about to follow Ted and George to coal-face. We got first 'aul in, ponies nearly got it back to shaft, and then there were this sound.' He coughed, and then spat on the ground. 'I thought they'd got out. Thought I 'eard 'em following, but they weren't ... When the fall stopped, we went back like – to get 'em – but it's blocked. There's no bloody way through –'

John could hear the panic in his voice and interrupted him.

'How far along the tunnel is the fall?'

''Bout a quarter-mile.'

'At the narrowest part of the tunnel?'

'Widest.'

'But surely the tunnel was shored up?'

'Aye. Like it always were,' Graham replied, frowning. 'We'd 'ad no trouble before, none at all. That pit were one of the easier ones.'

Without replying, John stared down into the mine, the yellow light flushing upwards and highlighting his angled face.

'There's *never* been a fall at this pit,' he said, almost to himself. 'I was told that when I bought it. "Safe as houses," they told me.' Quickly he glanced back to Graham. 'How much air have they got?'

'Enough to last 'em an hour, I reckon. Not longer.'

'If they're both alive,' John said evenly.

'Aye,' agreed the foreman, 'if they're both alive.'

Ignoring the miners watching him, John took off his jacket and moved towards the waiting lift, the men following him. In silence he pulled the gate closed behind them, the giant ebony-coloured wheel turning as the elevator lowered, the waiting women watching their men go in silence.

It shuddered to a halt at the bottom of the shaft, John opening the gate and then glancing down. Carefully he took off his gold watch and chain and wrapped it in his handkerchief before moving quickly towards the mouth of the tunnel. The cold and damp were pulverizing, the smell of wet coal overwhelming, making him cough as he cupped a hand around his candle and moved on. The tunnel widened, then narrowed, pit props holding up the shaft, the air moist and acrid with the ever-constant dripping of water.

In silence they walked for a couple of minutes, then John held up the candle and looked ahead. Where the first fall had been there was little debris, but as he moved on he could see a pony's leg jerking and twitching under a pile of coal. Alerted, the miners moved forward and began to dig, John glancing round, his head dipped down under the low ceiling.

'Careful!' he cautioned them. 'Make as little noise as possible. We don't want to set off another fall.'

In silence the foreman watched with him as the men dug out the ponies – one dead, the other lying with its eyes wide open, unresponsive.

His voice expressionless, John glanced at the man standing next to him. 'How much further in?'

Graham pointed ahead. ''Bout thirty yards.'

Nodding, John moved on, motioning for the other men to stay back, then he suddenly paused, listening. Nothing. Not a sound, apart from the slow, incessant dripping of water. Cautiously he called out the miners' names and then waited for a response. Again nothing. Only silence – and then a low, far-off rumble.

'Jesus! There's going to be another fall!' Graham said hoarsely, glancing over to his boss in terror.

But John Crossworth's face remained expressionless, and when the rumble finally ceased he moved on, only stopping when he reached the blocked part of the tunnel. The coal fall had banked off any entrance to the mine beyond – and any possible exit. From the floor to the six-foot-high ceiling there was nothing but dense black coal. Putting down his candle, John motioned for the foreman to do the same, and then walked over to the fall, pulling away the first loose pieces.

'Ted! . . . George!' he called. Then waited, pressing his ear against the coal slide. Nothing.

'We could use picks,' Graham suggested hopefully.

'And we could start another fall,' John replied. 'I know it would be quicker, but I don't want to risk it.'

Nodding, the foreman stared at him, his expensive trousers and the rolled up white shirt sleeves. He had had little to do with John Crossworth since he had bought the mine, had just been glad that the pit was being worked again, and even more grateful for the wage he could take home weekly. Crossworth was a fair boss, but an odd one really, married to a foreigner. A cold fish, he had said, and the other men had agreed.

The same men who were now stuck in the pit . . . They'd been wrong about their boss, as Graham had been wrong. After all, how many other owners came down the mines to help dig their workers out? How many others kept their distance – like old man Cotter and Dandry Fairclough? Denying responsibility, even refusing to keep up the widows' assistance payments? Fat cats in Up Holland and Upper Mill, light years away from the sweat and the cold of mining; up in the sun, never under the earth.

But John Crossworth was.

'Come on, help me,' he said to the foreman. 'Don't use the picks, we'll dig.'

In minutes, the sweat was pooling off them, the air stale, the cold sticking in their lungs along with the coal dust. Coughing, John wiped his mouth with the back of his hand and began to dig again, then paused, his head on one side.

'Listen – did you hear that?'

Graham stopped digging, breathing laboriously. 'What?'

'I thought I heard a voice.'

He stared at his boss, his voice low. 'There's not much time left,' he said simply. 'There's going to be no air in there before long. Why don't we use picks, Mr Crossworth? It'd be quicker.'

John weighed up the situation. He was sure he had heard

a voice a moment ago. Someone was still alive in there – but if they kept on digging manually they might not get there in time; and if they used the picks they might start off another coal fall . . . He had the foreman to think about, and the other men behind them in the tunnel, waiting for his call – as well as two trapped miners. He thought suddenly of Sarah, blinked, then stared ahead at the evil high banking of coal. I love you, he thought, I love you, but I have to do what I believe to be right.

Turning, he caught hold of a discarded pick, Graham hurriedly stopping him.

'Nay, you're no miner.'

John looked at the man steadily. 'I was a worker long before I was a boss. Now come on,' he said firmly. 'Let's dig them out.'

Despite what anyone said, Sarah was not going to remain at home. She had spent almost an hour staring out of the window and over the sound of the damning wind she could hear raised voices. The streets were freckled with light, lamps burning in all the windows, others held aloft as people hurried towards the pit. The news was out, and nearly every family in the town knew, or was related to, someone who worked in the mine.

She dressed absent-mindedly, then sat by the window again. Then stood up, then sat down, biting her hand. He wouldn't go down into the pit, surely? Oh, but he would, she knew that. He would feel obliged to go, to help his men. His men. His men! She thought furiously, what about his wife? His children? She touched her stomach, felt a movement, then tried to calm herself. John would come home. He had promised her, and he always kept his promises.

But she still couldn't rest and walked to the front door, pulling it open, the wind tearing at it and slamming it back against the wall behind. Startled, Sarah jumped, snatched up her coat and headed for the pit.

*   *   *

George Lyman was finding breathing difficult. Short, laboured, and he had stopped calling for help. It was not easy to die, he thought at first, but then, as he grew weaker and the air thicker, he found himself skipping in and out of reality. His wife was with him at one point, their youngest son – long dead of the flu – running a hoop down Gladstone Terrace. Then he was swimming in the Irwell, trying to catch a minnow in his cap.

Suddenly fully conscious again, George felt around for the candle and then tried to light it. But the matches were damp and never flared into life. Exhausted, he lay down again and thought about Ted lying beside him, wondering why he wasn't afraid of a corpse . . . Corpse, my arse! Ted said, aghast. It's your round when we get out of here.

Groggily George smiled into the darkness, the image of Ted fading, the reality of his death coming as black as the air around him, and try as he might, he couldn't stop the tears coming quick and unwanted under his lids.

The miners' wives saw Sarah coming, rushing over to her as she passed through the pit gates.

'You should be home, lass.'

'I have to be here!' she said firmly, moving towards the pithead, her tall figure unearthly, illuminated by the sulphurous light below. 'Where's my husband?'

They didn't answer her so she went further forward, peering down into the mine.

'Come away!' Martha Bennett said sharply. 'This is no place for you.'

'I have as much right to be here as you have!' Sarah countered furiously. 'My man is down there too.'

'Aye, and he wouldn't be pleased to know you were here in your condition,' Martha replied, her tone hard. 'I'll see you back home, Mrs Crossworth.'

Furiously, Sarah shook the hand off her arm, the wind snatching at the dark length of her hair.

'How many men are trapped?'

'Two. George Lyman and Ted Morris.'

She nodded, laid her hand on her stomach and pulled her coat around her.

'So no one's been brought out then?'

The oldest woman shook her head. Sarah knew her, Dora Coles, a widow who had lost her husband and her elder son. A woman whose last remaining child was down the mine now.

'They'll get them out,' Sarah said evenly, 'they *will*.'

'Aye.'

As she stood facing the miners' wives, the wind was making her unsteady on her feet, her pregnancy tiring her. Only determination was holding her upright.

'You've got a good man there,' Dora told her admiringly. 'Not many bosses would do what John Crossworth's done.' She glanced towards the huge black wheel dominating the night sky. 'You should go home and wait for him there.'

'He said he would be all right,' Sarah said stubbornly, 'and he will be. I'll wait for him here.'

'He might –'

'I'll wait for him here!' she repeated, pulling her coat around her and leaning against the casing of the wheel. 'We'll *all* wait here.'

His breathing was thick now, breathing treacle, letting his mind swim. Dying pore by pore. Maybe they wouldn't let his boy come down the pit now, George thought. It was a mug's game, after all. Work not fit for a dog, let alone a man. He thought suddenly of the pit ponies – bright little beggars – and hoped they'd got out. Didn't like to think of them caught, dying slow like him.

Then he heard it – the clink of a pick on coal. Like music. Dry-mouthed, George turned his head, nudging the dead man next to him. Someone's coming, he told Ted, not long now. But then another sound followed, a dark, uncaring crashing of drums, drowning the sweet music out.

Because – just as they were about to break through – there was another fall.

Sarah didn't hear it above ground – none of the miners' wives did – but they all sensed it and together gathered around the mine shaft, staring helplessly into the dark below. There was a crashing sound, then silence, then the noise of men shouting and a rush of air, coming foul up the shaft and into the stormy night.

'God!' Sarah said startled, and clinging to the wheel next to her. 'What was it – another fall?' She glanced around her, at the white faces chalked with moonlight. 'My husband's down there!'

Unmoving they watched her, seeing her lay her hands on her stomach as though protecting the children she carried, then together they all heard the sound of the lift being winched upwards, the vast black metal wheel creaking round, the sound sour and unearthly in the wild night.

Inch by inch they watched the lift come up. Each woman staring for her man, each face fixed, waiting for the one face above all others. And beside them, Sarah watched too. She saw the lift come up to the pithead, the ranks of men pressed against the gate, the rows of heads, and as they spilled out into the pit yard she studied each one.

They stumbled out, blackened and stunned, one by one claimed by their wives, the others silent and watchful. Then suddenly the lift was empty, and began its slow descent again. Breathing unevenly, Sarah stood in the wind and waited, saw the light lessen and heard the gates slam closed at the bottom again. Surely if John was trapped, they wouldn't leave him? He hadn't left them, so surely they wouldn't leave him? They must be bringing him up, she thought, suddenly elated. They were coming up! The two trapped miners were alive, and so was John.

Agonizingly slowly, the lift was winched up. Sarah's eyes fixed on the gate as the foreman slid it open. Slumped at the back of the lift was George Lyman, waxen but alive.

And beside him there were two stretchers: on one was the dead body of Ted Morris and on the other John Crossworth, a dark mark running across the left side of his forehead.

And in that instant Sarah blacked out.

'Push! Push!' Martha Bennett said firmly, 'Come on, Sarah, the babies are coming.'

She turned over, desperately trying to wave the woman away. 'No, not now –'

'They're coming whether you like it or not!' Martha replied, drawing the makeshift curtains in the pit hut and signalling to the woman next to her to bring some boiling water.

'John . . .' Sarah said brokenly, clutching at her stomach and moaning with pain. 'John . . .'

'He's all right.'

Sarah's eyes were black in the chalk-white face. 'I saw him!' she shouted. 'I saw him. He was dead.' She gritted her teeth suddenly against the pain, automatically drawing up her knees.

'Ted Morris was dead. Your husband's alive,' Martha said firmly. 'Now, concentrate on having your babies.'

'But I saw him!' Sarah insisted. 'He was on a stretcher. He was dead.'

'He was knocked out,' Martha replied, her tone emphatic. 'That second fall caught them just as they were coming out with George. A pit prop hit Mr Crossworth – but it didn't kill him,' she said, stroking Sarah's forehead. 'He's alive.'

She stared up at the woman helplessly. 'He's alive?'

Martha nodded.

'He's alive,' Sarah repeated, arching her back with pain, her mouth opening and closing silently.

He was alive . . . John Crossworth was alive. Her husband had kept his promise and had come home to her. Through the pain Sarah could only think of him, of the fact that the man whom she loved beyond life itself, was alive. Two hours later the first of her children was born. Ten minutes afterwards, the second came into the world. They were boys.

Jubilant, Martha laid them in their mother's arms. Then she suddenly frowned and leaned down towards them, her expression curious.

'What is it?' Sarah asked anxiously.

'I would never have believed it if I hadn't seen it with my own eyes,' Martha said gently. 'This one's his father's son all right . . .' She pulled back the rough blanket which covered the baby's head. 'Look.'

On the child's forehead – on the left-hand side – was a dark smudge, like a soot mark. And it was in exactly the same place where John Crossworth had been hit by the falling pit prop only hours before.

Chapter Eight

John closed the pit the day after the fall, swearing never to reopen it as the fall had weakened other seams and he was not prepared to risk further deaths. Ted Morris had died down there, and no one else's life was ever to be endangered. When they brought up George Lyman he was badly dehydrated and had internal injuries, but in time he recovered and when he asked John for help, his son was given an office job above ground. A soft job, George said, thank God for that. That terrible night, Iva Morris waited at the head of the pit until her husband's body was brought out. Then she moved over to the stretcher and put her shawl over his face so that no one else would see his injuries. After that, she walked home. She never remarried.

Ninety-nine miners were laid off that night. One died. For the sake of the one dead man, the ninety-nine were never again put at risk. They took the news badly, but John was adamant. They lost their jobs; John lost a fortune.

'I told you,' Dandry Fairclough said with triumph, 'that bugger was too lucky for it to last. He must have lost a mint.'

Old man Cotter was no less gleeful: he had been snubbed by John Crossworth, his plans for the future scuppered. And worse had followed; his doltish grandson falling in love with the sluttish Hettie Crossworth. Try as he had, nothing would convince Arnold to drop her; threats were no use, neither was reason. In the end old man Cotter told his grandson that he was cutting him out of the will. Recklessly, Arnold told him to go ahead; that it would make no difference to Hettie because she loved him and would stand by him. Hettie had other ideas.

White-hot with fury, she sidled over to see Cotter and explained how in love they were and how she would make Arnold a wonderful wife. Fine, Cotter replied sourly, you can still make him a wonderful wife without my money . . .

'. . . But, Mr Cotter, we love each other.'

Cotter regarded her coldly. 'Listen, my dear,' he said, his stoat's eyes alert, 'I know how much you ladies like to have pretty things. I understand, and what with the trouble with your brother and your rushed removal from Queen's Road, life must seem a little fraught at the moment.'

She was all sly attention.

'So I have a proposition to make,' Cotter went on. 'My grandson, Arnold . . .'

She smiled at the name.

'. . . is infatuated with you, and I understand why. But there are other considerations about his future, which I won't burden you with, but which force me to take certain steps.' He paused. 'Suffice it to say, I feel I can offer you a nice little nest egg if you will agree to give up the boy.'

Hettie glanced away, as though shocked. In reality she was thinking. Arnold was about to get disinherited, which was no use to her. Love in a cottage with Arnold was not how she saw her future; she had wanted the Cotter name and the Cotter fortune. If she accepted Cotter's offer she had some financial security *and* she was rid of his grandson in one fell swoop. After all, there was no point forcing Arnold to marry her if he was going to be cut off without a penny.

'Mr Cotter, I don't think –'

'But you *should* think of your future, Hettie,' he replied, cold-eyed and telling her in a glance that she was outmanoeuvred. 'This is the only offer I'm prepared to make.'

Of course she took it, and moved back to live with her father, blaming John for everything. After all, if he hadn't been so unpleasant to Mr Cotter she might well have been married to his grandson by now.

Although fully aware of her sister-in-law's simmering,

Sarah put Hettie to the back of her mind when John told her he was closing the mine.

'It could be serious . . .'

She was looking at the two sleeping boys, James and Frederick Crossworth, born to inherit *what* exactly?

'I've lost a lot of money, Sarah. If I don't get back on my feet soon we might have to sell the house and move somewhere smaller.'

Unperturbed, she looked up. 'If it comes to that, then we'll do it.'

He was immediately on the defensive. 'Of course it might not.'

She had learned how to handle his insecurities and was masterly at the technique.

'If you can't get back on your feet, John, we'll consolidate.'

Impatiently he glanced away. 'I'm not saying I can't –'

'Because it doesn't matter.'

'– I just wanted to warn you. *If* the worst happened.'

'We'll cope,' she said pragmatically, aware of the needled expression her husband had adopted.

'I suppose Dandry Fairclough and old man Cotter will have heard what happened by now,' Sarah said softly, still bending over the babies. 'No doubt they'll be pleased to see their rival beaten.'

'I didn't say I was beaten!' John snapped.

'Besides, you have plenty of houses, John,' Sarah went on blithely. 'We could live in one of the terraces you own. We'll hardly be turned out onto the street.'

'I didn't say we would! What *is* the matter with you?' he asked, finally exasperated.

Slowly Sarah straightened up and faced him.

'Are you seriously telling me that you can't recover from any loss you've taken?' Her eyes were steady. 'I don't care if you've lost a fortune, John, because better that than reopen a mine which might kill other men. I admire you for what you did – not many others would have made the same decision.' She smoothed her dress impassively. 'I don't want to hear another word about losses. You started from nothing and made a small fortune. If you lose money now, you'll make it again.' Her voice was suddenly steely: 'The important thing is *how* you make it, John. By closing that mine – even if it beggars us – you proved yourself to be honourable. That's what matters, not the money.'

He had listened to her in silence, watching her, thinking, and feeling his hopes rising as she spoke.

'There's always cotton.'

'Cotton?'

He nodded. 'There's a mill in Up Holland for sale. They're asking a stupid price, but it might be worth talking to them about it. Bargaining.' His doubts had vanished, he was planning again, thinking ahead, roping in another ambition. 'I won't sell the mine, not in the state it's in. It's too risky. So that leaves the terraces and the house.'

Silently, Sarah watched him.

'I can raise some money on the terraces and the shop, but the rest might have to come from mortgaging this house.'

'So mortgage it,' she said simply.

He was baffled by her lack of concern. 'Just like that?'

'Yes, just like that. You need the money, we have the money . . .' her arm went out in an expansive gesture, taking in the room, '. . . *here*. In the bricks and mortar. Do it, John. Raise whatever you need on the house.'

'Even if it meant that we might lose it?'

'It was your dream, my love, not mine,' she replied evenly, walking over to him. 'I want to see you succeed, John. Not for my sake, but for yours. I want to see you keep this house and outbuy and outlive the Faircloughs and the Cotters.' Her eyes were sharp with energy. 'I want to see our sons grow up knowing their father is the most successful and honourable man this town has ever seen. I want to be the wife of the man who never compromised his principles nor took the easy way out.' Her lips rested for a burning moment against his before she drew away from him. 'That's what I want, John – and I won't settle for anything less.'

The foreman, Graham Cox, came round to the Queen's Road house later that week, his expression anxious.

'The men . . . I mean, the miners . . . we wondered if you might be thinking of reopening the mine, Mr Crossworth?'

Surprised, John looked up. 'I told you I would never do that, Graham.'

'But there's always falls at pits,' he countered. 'It's the way of it. We need work, Mr Crossworth. If you don't reopen it, then sell it.'

The colour suddenly leaving his face, John held the man's gaze until Cox looked away.

'You really want me to sell that mine to someone like Fairclough or Cotter?' John's voice, unusually low and steady, was gathering in volume. He had been to the accountant's that afternoon to sort out his financial situation and had been told of the severity of his losses. Sell the mine, the accountant told him, let someone else work it.

'Have you forgotten that Ted Morris died in that mine?'

'Men die all the time,' Graham replied helplessly. 'The living still 'ave to eat.'

'Your two sons worked for me!' John said angrily. 'Should I put *them* back down too, Graham? Is that what you want? Maybe I should risk them –'

'We need work –'

'You'll have work!' John roared, rising abruptly to his feet, the foreman stepping back, startled by his employer's rage. 'But not in that mine. And I will not sell it. I WILL NOT SELL IT!' John repeated, his grey eyes riveted on the man. 'Do you understand? I'm not risking lives for jobs. Not now, never. And don't you ever – EVER – tell me what to do, Cox, or you'll never work for me again.'

Silence shuddered over them.

'I'm sorry,' Graham said at last.

'You should be,' John replied, turning away. 'Now get out and wait until you hear from me. I don't let people down.'

He put the wives to work first at the cotton mill. Odd way of going about it, people said, but still it was one wage coming in regular. When he had the money he would buy another pit, John told them, but in the meantime the women had to do the earning in the mill. Cotton was needed, and it was bought for high prices. Within a year – if he was lucky – John Crossworth might have a pit in which to put the miners back to work.

'Who's 'e bloody kidding?' one of the miners said pessimistically. 'This year, next year, sometime, never! I can't wait a bloody year for work.'

Others said the same, dribbling back to old man Cotter or Dandry Fairclough, tails between their legs, working long hours for minimum wages. Back to the old routine.

'You can't blame them,' John said one night to Sarah as she settled the babies to sleep. 'They want a wage –'

'Yes I can blame them!' she retorted hotly, then lowered her voice and tiptoed out of the nursery closing the door behind her. 'You set up a poor fund for them when the pit was running. There's enough money for the miners to get by on for a while.'

'It's a pittance –'

'I know. But they work for a pittance for the likes of Cotter!' she snapped back, walking downstairs and going to stand in front of the drawing-room fire.

Rumours and resentment had been rife, people nudging each other as they saw her pass, murmuring behind their hands. They had forgotten the death of Ted Morris all too easily; what they wanted now was work for the ninety-nine men laid off. Anxious, they saw their jobs withheld from them, taken away from them, and the villain was now John Crossworth.

'Sarah, calm down.'

'Don't tell me to calm down!' she replied coldly. 'They should be grateful to you.'

'They're angry.'

'And all this is *your* fault?' she retorted. '*You* caused the pit fall? You went down there to help dig them out, in case anyone has forgotten that.'

'They need jobs, it's been months now.'

'You've given the women jobs, John. They're working in the mill for you. And you've told the men you're trying to get another pit –'

'It's not enough.'

'NOT ENOUGH!' she roared. 'John, all this arguing is ridiculous. I will *not* see you working any harder than you are or you'll be ill. You have a responsibility to your family as well as your workers.'

'Sarah –'

She turned and put up her hands. 'No, hear me out. You are doing all you can. You cannot make the world run smoothly, John, you can only try and control your own portion of it. You want to help these people – well, you *are* doing. You cannot find money you don't have, or open a mine you don't yet own. For weeks I have seen you going out at all hours and coming home exhausted, and no better thought of. I've seen you sit up, driving yourself to distraction trying to understand and make sense of the situation. But you see, John, *it doesn't make sense.*'

He looked at her, baffled.

'You cannot take on a family of ninety-nine people. You are not responsible for your workers, you can only give them work when you have it. You can't make work for them. D'you think Fairclough or Cotter would have worried about this for one moment?' She glanced upwards, exasperated. 'What am I talking about? They wouldn't even have closed the mine. They wouldn't have cared if it was safe or not. What are a few miners' lives to them?' She leaned towards her husband. 'But you're different,

John, quite rightly you see the workers as people and so they *hurt* you as people.'

'I can't risk reopening the mine. I will *not* have the death of anyone else on my conscience.'

'I agree with you. Don't reopen the mine, or sell it. Keep it closed.'

'I'll get another pit.'

'Yes, you will,' Sarah agreed, 'but until then you'll have to stop worrying for ninety-nine people – when there are three of us at home who need you more.'

Chapter Nine

1919

He was screaming again, throwing himself against the wall and banging his head repeatedly. Struggling to hold him, Sarah called for help, John hurrying up the stairs and catching hold of his son.

'Calm down. Come on, Freddie, calm down.'

Uncontrollable, the boy continued to scream, saliva collecting in the corners of his mouth.

'Freddie,' John repeated, keeping his tone even. 'Calm down.' Adeptly, he pinioned the child's arms down by his sides, and then picked Freddie up, rocking him steadily. 'There, there,' John said, 'there, there . . .'

Smoothing her hair, Sarah turned and caught Jim standing by the door. As quiet as his brother was nervous. Her hand went out to him.

'Hello, sweetheart.'

At once, he moved over to her. 'What's the matter?'

'Nothing now,' John said evenly, still holding Freddie. 'Everything's fine now.'

The doctor had told her that it was just a stage of growing up. He'll grow out of it, children always do. It's just tantrums, a way of striving for attention. But it wasn't, it was something much deeper than a tantrum, something more disturbing. As John continued to rock Freddie, Sarah sat down and pulled Jim onto her lap. The boy was quiet, leaning against her, the birthmark on his head as vivid as the day he was born. Over the years John's mark had faded, the wound closing and leaving no scar, but the brand stayed on Jim's forehead and grew with him, marking him for ever as his father's child.

You'd never think they were twins, Sarah thought to herself. Oh yes, they were physically alike, but that made the difference in their characters all the more unsettling. She glanced over to her husband, Freddie now still against his father's shoulder, his hands limp. Slowly she studied her son; the long-boned limbs, the dark hair, and the closed lids hiding his father's eyes. Then she glanced at the child on her lap; same body, same face, but this child was looking at her; eyes wide open, hiding nothing.

'I think I should have another talk with his school teacher,' John said quietly.

'He says what he always says – that Freddie will settle down in time,' Sarah replied. 'You settled, didn't you, Jim?'

He nodded in agreement. Never one to waste words: like his father for that.

'Perhaps we should have him taught at home?'

Sarah balked at the suggestion. Freddie needed to learn how to cope with people; not be segregated from them.

'No, I don't think that would be a good idea.'

'We'll have to talk about it later,' John said after another moment. 'I have to go now.' At once, Freddie clung onto him, John trying patiently to escape from his son's grip. 'Now, come on. Be a good boy. Freddie, let me go to work!'

At once, a muted wail emanated from between the child's teeth. Sarah put Jim down and walked over to her husband. Firmly she took hold of Freddie, felt him tighten and then suddenly relax, his head nestling against hers. That was what made it so difficult: all the temper, all the violence was somehow made bearable by the sweetness he could show her when he chose to.

'How long will you be gone?' she asked, over her son's head.

'I'm not sure,' John replied honestly. 'I have to call at the mill and then go on to the mine.'

'You should delegate more,' Sarah told him. 'Get Sammy Upton to call at the mill for you.'

He reached out; touched her face. Something of Freddie was in the gesture.

'You know what I'm like. I have to check everything out for myself,' he said. 'I don't want any mistakes.'

Not that there had been. Eighteen months after John had closed the first pit, he had bought his second on the outskirts of the town, some of the men he had hired coming back to work for him eagerly. Others, ashamed at having thrown in their lot with Cotter and Fairclough, came back timidly. A few stayed away.

John had been deeply hurt by their behaviour at first; and their animosity when he closed the mine had been violent and unexpected. It seemed that only a few understood what he had done and the others' lack of faith embittered him. Sarah responded differently, and seeing her husband exhausting himself financially and emotionally, she decided on her own course of action.

It was a sullen spring morning when she called at the Ash mill. Fully aware that John was at the bank trying to raise funds, Sarah walked into the mill and stood for a while, unseen, in her husband's office. Below her, the weaving shed stretched into the distance, the pulleys shunting backwards and forwards, the cotton dust hanging thick in the air. The noise was dense, communication achieved by lip-reading, the 'mee-mawing' of the women telling stories as they worked.

Sarah knew many of the women by sight. There was Bob Holmes's wife, Minnie Ginnins, Lily Gurney, and a row beyond, Mollie Lyman. George Lyman had been one of the few not to complain, Sarah remembered; he knew that his life had been saved by John and whole-heartedly backed his employer's decision to close the mine.

'It's an unlucky place,' he'd said. 'It *should* be closed and *stay* closed.'

Then Sarah caught sight of someone else she knew. Myra Harrop, a worn-down, overanxious woman, who had – Sarah was certain – never condoned her husband's march.

She could remember the day all too well. John had been desperate to raise money, had mortgaged the house and was even considering selling one of the terraces when Mick Harrop came to Queen's Road. But he didn't come alone; he came with over three dozen disaffected miners and stood shouting at the gate for John to come out and face them.

The babies had been alarmed, crying at the noise, Sarah remembered. She had tried to stop John going out, but he had gone anyway, standing on the front steps and facing them. Many had been drinking, their faces sour in the semi-dark. In the houses around them, lights were going on, neighbours looking out anxiously, a coachman turning his horses at the head of the street. She didn't know if John was afraid; he didn't look it, but then he always disguised his feelings. He just stood on the steps and intimidated them by his stillness. His silence. In the upstairs window, in front of the babies' cot, Sarah watched the men fall silent, Mick Harrop stepping forwards suddenly, his tone belligerent.

'We want a word with you, Crossworth.'

No 'Mister' any more. Just Crossworth – as though he were an enemy. Sarah could feel her anger mounting.

'So say what you came to say, and then leave,' John had replied.

How did he keep his voice so steady? she had wondered, watching as he moved down from the front door steps and came into her line of vision. She could see the top of his hair, the way his hair parted at the crown, and then she glanced over to Harrop.

'We want you to reopen the mine, or sell it, Crossworth.'

'You can't dictate terms to me, Mr Harrop,' John replied evenly, his composure awesome. 'I've made my decision, and I won't change my mind.'

Out of the corner of her eye Sarah could see the lights go on in the house next to theirs. Police would be called. Go on, she willed her neighbour, call them, call them. Get help.

'We need work!' one man cried out from the back of the pack.

'WE NEED WORK!' went up the cry, Harrop turning back to John triumphantly.

'It's all right for you, you're all comfy in your big 'ouse. We've got nowt now you've laid us off.'

'I set up a poor fund for you –'

John's words were immediately drowned out by a storm of angry shouting.

Go and get the police! Sarah prayed. Someone, get help . . . Automatically, she had pushed the babies' cot back from the window, afraid that someone would throw something at the house.

'The poor fund's not enough!' Harrop said savagely. 'You're not living off a bloody poor fund, Crossworth!'

Upstairs, Sarah watched her husband face them. Only she knew how little money John had left, how much he had lost with the closure of the pit.

'You let us down, Crossworth. You're no better than the likes of Fairclough and old man Cotter!'

One man facing nearly forty angry miners, John stood up to them.

'I know *you*,' he said, pointing to one man on the edge of the group. 'I let you have two weeks' rent on tick, and *you*,' he pointed to another. 'You had extra overtime when you asked for it after your last child was born.' He scanned the faces. 'I know you, and you, and you. I can look at your faces and remember your names and count the favours I've done for you –'

Harrop was unwilling to lose his advantage. 'Be that as it may –'

'And I gave *you* a job after your last boss threw you out. He told me you were a troublemaker,' John smiled grimly. 'He was right. You *are* a troublemaker, Harrop, and you . . .' he glanced at the men in front of him, '. . . are all fools to listen to him.'

A roar went up from the miners, John putting up his

hands to silence them. From her vantage point at the upper window, Sarah could feel her palms sweat. Be careful, she willed her husband, be careful, this is no time to lose your temper . . .

'Yes, you're fools!' John repeated angrily. 'Fools not to think for yourselves. Fools to let a no-hoper like Harrop stir you up.' He moved a step towards them. Incredibly, the men moved a step backwards. 'I closed the mine because it killed Ted Morris and because it's unsafe. *I will not open it again.*' He let the words sink into the cold, still air. The houses on the terrace were ablaze with lights; it seemed that everyone listened to him. 'But I *will* buy another pit –'

'Oh aye!' Harrop said scornfully.

John's anger was as sour as vinegar. '*Yes, I will.* When I have the money, I'll buy another pit and I'll be hiring again. I'll need miners.' He paused. 'I'll need sound men. Men I can trust. Men I can count on, in the good times *and* in times of trouble.' The mob was silent now, listening to him. 'I'm looking at all of you. I'm memorizing each face. Each name. I'm marking you out and I know my enemies.'

The street was as silent as the men.

'I know my enemies,' John repeated, 'but if you men turn away now and go home, I can forget. I can forget your faces and your names.' He stared at them. 'When the time comes – and it will – I'll remember nothing of the men who leave now.'

One by one the miners began to file off, walking into the darkness, Harrop shouting after them, John watching dispassionately.

'. . . But those who remain; those who come here and try to intimidate me and my family; those I'll remember. And you,' he pointed directly at Harrop, 'you I will *never* forget.'

Sarah remembered the night as though she were reliving it . . . and the incident which followed soon after . . . She had stood looking down at the mill weaving shed and then slowly descended the steps which led to the women. A whistle blew, just as she knew it would, for the tea break. Silence, sudden and intimidating, fell over the mill.

They saw her then. Stopped and watched her. The boss's wife, tall and handsome, standing at the head of the row of looms. She was dressed in an unpatterned dark green suit, a black hat covering her hair, her hands gloved. Her face was composed, her understated elegance formidable. She wore no jewellery, and no perfume: she had come to talk, to win over the workers, not alienate them. Around her the women watched, their sleeves rolled up, coarse aprons over their dresses, arms and hair flecked with cotton dust.

Sarah had seen her husband stand up to the men and now it was her turn. Only *her* intervention was to be private, between the women and herself.

'You all know me,' she said, raising her voice, 'and I imagine some of you can guess why I've come. The other night many of your men came to see my husband.' She paused. They were listening, fascinated and curious. 'They wanted work. They were angry, disbelieving. When they left they were quietened, but for how long?' She moved down the aisle slowly, the women watching her from both sides. 'I came here to ask for your help. To ask for you to back me.'

'What?' someone said incredulously.

Sarah turned, faced the woman. 'To back me,' she repeated, 'to help me to help you.' Her eyes scanned the mill workers. 'My husband will be doing everything in his power to get your men back to work. He'll do it, because he promised to. But I don't know when he'll get his next mine. I don't know how soon it will be. So in the meantime, we can give only you work. Secure work, in this mill.' Her voice, with its foreign accent, was mesmeric. 'My husband doesn't know I'm talking to you; your husbands don't need to know what's been said today; this is between us. We are all women, we all have families, responsibilities. I, no less than you.' Her eyes fixed on Mollie Lyman. 'My husband is a good man, *you* know that. He's not like old man Cotter or Dandry Fairclough . . .' she turned, taking in the other women's faces, '. . . he's an honourable man and that should count for something. He doesn't deserve the treatment he's been getting. It's cruel and unjust.' She gave them time to take in her words. 'I'm asking for your patience, for your backing. I'm asking you to sit it out and keep your men hopeful until the day comes when there *is* work for them again.'

Frowning, Mollie stared at Sarah. 'None of us knew about the other night.'

'That's true!' a number of them chorused.

Sarah nodded. 'No matter. It's passed. Over,' she said quietly. 'But I don't want any more unpleasantness. John is doing all he can for all of you. You should trust him more – and I'll do everything I can for you. In return I only ask you to keep this to yourselves.' She looked over to Myra Harrop, half hidden behind a pulley. 'Especially you, Myra.'

'I knew nothing about the other night, Mrs Crossworth!' she said timidly. 'I swear I didn't.'

'I believe you,' Sarah replied, 'but if you want to continue working here you have to promise to say nothing about this to your husband.'

'I promise,' she said, close to tears. 'I promise.'

Nodding, Sarah turned away, the women watching her as she mounted the steps to the office and left by the back door. In that instant they realized where the power lay, and threw in their lot with Sarah Crossworth.

That had been almost five years ago, when the twins were still babies. Five years in which John struggled and fought to save the mill and buy the new mine; five years in which Sarah brought up her sons almost single-handed. Leaving before seven in the morning, John was seldom home before ten, and when the war broke out, she, like most of the other women in Oldham, was left at home whilst the men went off to fight.

It was then that Sarah learned about loneliness. She might have been an outcast before, but she had had her father with her, and later, John. This time, in the long four years of the Great War, she was left almost isolated in Queen's Road. The house, with its grand stairs and five floors, was sometimes painfully cold; fuel scarce, food rationed, the children receiving most of their mother's ration. She had no help in the house now, only one old woman to clean, and at the front entrance the railings had been requisitioned by the army, the garden barren and empty of flowers. It seemed as though all the security Sarah had treasured was now gone. John was away fighting, and the children were too young to be companions.

News came slow from the Front.

When war had been declared Sarah had known at once that John would go off to fight; that he would be one of the first to volunteer. It was typical of him, his sense of duty forcing him to act. And, just as typically, Sarah never attempted to persuade him otherwise.

The night before he left he was restless, turning repeatedly in bed.

'What time is it?' His voice was controlled, steady.

'Not even two,' she answered in the darkness.

'Will you manage?'

'Yes.'

His hand moved over hers. He felt, for an instant, that he might break down.

'Will you write?'

'Every day.'

'No more than that?'

They laughed suddenly, desperately, he wrapping his legs around hers and laying his head on her shoulder.

'I'll come home.'

She wondered then how she would sleep without him;

without hearing his breathing next to hers. Tears, unshed, lay on her tongue like acid.

'I promise you, Sarah. I'll come home.'

'Soon?'

'Soon.'

'How long will it last?'

'Only months,' he replied softly. 'They all say it will only go on a little while.'

'Hardly worth going then.'

He smiled against her shoulder.

'Sammy Upton will help you with the business,' John said for the third time. Sammy had been declared unfit for service, tuberculosis making a coward out of him. 'He's a sound man.'

'You've told me already,' Sarah said, gently chastising him.

The dark was thick with dread.

'Look after the boys.'

'Yes . . .'

'Write and tell me how they're doing,' John went on, then pressed his lips hard against her shoulder. 'You are my life.'

'You'll come back,' Sarah said firmly, reaching up and stroking his head. 'Remember how you used to think of Queen's Road when you were a boy, and how that thought kept you going?' He nodded dumbly. 'Well, now you have a house on Queen's Road to come home to, and a wife and a family. It's not a dream any longer, John. It's real.'

He could hardly speak. 'What time is it?'

'Two o'clock.'

'Do you remember the day we came back to Oldham?'

She nodded. Thought of Howard, and of Hettie, both sleeping across the park in Brompton Street. Sleeping like the just.

'We've had some times together, Sarah,' he said simply.

'And we'll have more,' she answered him.

'Yes, more. Many, many more.'

The time wound on, crept towards dawn. Outside, the town was quiet, and at five thirty, John left.

Thinking back, Sarah wondered if it was due to John's absence that Freddie behaved so erratically. Perhaps he missed his father, or needed a man around to discipline him. Yet she hadn't been soft with either of her sons. Loving, naturally, but always firm. Jim had responded, developed at a normal rate, Freddie smaller, slower to mature. Yet by the time they were three the boys were physically identical, only their characters becoming more and more diverse.

Jim was her security, steady, reliable, never jealous. She might pick him up and love him, but he was seldom fractious when she put him down. Not like Freddie. He saw his brother as his rival from the first: his rival for affection and attention. Charming and loving when he pleased, Freddie commanded attention from his mother persistently, Jim often unfairly relegated to second place.

Aware of the situation, Sarah compensated by spending time with Jim when Freddie slept – which he did longer and more frequently than his brother. From the first they had had to sleep apart; Freddie screaming and kicking out at Jim if they were placed together.

Having hired Mollie Lyman to help her manage the boys, Sarah, baffled by her son's aggression, was quick to confide.

'I don't understand it, Jim is never violent.'

Mollie looked at Freddie sitting in front of the fire. He was playing with wooden bricks, his head bowed. A little way off, Jim was reading a rag book. Quiet, solitary.

'That one's like 'is father,' Mollie said, pointing to Jim.

Sarah nodded. 'And Freddie? Who's he like?'

Mollie didn't want to say. Freddie was a little of Howard Crossworth and rather more of Hettie – certainly nothing of his mother, and of his father. Well, only in looks.

'Children change all the time,' Mollie replied diplomatically. 'Freddie'll settle down.'

But he *didn't* settle. He grew worse, and angry, and petulant, and at times, cruel.

'Now this has to stop!' Sarah said, grabbing her son by the arm one morning and hoisting him to his feet after he had savagely pinched his brother. '*Don't* do that, Freddie.'

He was limp with remorse, hanging his head and clinging to her skirts. Incensed, Sarah pulled him off and called Jim over to her, Freddie hanging back, staring, sullen.

'You should have seen 'is face,' Mollie said to George later. ''E had a right look about 'im. If you ask me that child's got all the worst of the Crossworths in 'im, and none of the good . . .' Many others said the same as Freddie started to grow up.

The children were five when John thankfully returned from the war and began running the business again. Sammy Upton had done a fair job, and within months the pit was functioning once more, the war survivors eager for work. It seemed to John – euphoric at returning home safely – that his life was blessed. The business was flourishing, he was financially secure, and he was home with his family.

Only the thought of Hettie could mar John's peace of mind. His sister had caused a scandal, being set up by old man Cotter's son, Arnold, in a house in Up Holland. Yet although she was publicly reviled, Hettie walked around the town without shame, proud in her opulent clothes, as full of herself as ever. Once Sarah had seen her pass on the High Street and been astonished to find herself snubbed by the girl she had given a home to. Hettie Crossworth, living up to her reputation at last.

But Freddie was a different matter. For as long as she could, Sarah kept her anxieties to herself, but gradually, as his moods worsened, she felt compelled to confide. Yet for some reason the moment was never right; John was always busy, going somewhere, hurrying off. Time and again Sarah promised herself that she would talk to him, and time and again she held back. Until – after Freddie had had a particularly violent outburst – she finally confronted John.

'We have to do something about him.'

John looked at her, wanting to be off to the mine. But not this time, Sarah thought. No, this time, we talk.

'I don't think there's anything to really worry about,' John said calmly. 'Freddie just gets jumpy sometimes. He gets overexcited.'

'He was hysterical,' Sarah replied, her tone calm.

John shrugged his shoulders. 'Childhood tantrums. He'll grow out of it.'

'How would you know?' she countered angrily. 'You've been away for years. You've no idea how difficult Freddie's been. And don't you *dare* tell me how to bring up our sons. It seems to me that I did a good enough job whilst you were away.' Her face had flushed, her sloe eyes sharp.

'I wasn't criticizing you,' John replied quietly. 'I was just remarking –'

'On how our son would grow out of his moods. Well, what if he doesn't?' she asked bluntly. 'What if he remains a problem? What if he gets worse? He's always been the same, John. I don't know why. He gets so jealous, so angry about things.'

'You never said anything about this before.'

'Why worry you? I also thought he might grow out of it. Besides, he was always on his best behaviour when you were home on leave.' She stared at her husband. 'I don't like spoiled children, and I didn't spoil him, believe me. Well, look at Jim, he's all right.'

'You've done a fine job,' John assured her, but he was worried, thinking back to the outburst he had just witnessed.

He had never seen anyone – let alone a child – react so violently. The noise of Freddie's head banging had reverberated around the house. He had been reading in the study and had thought someone was hammering in a nail to hang a picture. Nothing had prepared him for the sight of his son, white-faced, blue-lipped, repeatedly slamming his forehead against the wall.

'How long has he been banging his head?'

'Today was the first time,' Sarah replied. 'Before the head banging, he used to hold his breath.'

'Hettie used to do that.'

Sarah said nothing.

'Perhaps we ought to let a doctor look at him?'

'He has.'

'I don't mean *our* doctor, I mean a specialist.'

'In what, head banging?' Sarah retorted acidly, then sighed. 'Jim gets so little attention in comparison. I feel guilty about that.' She reached out for her husband's hand and squeezed it, seeking comfort. 'But now there are two of us it will be easier.'

He thought he might, he might, try to climb into it. It was easy really. Just climb into the dumbwaiter and wait for someone to let it down. No one would know he was in there; they would all be looking for him . . . Freddie glanced out of the playroom window. Jim was in the garden, playing with a wooden train set. No one else was around. Spurred on, Freddie squirmed off the window seat and moved over to the trapdoor.

It was heavy, difficult to push up. He tried again, then pushed once more. The door slid upwards reluctantly, the dumbwaiter half exposed. Hurriedly Freddie climbed in and then slid the opening closed again.

Darkness surrounded him. Below he could hear people in the kitchen and the faint sound of someone sweeping the basement steps. All he had to do was to sit and wait. Soon someone would pull the dumbwaiter down and he'd jump out and frighten them, Freddie thought, smiling to himself. Or they'd suddenly notice he was gone and search for him everywhere.

It would be fun to hear them all calling for him, waiting in the darkness. It would be funny to hear them looking everywhere. Everywhere but here.

Chapter Ten

1929

Whatever you said about it, was true, Jim decided. The business was incredible. He paused by the pithead, looking down at the mine shaft. In the office across the yard his father was working. Jim could see him through the window, the prematurely greying head of John Crossworth bent over a ledger. He hadn't changed the office in all the years since he had first bought the mine; liked to look out and knew that the men liked to be able to look in and see him. It made him approachable.

Approachable. Jim raised his eyebrows at the word. His father was many things, but approachable? No, he didn't think so. He was too naturally reserved for that. Suddenly catching his father's eye, Jim waved. John paused, then waved less ebulliently in response. Behind him on the wall was a photograph of his mother and beneath that, a photograph of his sons.

Freddie and me . . . Jim frowned, his good temper threatened. Only the night before he had caught Freddie coming in late, stumbling over the window ledge of the library in Queen's Road.

Hearing the noise Jim had come downstairs and snapped on the light. 'What the hell! Freddie?'

'Who'd you think it was, Father bloody Christmas?' his brother had remarked sourly. 'Well, don't just stand there, give us a hand.'

Reluctantly he had done, Freddie lumbering into the room and slumping into the nearest chair. He was slightly heavier than Jim, and weighty in his movements, his long arms, with their rolled-up sleeves, powerfully built.

'Drunk?'

'Sober.'

'What happened?' Jim asked drily. 'You run out of money?'

Freddie raised his eyebrows, then grinned. That was the trouble with Freddie, you couldn't hate him for long. Or maybe that was because he was his brother; because he saw too much of himself in Freddie; because they had shared the same womb for nine months. Whatever it was, it mattered.

'I thought you were staying in tonight.'

'I got bored.'

'Father was looking for you,' Jim said, sitting next to his brother, his body slim in a business suit. 'He looked everywhere.'

People were always looking for Freddie. Ever since the day he got stuck in the dumbwaiter and had everyone in the house panicking. Ever since then . . . Jim thought back. The dumbwaiter had jammed between floors, Freddie falling asleep, their mother certain that he had run away, their father trying to calm her. Hours had passed, all Freddie's misdemeanours forgotten at the thought that he might be dead somewhere. They had all run around frantically inside and out, Freddie finally emerging with a sly smile on his face at dinner time, when the cook lowered the dumbwaiter into the kitchen and then dropped the tureen she was carrying when he jumped out. It wasn't funny – or was it? Jim wasn't sure, he just wished he had thought of it first. But then he never thought of anything like that. He wasn't supposed to; that was Freddie's way, not his.

'I went to the mine today.'

'Uh-huh.'

'Father showed me the books,' Jim said, trying to elicit some response. 'It's –'

'Boring.'

Jim glanced away. 'So where have you been that was so interesting?'

'Over at Hettie's.'

'Hettie's?' Jim echoed. 'Aunt Hettie's?'

Freddie nodded.

'Mother will go mad if she finds out.'

'Hettie makes me laugh,' Freddie said, by way of explanation. 'I like her.'

Without answering, Jim thought of his aunt, her hair dyed, her face made up like the women at the pictures. Only Hettie didn't look like Mae West, she looked large-pored and gaudy, like her house with its photographs of Arnold everywhere. Against all the odds she had stayed with him; not as his wife, but as his mistress, shored away from the town, Arnold visiting her as often as he could get away from his wife. The talk of the town, the butt of jokes, as remote from the decent people of Oldham as a Chinese concubine.

'She gave me this,' Freddie said, pulling out a ring and staring at it critically. 'I don't suppose it's worth much. Said it was grandmother's.'

Jim put out his hand, but Freddie snatched his away. 'She gave it to me, not you. You won't even go and see her.'

Because I don't like her, Jim thought to himself. Because she's jealous and critical and dangerous.

'I don't think you should take it.'

'Why not? Arnold gives her plenty of jewellery.'

Old man Cotter was dying; had lost his grip on the business and on Arnold. Too sick to be able to stop anything any more, he was holed up in Marstone Hall, trying to die and failing.

'When Father was looking for you earlier,' Jim said after a moment, 'I told him you were fishing.'

'Fishing . . .' Freddie echoed, amused. He had given up fishing a year earlier, too mature at fifteen to spend time trying to catch the odd trout which found its misplaced way up the Irwell. No, Freddie wasn't interested in fish any more, he had other things to hook. Like girls.

Jim was watching him think, knowing fairly accurately how his brother's mind was working. That was the advantage of being a twin, you had a perpetual insight into the other's mind, the ability to become a mental Peeping Tom. Leaning against the back of his chair, his eyes closed, their lids transparent, there was something faintly unreal about Freddie; something his dark hair and eyes did nothing to dispel. Jim might have the same colouring as his brother, but Freddie's skin was finer, translucent under his eyes, giving him a foreign look.

His mother's son, all right.

'He wanted to talk to you about the business,' Jim went on, trying helplessly to provoke some interest. It was a good business, with a good income; they were envied – the Crossworth boys, sure to succeed. Not that Freddie saw it that way. He didn't want to succeed in anything; wasn't really interested in anything; just swung through life recklessly.

Jim was envious of that. Desperately so.

'Why did the old man want to talk to me?' Freddie asked, with that lazy tone he always assumed when anyone wanted him to do anything.

'He said it was time you – *we* – got more involved.'

'Ready to inherit one day?' Freddie asked, opening one eye, about to wink.

But the wink never materialized, Freddie glancing away instead. It was strange, but although Jim was thought of as good-natured and reliable, there was always something under the surface which prevented Freddie from pushing his luck with his brother. Some intimation of steel which warned him off.

He had learned his lesson when they were ten. Jim had been smitten by the daughter of one of their neighbours, a tiny girl of about nine. Every morning Jim used to leave something on her doorstep as a present. A few flowers, some chocolate. He was very sensitive about it and kept his gifts a secret, until Freddie told their parents. He thought it was funny, you see. Well, it was, wasn't it? And stupidly, Freddie thought that because it was Jim – easy-going Jim – he would get away with it.

For a while, he did. A few mornings passed and Freddie kept riling his brother, and his brother kept ignoring him and then one morning Freddie decided to follow his twin to the girl's house. He stood laughing as she came out to talk to his brother ... Freddie winced, pained by the memory. He had been as big as his brother, they could always match each other physically as they were growing up, but he still hadn't expected the force with which Jim ran into him and knocked him over the wall.

The fall didn't hurt half as much as his pride as Freddie scrambled to his feet and put his fists up. Then stopped dead – because he saw an expression on Jim's face at that moment which he had never seen before or since; an expression which he never wanted to see again. Cowed, he ran home.

So Freddie never pushed his brother too far again ... Thoughtfully, he looked over to Jim. The birthmark had seemed to darken over the years, slanting from his brother's hairline to his left temple. It gave him, Freddie thought jealously, a roguish look. *He* should have inherited it; he could have carried it off much better, he thought. It was too romantic, too cavalier for Jim. It should have been his personal mark of Cain.

'Of course, I might not stay around to inherit the family empire.'

'Really?' Jim replied drily. 'What are you going to do instead?'

'I might run away and make my fortune.'

'Like Father?'

'Why not?' Freddie mused. 'Adventure runs in the blood.'

Not in yours, Jim thought wryly. You'd never make it

to the end of the road, away from the soft sheets and the soft words. Away from the admiration and petting. He stared at his brother's hands. His parents had bought Freddie a piano after he had seen someone playing at the music hall. He fancied himself as that man, leaving the women limp with admiration, the whole auditorium paying homage to his skill. But after a few half-hearted lessons, Freddie gave it up. It was boring, he said. Better to say it was boring than admit it was beyond him.

'So where will you be going, Freddie?'

He gazed across the room, his eyes fixed on some imaginary horizon. 'India.'

'Oh, *India* . . .'

'Why not?' Freddie countered, suddenly defensive. 'I could make a million out there.'

'Doing what?'

'Talking,' a voice said behind them.

Startled, Freddie spun round. In the doorway stood John, watching his sons.

'I didn't see you, Father.'

'I gathered that,' John replied, walking into the room and glancing round. The window was still open, the night air dank. 'Only thieves come in at the window.'

Freddie glanced away. 'I was late –'

'I know that. But what I don't know is *why* you were late.'

'I was talking.'

'To the fishes?' John countered.

Jim avoided both his gaze and the lie.

'What were you hoping to catch so late, Freddie?'

'We'd stopped fishing, and we got talking – me and the other lads,' he spluttered, then picked up speed rapidly. 'About things. You know, this and that.'

'No, explain it to me.'

'About things . . .' Freddie trailed off, glancing helplessly over to his brother.

'I wanted to talk to you tonight,' their father continued.

'In fact, I waited at the office for you. I didn't realize I would have to make an appointment to see my own son or I would have made sure it was convenient for you.' The sarcasm was pungent.

'Sorry, Father.'

'So where were you?'

'Fishing –'

'Don't lie to me! And you shouldn't cover up for him either!' he snapped at Jim. 'Let your brother lie for himself, he's had enough practice.'

'I was going to come to the office. *Really* I was.'

Ignoring him, John repeated his previous question. 'Where were you?'

'Nowhere special.'

'So if it was nowhere special, you won't mind telling me.'

Freddie's colour was heating up. 'At a friend's.'

'Which friend?'

'Just a friend.'

Slowly, John walked over to his son and pulled him to his feet. He thought for a moment that he might hit him, but resisted. Violence never had any effect, it merely gave Freddie an excuse for sullen withdrawal which might last for days. John couldn't – as he looked at his son – feel anything but dislike for him. The head-banging child of the past had developed into this indolent liar. Charming at times, but feckless.

'I'll ask you once more. Where were you?'

Freddie's expression had hardened. He knew he was in trouble and had dropped any pretence of charm.

'At Hettie's.'

The name struck out like a boxer's glove.

'*Hettie's?*' John repeated incredulously, his grip tightening on Freddie's collar. 'Are you quite mad?'

'She's my aunt –'

'She's worthless!' John replied, letting go of his son, his disgust evident. 'Have you heard nothing?'

'What?'

'All these years? As you sat at our table and listened to our conversations, have you heard *nothing*, Freddie?'

He was mute, uncertain.

'Your aunt has tried to undermine me for years. She has been jealous and envious, and worse – she has a reputation of which no one could be proud.'

John drew in a breath. Why was he having to explain? Surely Freddie understood? Surely he wasn't the only person in Oldham to fail to see Hettie for what she was? His thoughts scalded him. Maybe his sister had been manipulating the boy, turning him against his family. But no, Freddie had *always* been against his father; against his family, against the business, against convention of any form.

'*Why* did you go to see her?'

'I like her.'

The answer was so unexpected, and delivered in so sullen a tone, that it left John momentarily speechless.

'*You like her!*' he repeated at last.

Both boys winced.

'You like the town whore?' John went on furiously, turning away from his son and looking round at the expensively furnished room. 'Why don't you like *this*, Freddie?' he asked, banging his fist into the back of the couch. '*Or this?*' he asked, pointing to the fireplace and the pictures. 'I worked for these things. As did your mother. Hard work, cold work, in all weathers, sometimes when all the cards were stacked against me and I wondered how in God's name I would survive. But I worked for it honourably. I didn't earn it on my back.' He was shouting now.

Suddenly Sarah was watching them from the doorway. 'What's going on?'

John spun round to face her, ashen with rage. 'Your son has been seeing my sister. Hettie Crossworth. And d'you know why? Because he *likes* her!'

Sarah kept her voice calm. 'How long have you been seeing her, Freddie?'

'What's that got to do with it?' John snapped.

'Quite a lot, I would have thought,' Sarah replied pragmatically, turning back to her son. 'Well, how long?'

'A few months.'

'Jesus!' John said, throwing up his hands in despair. 'Perhaps you'd like to go and live with her –'

'Stop it, both of you!' Sarah snapped, Freddie hanging his head, Jim silent beside the window. 'Your aunt is a troublemaker, Freddie,' she said simply. 'Common sense should tell you to keep away from her.'

'And how do I explain that to her?' Freddie asked, standing up to his mother. 'After all, she's been very kind to me. She gave me . . .' He trailed off, flushing.

John walked over to him slowly. 'She gave you *what*, exactly?'

'A ring,' Freddie admitted at last.

Without speaking, John put out his hand and reluctantly, Freddie dropped the ring into his palm.

I want you to give this to your wife when you marry, Peggy had told him when he was Freddie's age. Treasure it. It's not much, but it's not worthless either. She had smiled encouragingly, even though the kitchen was piled with washing, a folded stack waiting to be ironed. Hard work, circular work, coming, going, returning, day after day. Taking her down with it, until she was drowning in a white mire of other people's linen. I'll come back for you, he had promised her. I'll go away and make money and then I'll make it all right for you. I promise, I promise . . .

'John?' Sarah asked, concerned as she watched her husband's face.

I've always kept it safe, Peggy had said about the ring. Ready for you. All you have to do is to find someone you want to wear it. Don't tell your father, he'd not understand and want me to sell it instead. Then maybe you should,

John had answered her. Never, his mother had replied, you don't sell your luck, or give it away . . .

'John, are you all right?' Sarah repeated, touching his arm.

He had asked Hettie about the ring when he came back to Oldham with his bride and she had told him that they had been forced to sell it. We were so short of cash, John, she'd said pitifully. I know it was meant to be yours, but Mum had no choice . . . And he'd believed her, never thinking that she'd kept it, trying it on in secret, too jealous to give it up, too immoral to grant the wish of a dead woman.

Fiercely, John's fingers closed over the ring.

'I forbid you to see that woman ever again,' he told Freddie. 'Do you understand?'

'But –'

'I WILL HAVE NO BUTS!' he roared, as Sarah flinched. 'I will have no more defiance in this house. No more deceit, no more treachery. You live by my standards of decency, Freddie, or else.' He turned away, exasperated.

'Go upstairs,' Sarah said quickly to her son, then nodded to Jim. 'You too.'

Softly the door closed after them. John was unmoving, his fist clenched. He seemed past rage, his expression injured – just as it had been the day his father told him about his mother's death. It was the look of disbelief, or disappointment. Of loss.

'John, sit down, you're getting yourself all worked up,' Sarah said soothingly.

When he was younger he had seldom shown his feelings, except to her: had always been in control. But Freddie had taken away his composure, managing to achieve what no one else ever had.

'I can't understand that boy –'

'Sssh,' she soothed him. 'I'll have a word with Freddie later.'

He stared at her for a long moment. 'I don't like him,' he

said at last. 'God forgive me, but I don't like my own son.'

Her hand tightened over his. 'You're just upset –'

'No,' John replied firmly. 'I'm telling you the truth. I never thought I would admit it, I thought it would change, that *he* would change. But he hasn't, and neither have my feelings for him.'

'John, listen to me –'

'He has no *honour*,' John said incredulously. 'Stupidity I would have forgiven, even idleness, but a liar, no . . . and he is a liar, Sarah. And it's only now that I'm beginning to realize how *much* he lies – and I'm also beginning to wonder how *long* he's been lying to us.' His voice faltered for an instant. 'I don't know what to do with him.'

Sarah didn't know either; she had tried affection, discipline and reason, none of which had had any lasting effect. Freddie was feckless, shiftless and aimless. He had sidled through his childhood relying on charm and temper; he had exhausted people with his demands and provoked them with his thoughtlessness. He had been cruel and obstructive and at times peevish . . .

And he had been loving. He had crept up behind his mother and covered her eyes with his hands, breathing softly against her cheek. At other times he had known she was watching him and suddenly looked up, winking; or he had paused by her window and pulled faces, making her laugh; or mimicked his father's walk as John left the house. He had been wicked and vicious, tender and gentle.

He had been her son. And he still was.

'He can't be all bad,' Sarah said simply. 'No one is.'

'He's too like my sister,' John replied, his tone bitter. 'Bad blood.'

'It's your blood too.'

'So this is all *my* fault?' he snapped, then shook his head apologetically. 'Sorry. Sorry, Sarah. I didn't mean to say that . . . Do you see how we always quarrel when we talk about Freddie? He even manages to come between us.'

'John, nothing and no one can come between us,' she

said firmly, moving over to him and smoothing the back of his hair. 'You've been working too hard –'

'I have to.'

'I know, I know,' she chided him. 'There's always a reason why you have to do everything; always an excuse not to delegate.' Her fingers ran down his neck lightly, soothing him. 'The boys are sixteen, nearly seventeen, they will be able to help you soon.'

'You mean Jim will,' John replied. 'Freddie will never be any good in the business, and you know it.'

'He might, in time.'

'Never.' John reached out and caught hold of his wife's hands. Gently he drew them to his mouth and kissed each palm. 'No more.'

'No more *what*?' she asked, frowning.

'No more talking about our son,' John replied. 'I want to talk about us. About you.'

She laughed, bent down to nuzzle his hair. 'What about me?'

'Which flowers do you like, Sarah?' he asked, pulling her onto his lap.

'You know which flowers I like!'

'I know I do, but I want you to tell me – as though we'd only just met and it's all new to me.' He stared at her face; she felt herself warming with excitement. 'What kind of food do you like, Sarah?'

'Hot food.'

'Wine?'

She nodded, her gaze lingering for an instant on his mouth.

'And what kind of clothes, Sarah?' he asked her, his tone low, intimate, as he stroked her hair and then let his hand slide down her throat to her breast.

Her head fell backwards then as she held on to him, her mouth opening. For a short time Freddie was all but forgotten.

*   *   *

Dandry Fairclough's blood pressure was rising, not due to excitement, but food. Too *much* food. He liked eating – always had – but in the past he had managed to control his weight; he had always been stout, but now he was obese. He wheezed with food. He sweated food; from his open pores he oozed port and grease; from his finger ends, chicken fat, and all his clothes smelled of old meals and sour wine.

He was too fat to move easily now. Sat stuffed in his armchair with his jacket off because he was always too hot. The office was cool for everyone else; but not Fairclough, he was sweating, his fingers leaving damp prints on the papers Forecourt handed him.

His minion had stayed with him. Couldn't leave after a while, *had* to stick it out. Besides, Forecourt said to his wife, it was worth it just to see Fairclough squirm. And he had done a lot of squirming over the past decade as his power subsided and he saw John Crossworth nibbling away at his empire. Bit by bit, the influence he had taken for granted for so long was crumbling.

The trouble was that Fairclough had never expected John Crossworth to survive the mine closure. He had been elated to hear about the discontent from the laid off workers, and triumphant when some came back to work for him: *You see, lads, you ought to stay where the real power is. You don't need some cocky newcomer coming in and buggering up the works. Better stick to the devil you know* ... But the devil was losing his touch; and when old man Cotter began his prolonged dying, Fairclough's position started to look more than a little shaky.

The long planned meeting of their dynasties had not materialized. Cotter's moronic grandson had married some out-of-town heiress and Fairclough's daughter – for all her father's money – was looking hard to shift. Suitors weren't exactly clamouring at the door ... Forecourt would have told him why; it's not that your daughter's fat and spoiled, he would have said, but she carries a bad name, and no one wants to marry into that.

But Fairclough didn't ask his accountant's opinion, and instead he decided that all his misfortunes were due to one man, and one man only. Crossworth. It hadn't helped him when he saw Crossworth's wife; handsome and autocratic as a Tsarina; or when he heard that she had given birth to twins. Two boys. Not just one. Oh no, not for Crossworth, he had to have *two* sons.

His jealousy simmered like a slow stew, picking up flavour over the years that Crossworth prospered. From a distance Fairclough saw him buy the Ash mill and then his second pit; and then witnessed the humiliating fallout of his own men as they defected back to their old boss. Even his name seemed to be everywhere. Crossworth's tobacconist's, Crossworth's houses, Crossworth's pit and Crossworth's mill . . . Fairclough raged, his heartbeat singing a mantra in his ears, Crossworth, Crossworth, Crossworth.

Then a few years after Crossworth bought the new pit, Fairclough's wife died. He missed her; not for herself particularly, but for the conscience she had carried for him. Whilst she had lived, she had backed everything he had ever done and absolved him of all guilt. She actually *approved* of him. So even when his conscience might occasionally trouble him – as it did after he fired a man for simply arguing with him – Fairclough's wife told him he was right. And he chose to believe her.

But when she died he wasn't quite so sure any more; and besides, the house was very quiet most of the time and there was no one left who chose to spend time with him. Not even his daughter. She merely endured him until he could marry her off. It had been a bad time, Fairclough remembered; no old man Cotter around to plot with, no wife, with all his ambitions held to ransom by bloody Crossworth.

But now things might not be quite so hopeless. The two

bright Crossworth boys weren't quite what they seemed. Admittedly, Jim was alert and pleasant enough, but Freddie . . . Fairclough could feel his blood pressure dropping . . . Freddie was no good. No good at all. Fairclough knew all the signs, because he recognized himself in Freddie Crossworth – the same lack of feeling, the same unconcern for others. He even knew the walk, that saunter which came from the hips, not from the shoulders like other men. Before he had got fat, *he* had walked that way . . .

Oh yes, Freddie Crossworth was going to be trouble. Big trouble. Fairclough had already begun to hear rumours: Freddie skipping off school, chatting up the girls, drinking a little, skiving a lot. He'd even had his first flutter on the horses the other week, using one of Fairclough's bookies – and had been violently angry when he lost.

Oh yes, Fairclough thought to himself, things weren't looking too bad after all. Crossworth's luck – so bloody charmed – might finally have begun to run out.

'Sir?'

Fairclough glanced up. He had forgotten Forecourt was there.

'What is it?'

'The bills, sir. You called me in to show you them.'

'Bad?'

'Not particularly.'

'Anything likely to put up a man's blood pressure?'

'No. Just minor irritations.'

Fairclough nodded. *Just minor irritations.* Like Crossworth's son was now. A minor irritation – with all the potential of becoming a full-blown drama. It hurt Fairclough less to think of Crossworth's success, knowing that his son might just ruin him on his behalf.

Chapter Eleven

1934

'Dry up,' Freddie said simply, tossing aside the butt of his cigarette and glancing over the hills outside Oldham. To the left was Upper Mill, to the right the far-off peaks of the Pennines, and below, the cluster of mill chimneys and terraces gridded over the earth. Smoke snaked from the ragged line of chimneys and the noise of a mill hooter sounded distantly from below. The sky was low with haze, rain stomping the horizon, the sun making dirty tears of light through the seamless cloud.

'It's your own fault –'

'Oh Christ!' Freddie replied, turning to look at his brother. 'That's all you ever say.'

Jim frowned and looked away. 'I don't have to be here –'

'So go!'

Immediately Jim turned and began to walk off, Freddie, panicked, calling after him.

'Aw, come on, I didn't mean it. Jim. JIM!'

He turned. 'What now?'

'I didn't mean it.'

'You're the one in the mess.'

'I know, I know,' Freddie said soothingly.

'I should let you rot.'

'But you won't.'

'Why not?'

Freddie tried a smile. 'Because we're brothers?'

'Because I'm the only one who'll help you out, more like.'

There was a wind blowing down from the hills. Soon it

would snow. February snow coming over the Northern hills. The next day was to be their twenty-first birthday, a cause for celebration. At least it should have been. When they were born, John had set out a trust for them; on their coming of age his sons were to inherit ten per cent of the business each. A partial and gradual passing over would follow year by year, the boys steadily taking over the mill, the mine, and the property that John Crossworth had so assiduously accumulated.

That had been his plan – but circumstances had caused him to revise it. Jim had gone to work with him at the mine and later John had eased him into the cotton mill business – but not Freddie. Instead, at seventeen Freddie had run off, disappearing without a word. For months Sarah had sat by the window waiting, just as Peggy Crossworth had done so many years before. She had known the bitter anxiety of a lost child and yet she never, in a look or by a word, lost hope.

'It's my punishment,' John had said simply. 'I know what it feels like now. Until now I never realized what I put my mother through.'

Sarah said nothing, simply turned back to the window.

'You think I was too hard with him, don't you?'

Her head remained firmly turned away from him.

'Our son stole, Sarah. He *stole* from us.'

'We are his parents,' she said simply, tired of the argument. 'I don't condone it, but –'

'But *what*?' her husband challenged her. 'I should have let him off? Forgiven him? What good would that have done, Sarah? We've forgiven him too much for too long.'

'Well, he's gone now,' she replied dully. 'I suppose we should be grateful that we don't have to worry about him any longer.'

Freddie had been betting, losing money. Or so John discovered later. He had been to the dogs – gone to the dogs literally, John thought grimly – and Dandry Fairclough had been behind it. So Sammy Upton told him. Fairclough had loaned Freddie money to pay off his first debts and then continued to loan him money to cover the next, and the next, winching him in like a hooked carp.

Money had slid through Freddie's fingers like grease. Money from his father and his mother; first his allowance, then, when they stopped that, he stole from them. Broke into the safe at the pit and took the men's wages for the week. Their *wages* . . . John shook his head incredulously. To take the miners' money; the money good men had worked hard for. Money to pay rents and feed children. To take it, without conscience. And then to run away.

That was the hardest part to bear: the cowardice. For years John had tried to pull his son into line; for years Sarah had persevered, trying to develop a conscience where there was none. And no one had tried harder than Jim – Freddie was his brother, after all. Freddie was ungovernable, amoral: the head-banging child who had grown up banging his head against the world. Charm – his most adept weapon – he employed with all the skill of a butcher filleting a carcass. He knew enough about everything to gain attention and too little about everything to hold respect. Nothing suited him for long; no clothes, no places, no interests. He was, for a considerable time before his disgrace, marking time towards disaster.

He was too old to hit, or reason with. Over six feet, like his brother, Freddie had been well-built, handsome, attracting interest effortlessly. When he left he had wanted for nothing, and had therefore aimed for nothing.

For three months he had stayed away, during which time he sent no word. Then one day in early April, Freddie Crossworth came home. Sarah had been waiting for him for so long that when he finally did walk up the path she remained motionless by the window without blinking, afraid that if she did so, he would disappear.

He came in whistling – and explained nothing.

'*Why*, Freddie?' Jim asked at last as he glanced over to his brother and remembered that day four years ago.

'Why *what*?'

'Why don't you consider other people?'

The rain had finally started, coming sweet as bile, Jim turning up the collar of his coat.

'Oh hell, I try to be thoughtful, honest I do. It just isn't easy for me. I don't want to be like everyone else. You know what I mean, Jim . . .' He trailed off, bored by trying to explain, his thoughts turning back to the morning. 'I have to say, though – I never thought the old bugger would do it.'

Only hours earlier his father had called him into his study and told him, without emotion, that he was cutting him out of his will. There was to be no trust fund for Frederick Crossworth – not until he had proved himself. If he pulled himself together, worked in the business and made progress, then John would reconsider, but not until then.

Freddie had stayed silent. He had expected it, of course, and yet in a way he had thought he might get away with it as he had done so many times before. But, foolishly, he had underestimated his father. As he spoke, John had drawn out a sheet of paper on which he had written every one of his son's misdemeanours. It was so like him, Freddie had thought at the time, so very businesslike. The list was unflattering. Betting, fighting, lying. It made him sound like a comic music-hall villain, Freddie thought, almost amused.

But it wasn't funny for long.

'I don't know how you can act so surprised, you had to see it coming,' Jim said bluntly. 'It's your own fault –'

'You've already said that!' Freddie snapped.

Jim studied his brother for a long moment before he spoke again. 'Just tell me honestly – what did you *expect*? Did you think Father would still let you have the money? After all, Freddie, what have you ever done to earn it?'

'I suppose you think you've done plenty for your share,' Freddie replied acidly, pushing his hands into his coat pockets and squinting against the cold.

'Actually I do,' Jim replied simply. 'I work hard and like the business –'

'Well, bully for you, because I bloody don't!'

'So how can you expect to live off it, if you don't contribute to it?'

Freddie's expression was sour as he turned back to his brother. 'It's all so simple for you, isn't it? The preferred son, the doting little favourite, hanging on Daddy's coat-tails –'

'Watch it,' Jim said warningly. 'Remember that you're asking me for help.'

Superficially contrite, Freddie's tone softened. 'Listen, I'm not like you, Jim. I don't like this bloody town. I don't like mills and pits –'

'I've noticed.'

'I'm not you.'

Suddenly Jim wanted to walk away. He realized that his feelings for Freddie had changed; he no longer admired his brother or envied his recklessness. Standing on that hillside, Freddie was suddenly revealed for what he really was, a grasping, insensitive lout.

'Jim, come on, tell me what I should do.'

'Tell Father.'

'Naturally!' Freddie said with derision.

'So what else *can* you do? Run away?'

'It was an accident.'

Jim stared down at his shoes. The rain had soaked into the leather, making it dark around the soles. Far away another hooter sounded from one of the furthest mills; change of shift. Soon the looms would stop for a minute, the cotton-dusted air settling like a snowfall.

'How's she taking it?'

'Not well . . .' Freddie said sullenly.

'Told her parents?'

'Do me a favour! I told her to keep quiet.'

Jim stared ahead; he wanted to be gone, to get back to the things he understood. I don't want to hear about it,

Freddie, he wanted to say. Go away, run off again, but don't involve me. I don't want to know any more.

'Who is it?'

'Sally Rimmer.'

Unexpectedly, Jim laughed.

'I'm glad you think this is funny!'

'You made a bad choice there. Have you seen the size of her brother?'

Impatiently, Freddie moved closer. 'If you could just lend me the money, I could sort it out.'

Jim shook his head. 'I don't have it –'

'Liar!'

Jim's expression hardened. '*I don't have it.* Besides, what d'you need money for?'

'An abortion.'

A bird flew over them; high on the February air tides. A kestrel, Jim thought absently.

'Are you mad?'

'I've no choice,' Freddie answered. 'Oh Jim, don't look at me that way! It's not that bad. She'll get over it –'

'Haven't you done enough?'

'It was an accident –'

'Which you now want to cover up. Get some money off your soft brother and pay for an abortion. Then no one would be any the wiser, would they?' Jim's face had hardened, the birthmark on his temple dark against the cold skin. 'Well, you can go to hell, Freddie. This time you're on your own.'

'Jesus! What's the problem?' his brother asked, genuinely mystified. 'It happens every day.'

'Not to Sally Rimmer, it doesn't.'

Freddie was incredulous; 'What's she to you? You don't even know her!'

'I don't have to know her to know that it's wrong.'

'Christ!'

'Yes, go on, lose your temper, Freddie. Shout like you usually do. Then you can go on and on about your hard

131

bloody luck. That's the way it normally goes, isn't it? Well, this time I don't want to listen to you. This time, you can listen to *me*.' The wind was starting up and pelting them with sleet. 'What you're doing is wrong. You got that girl into trouble and you can't buy your way out of it.'

'So what do you suggest? That I marry her?'

'Yes,' Jim replied flatly.

Throwing up his hands in exasperation, Freddie moved away and then turned back. His hair was wet, plastered to his head, his fine face baffled. He looked, Jim thought, just as he had done when he was thwarted as a child.

'I *can't* get married.'

'Why not?'

'I just can't.'

Huddling into his coat, Jim shivered: the sleet was settling, snow following on its cold heels.

'You slept with her –'

'Which is more than you've ever done with any girl, isn't it?' Freddie said peevishly.

Provoked, Jim moved towards him, his brother smiling and skipping back, ducking and diving as though he were sparring at a boxing match.

'What's the matter, brother, not getting your oats? You want to leave Daddy to run the business and work off all that excess energy more pleasantly –'

Incensed, Jim swung out at him, missing his head and landing his fist into his shoulder. Wincing in surprise, Freddie cursed and struck back, completely missing his brother as Jim delivered another swift blow to his abdomen. Immediately he doubled over, his eyes widened, his face ashen, the sound of air leaving his lungs as he slumped onto the hard ground.

Panting heavily, Jim stood over him.

'You want to fight some more?' he asked coldly. 'If you do, just let me know, I could happily continue.'

Crouched on his haunches Freddie shook his head, grabbing at breaths.

'You've . . . no . . . sense . . . of . . . humour.'

Still looming over his brother Jim could see the shadows under Freddie's cheekbones and the long narrow nose, white as a piece of chalk. His face was so similar to his own that it seemed he was looking in a mirror; and that, by striking his brother, he had in fact injured himself. Empty with past anger, he put out his hand.

'Get up.'

Freddie grasped it willingly, allowing Jim to pull him to his feet.

'Stop the act, Freddie, you're not really hurt.'

His brother gave him a slow look, then unexpectedly smiled. 'Bully.'

'A bully is someone who picks on someone smaller than himself.'

Idly, Freddie rubbed his solar plexus. His hands were bony, pliant, double-jointed at the thumbs. 'So, *will* you help me?'

'You mean, will I give you the money?'

'Yes.'

Jim shook his head. 'No, I won't.'

'So what the hell am I supposed to do?' Freddie snapped.

'Tell Father. Ask him for help.'

'For *money*?' Freddie asked, blinking against the wind.

'No, for *help*,' Jim replied, thinking ahead, automatically trying – as he had done so many times before – to get his brother out of trouble. 'Tell him you're sorry, that you want to turn over a new leaf –'

'He'd never believe me!'

'He might – if you meant it.'

Freddie's teeth were chattering. He looked nauseous, threatened. He looked, Jim thought, vaguely unpleasant. Why do I help you? he wanted to ask. Why do I do it so many times, when I know you would never help me? Or *would* you? . . . Despite himself he felt the usual draw towards Freddie. Smile at me, impress me. Let me live a little through your recklessness.

He had known from the beginning, at least from the time he had known how to reason, that in Freddie he lived vicariously. He did not want to be his brother, or to emulate him, but the sheer bravado, the bloody-minded arrogance of his twin let him indulge in some strange form of life change. Jim could listen to Freddie and hear about his misdeeds and slide easily – so very easily – into his role. He borrowed Freddie's life and could see himself – looking and sounding the same – acting as Freddie.

Which was why he needed his brother as much as Freddie needed him. Jim would never tell him this, would let his twin think that he was helping him because of their blood ties; would never let go of the only advantage he had over him. But when life seemed dull – and it could seem *so* dull – then it was a kind of comfort to pretend and appropriate Freddie's life for a while.

'Tell Father what you've been thinking, and that it's about time you settled down –'

'Hah!'

'Freddie,' Jim said patiently, 'I don't have to be here. Either listen to me, or I leave. The choice is yours.'

'Oh, go on!'

'Tell him you want to work in the business, that you're sorry for the past and want to make up for it. He might help you then.'

'Does he realize that I've been going out with Sally Rimmer?'

'I don't know, but he seems to hear about most things.'

'Bloody Sammy Upton!' Freddie said darkly. 'Sodding spy.'

The kestrel passed over them again; a shape against the dark sky.

'Are you in love with her?'

'I like her,' Freddie admitted. 'She's fun.'

Jim had heard her described in other ways, flighty being the most common. Pretty Sally Rimmer, curly-haired, long-legged, one of the best dancers in town. Always ready to go out, her brother following her like a guard dog. But not always, Jim realized. Her brother must have relaxed his watch or otherwise Sally wouldn't be pregnant ... The kestrel stooped a way off, finding a lone mouse in the wet tangle of hill gorse.

Dear God, Jim thought suddenly, what would their mother say when she heard about this? An image of Sarah materialized in front of him, blocking out the hills and the kestrel. She had had her hair cut shorter, her clothes made by her own private costumier. Always elegant, she had metamorphosed into someone so soignée that people stared at her wherever she went. In his mind Jim held up his image of his mother and then compared it with Sally Rimmer with her silly hair and silly clothes. *Silly Sally Rimmer* – but harmless for all that, and probably all too aware of the disgrace which was awaiting her.

'Well, what d'you think?'

Jim blinked, turning to his brother. 'About what?'

'I was wondering what Mother would say.'

They had picked up each other's thoughts. As usual.

'I don't know,' Jim replied honestly. 'But she doesn't like scandal. She's had too much of it in the past.'

Far too much. Too much as a foreigner, too much as the mother of Freddie Crossworth.

'She'll play hell.'

Jim nodded. 'Probably.'

Sighing, Freddie lit up another cigarette. 'Funnily enough, I'm more worried about telling her than Father.'

His brother understood why. For John Crossworth it was just another betrayal to come on top of all the others; to Sarah it would seem like an emotional deceit. Something immoral and spiritually cheap.

'You couldn't tell her for me, could you?'

'No.'

Freddie had the sense not to pursue it.

'I suppose I *could* try and talk to the old man,' he said at last, staring down at the town below them.

What else *could* he do? Run away again? To *what*? He wasn't likely to make his fortune alone. He hadn't the skill or the tenacity. His best chance – his *only* chance – was here. Unlikely as it seemed, perhaps he really *could* save the situation . . . Idly, Freddie puffed cigarette smoke from between his lips. If he buckled down for a while and made it look as though he were trying to make a go of it, he could sneak back into his father's good books and then back into his will . . . Straining his eyes, Freddie could see the huge letters ASH printed on the side of the mill. It *was* his inheritance, after all. He was entitled to it as much as his brother.

Yes, he would talk to his father, beg forgiveness, go to work in the bloody business, and then explain about Sally. His father had contacts, knew everyone in the town; he was bound to know someone who would marry her and give a name to the child. After all, John Crossworth wouldn't want Sally Rimmer as a daughter-in-law. He was too proud, too aware of his position as one of the town's worthies to endanger his own standing . . . Freddie smiled, his humour picking up. His father would sort it all out.

And all the time Freddie plotted, Jim was also thinking about their father. *You have to marry well. Not for money, but you have to choose someone you can respect. It matters . . . Love is the hardest thing to find and the easiest thing to lose.* He had said those words to him only months before, embarrassed to be talking about affection, unusually hesitant. *I was lucky with your mother. She made my life. The right partner can do that. The wrong one can ruin everything.* He had paused, fiddling through some swatches of material as though the words he sought were to be found amongst them. *If I ever did an honourable thing, it was due to your mother. If I ever behaved well, it was because I was afraid to lose face in her eyes. Remember what I say, Jim, and choose someone who, by loving you, makes you a better man.*

'I *am* going to talk to him,' Freddie said finally, cutting into his brother's thoughts and grinding out his cigarette. 'I reckon I can pull it off.' He smiled, then began to walk down the hillside to the town. 'Yes, I reckon I can really pull it off.'

She had been crying for so long that she had lost track of time. Nothing was funny any more; nothing was light-hearted or silly. It was real. She was pregnant. The word snapped at her, with all its sickening implications. An unmarried woman, pregnant with Freddie Crossworth's child. Fiercely she pressed her fingers into her stomach, her nails scratching into her skin. *Pregnant* . . . It had been a wonderful evening, they'd been dancing, and he'd looked so handsome that when he kissed her . . .

The moon had been high and full; yellow as sulphur over the hills. Far below them the town had been strung with lights, on Oldham Heights the air cool, his lips cold against hers. They had been dancing to a band, Sally letting her skirt fly up, her legs – the best in the town – on full view. For once her brother hadn't been there; hadn't been watching from the sidelines, set on guard by their widowed mother. He had flu and was at home in bed . . . So she'd danced and drunk a little and watched the yellow moon climb up and shine through the dance-hall windows.

Later she watched the same moon over Freddie's shoulder as she lay under him. The ground was dry but cold – it hadn't rained for days – and far away she could hear the sound of an animal in the grass. Laughing, Freddie had teased her, told her he adored her, taken off her blouse under the yellow moon. It had been the most natural thing to do, and it proved that she loved him . . . that was what he had said, anyway. Only he hadn't said that he loved her.

The moon seemed a lot less bright afterwards; a sickly disc without magic. And the music had stopped, the dance hall closed as he walked her home. No more voices, no more laughter, only the sly creeping in after everyone was asleep. Her house had been cold, a pot of tea left out to welcome her back. It was then she had started to cry, looking at the earthenware pot and shivering by the dead ashes of the fire.

She had thought that you didn't get pregnant the first time, but weeks later her period hadn't come and Sally knew – without doubt – what had happened. At work in the shoe shop she was silent, withdrawn, no banter, grey-faced in her uniform. She caught the bus at another stop to avoid seeing her friends and when Freddie came calling she clung to him frantically.

'Hey, what was that for?' he asked her, pulling away and staring into her face. She wore no make-up, her hair lank. 'You look awful.'

Self-consciously, she glanced away. 'I'm OK.'

'We could go to the pictures later . . .' he said, but she could see that he was annoyed by her appearance and unwilling to be seen with her, '. . . if you fix yourself up.'

She wanted to tell him then, but hesitated. Later she told herself that she wanted to be sure she was pregnant before she worried him, but she knew the real reason she didn't tell him was because when she did he would be angry and she couldn't risk that.

So she kept quiet and avoided her mother's eyes and felt each act of kindness as a blow. Her brother recovered and went everywhere with her again and she wanted to laugh – to *laugh* – and tell him that he was too late, far too late. But she didn't, and soon she stopped going to dances and lengthened her skirts and never once looked up at the moon, yellow or otherwise.

Then six weeks later, she told Freddie.

'What! You're joking!' He was agitated, already eager to be gone.

'We have to do something,' Sally said hurriedly, trying to sound serious.

But he didn't know the serious girl, only the silly one.

'Hey, come on, Sally, you *must* be wrong,' he'd chivvied her. 'Wait a bit and see.'

'I'm *not* wrong,' she'd insisted, using a tone of voice he had never heard before, her face peaky, her allure gone.

'I have to think,' he said angrily, moving to the door and bumping into her mother. 'Oh, hello there, Mrs Rimmer, how are you?'

She almost hated him then. In that one moment when he sounded so unconcerned; when he acted so plausibly, as though there was nothing wrong. But what could she do? It was his child, Freddie Crossworth had to take responsibility ... So she followed him out and walked down the street with him, pausing at the corner when he did.

'You have to stand by me –'

His face hardened: 'Now, just a minute.'

But she was determined, trapped, attached to him not through passion, but necessity. 'You have to do something,' she repeated, not knowing how to continue, her limited intelligence only taking her so far. 'You have to – or I'll go and talk to your mother.'

His face had altered then from unconcern to slyness. She saw the change and was momentarily threatened.

'Freddie,' she said, touching his arm to soothe him. '*Please* ...'

'Don't you dare to go near my mother!' he hissed. 'Don't you dare.'

'I won't! I won't!' Sally assured him, already sorry for what she had said. If he left her she had nothing, and who was to say that his mother would help her? The Rimmers were nobodies from the poorer side of town. What chance did they have against the Crossworths? She had been hasty and silly ...

Wetting her lips, Sally pushed back her hair and tried to smile.

'I didn't mean it, I'm just scared,' she said timidly, trying to flirt and then faltering. 'Freddie ... we *have* to do something.'

'Leave it to me,' he said finally, turning away. 'I've got to think.'

She hurried after him down the street.

'When will I see you again?'

He didn't pause, or turn.

'Soon. '

'*How* soon?' she asked, close to tears, a bus passing by them and causing a draught which caught at their clothes.

'For God's sake!' he shouted angrily. 'Give me a chance.'

She stopped, cold in a thin dress, crying, and knowing that her mother would want to know why when she got back. But it didn't seem to matter any more; all that mattered was that Freddie was angry.

'Freddie, don't shout at me –'

He had the upper hand and knew it. 'Why not?' he queried, turning to look at her with an expression of irritation. 'You follow me around all the time –'

'I just wanted to talk to you –'

'– and make me look a fool.' He stared at her. 'You should do something with yourself, you look terrible.'

Her tears were unstoppable, her voice faltering. 'Don't be angry.'

A man walked past, staring hard at both of them. Annoyed, Freddie pulled Sally towards him and dropped his voice.

'You're making a spectacle of yourself.'

'I don't care –'

'Well, I do!' he replied savagely. 'How could you let this happen?'

'What?'

'How could you let yourself get pregnant?'

Her face slackened, bewilderment in her eyes. '*How could I let it happen?*' she repeated blankly. 'I thought . . . I didn't know about . . . Oh, Freddie, you were the first man I ever went with.'

'I bet!'

She could feel her legs go limp, her mouth drying.

'You *were*,' she whispered. 'You *were*.'

He realized then she was telling the truth and felt even more cornered as he led her on, hurrying her down the street. Blindly she stumbled along with him, her mind reeling. He thought she was a tart, a cheap tart. Everything he had ever said or done had been a lie. He had just wanted to sleep with her, and nothing more. Suddenly dizzy, Sally stopped by a lamppost and clung on to it. The iron was cold against her hands, chilling her face when she laid her cheek against it.

'What is it? Are you sick?'

She said nothing.

'Sally, are you sick?' he repeated.

Silence.

In those few moments – as she held on to that lamppost – Silly Sally Rimmer grew up. Everything she had believed, everything she had enjoyed, everything she had hoped for, was suddenly seen for what it was – a sham. The only reality was that she was pregnant by this man.

Slowly she glanced over to Freddie, her gaze unreadable. 'Take me home.'

He was more disturbed by her now than he had been before.

'Listen, Sally, we'll sort it out –'

'I just want to go home,' she replied, pushing herself from the lamppost and walking away.

Hurriedly he ran after her, taking off his coat and putting it round her shoulders.

She would have been so glad of the gesture before, but now it was meaningless. Something done out of guilt, no more.

'Sally, we have to talk –'

'Not now,' she said simply, striding ahead, her eyes fixed on the street. The air was very cold, drying her tears and taking down the swelling round her eyes. With luck, no one would notice anything unusual when she got back.

'I'll call by tomorrow.'

'Yes,' she said quietly. 'Do that.'

'Then we'll talk.'

Her shoes were making a lot of noise – *such* a lot of noise – on the street. Funny how she had never noticed that before.

'I have to go now,' Freddie said as they reached the corner. 'Will you be all right?'

She nodded, then walked on without looking back. He was sorry now, Sally thought, sorry for what he had done and what he had said. He was wondering what she was going to do . . . Suddenly she paused, struggling to prevent further tears, her teeth biting into her bottom lip. He was thinking of how he could get out of it, she realized, how he could escape . . . The street swam in front of her, the hated moon making another entrance over the terraces. But he couldn't, he *wouldn't*, get away with it.

She had wanted to love him, but he had spoiled that. He had all but called her a tart, and killed any innocence with a few short, spiteful, thoughtless words; and he would, Sally swore in that moment, learn just how costly a few cruel syllables could be.

Chapter Twelve

Freddie had gone to the pit to find his father, but John had left, moving on to the mill. Walking with his head down, Freddie then crossed town and made for the Ash mill, pausing in the yard to collect his thoughts. What had seemed so simple on Oldham Heights was more daunting now. A whistle blew suddenly and Freddie jumped, one of the mill workers laughing and winking as she passed.

For once Freddie didn't respond, he just stood looking at the mill uneasily. The vast chimney rose up above him, steam coming from a doorway. His father's office was situated round the back. He was glad of that, for it meant John hadn't seen him coming. It meant he could leave if he wanted to. But how *could* he? Freddie wondered, taking out a cigarette and lighting it. God, what a mess.

'Freddie?'

He jumped at the sound of his name, unusually nervous.

Sammy Upton was staring at him; 'You lost, or summat?'

'Huh?'

'Well, you must be. You'd never come here by choice,' Upton replied slyly.

Narrowing his eyes, Freddie ignored the comment. 'Is my father in?'

Upton jerked his head to the right: 'In the office. You do know where that is, don't you?'

They had always detested each other; Upton seeing Freddie as the idle wastrel son, Freddie seeing Upton as his father's spy.

'You get funnier every time I see you,' Freddie said coldly. 'You should go on the stage.'

'So should you – as the amazing disappearing Crossworth,' Upton replied shortly, walking off.

Seething, Freddie walked round the back of the mill, avoiding the curious stares and the odd light-hearted wolf whistle from the mill girls. His steps seemed to drag, each one slower as he drew closer to his father's office. Every word he had rehearsed so perfectly now sounded ludicrous, as transparently false as a badly written play. Freddie paused, took a last puff of his cigarette and then walked in.

He wasn't going to find it easy playing the prodigal; and his father wasn't going to find it easy believing him. For an instant Freddie thought of his brother. Jim had no trouble talking to their father; and he was liked, even respected, by the workers. Freddie felt – to his amazement – a sudden and unpleasant tweak of jealousy. *Jealous of Jim!* Freddie thought incredulously. How *could* he be? His brother was tied in to this town, to the business: he was boring, reliable. He was Jim . . .

He was loved . . . Freddie felt himself falter, his skin clammy. No one really loved him, even his mother was cool with him now, exhausted by his exploits. And as for Sally Rimmer, she had trapped him with the oldest trick in the book, forcing him here today and making him beg. His temper seeped into every pore. He shouldn't have to ask his father to forgive him! He didn't regret anything he had done, so what was he asking forgiveness for?

But if he didn't beg, he was out. Freddie's right foot tapped on the yard cobbles. Tap, tap, tap, tap . . . The sound drummed into him, pitter-pattered on his nerve endings. He had to have money and he had to get out of the mess with Sally Rimmer. He had no choice.

But he wasn't used to asking for anything. Taking, yes. Asking, no. Freddie stared at the red brick walls, hearing the loud voices from the weaving shed. If I don't go in, I lose everything . . . He thought of the house on Queen's Road, of all the other property his father owned, of the furniture, the silver, the mill, the pit: the images heaped up like food in front of a starving man.

It's mine by rights; I was born to it, Freddie thought, his eyes burning with the vision inside his head. He was mesmerized by the image, so transfixed that he jumped, startled, when he heard his name called.

'Freddie?'

John was walking towards him with a look of caution, his eyes steady and deep-set, his left hand fingering the gold watch he always wore. A prosperous man of business, the mill rising behind him like a maharajah's palace.

'Father,' Freddie said, and then paused. He was so bad-tempered he could hardly speak.

'It's good to see you,' John said sincerely. 'Come in.'

'I wanted to talk to you,' his son continued, the words coming like stale bread in a dry mouth.

'Good. It's time we talked,' John said simply, guiding his son towards his office and then sitting down. 'What is it?'

Idly Freddie slumped into a chair opposite his father's desk.

'I wanted to say I was . . .' The word *sorry* scalded his tongue. It dug its claws into his lips and refused to be said.

'Yes?' John queried, watching his son curiously.

The cold air had been unkind to Freddie, blanching his skin to make his hair look artificially dark, his eyelids puffy from lack of sleep. He would, John realized, age quickly, his good looks usurped by his nature.

'I wanted to say I was sorry,' Freddie managed at last, but the words were so insincere that they came out almost as an insult.

'You don't sound it.'

'I mean it!' Freddie snapped. 'I suppose if Jim had said it, it would have sounded right.'

'The question is – would Jim have *needed* to say it?'

Freddie's face was sullen. 'Oh no, not Jim. My brother never does anything wrong.'

'Have you come here just to argue with me?' John asked wearily, 'because if you have, I don't have the time, or the inclination.'

Freddie's gaze rested for a moment on the view outside the window. The rain had settled, a lonely sun was making its presence felt, the cobbles steaming.

'I don't want to fight.'

'Good.'

'I want to come and work in the business,' he said finally, looking back to his father. But he couldn't hold John's gaze and glanced away again.

'Why did you *really* come?'

Freddie's eyes closed. He had been an idiot to think for an instant that he could fool his father. No one ever did. His mind wandered blindly and he felt suddenly desperately tired, wearied by lying.

'I'm in trouble.'

There was no response.

'Big trouble.'

'What is it this time?' John asked, his tone of voice expressionless.

'I –'

Freddie was unexpectedly caught off balance by the door opening and Sarah entering. She came in smiling, dressed in brown velvet, a cream blouse high at her neck. Class was in every inch of her clothing, and her manner, only her voice still betraying her foreign history.

'Freddie,' she said, bending down and kissing his cheek. Shame made him flush hotly. 'How good to see you here.' She glanced over to John. 'Am I disturbing something?' She said it with the tone of someone desperately hoping that she was wrong, that trouble could on this occasion be circumvented.

John felt for the first time, as he looked at her, a desire to lie.

'Freddie came to talk.'

Sitting down, Sarah crossed her legs and leaned back in

her chair. Looking at her Freddie realized again the difference between his mother and his girlfriend, and flinched.

'So what do you want to talk about?' Sarah asked her son, pulling off her leather gloves and laying them on her lap. Freddie felt – crushingly and abruptly – overawed by her.

'I'm in trouble.'

Sighing, John looked down at his desk.

Calmly, Sarah looked over to her husband. 'Do you know what this is about?'

'You know as much as I do. Frederick was about to explain when you came in.'

'Then perhaps he would be good enough to continue,' Sarah said coldly, turning back to her son. 'Is it gambling?'

'No.'

'So what is it?'

Freddie's flush deepened; he lit up another cigarette.

'I've . . . got someone else in trouble.'

'I suppose that was the next step,' Sarah said, her tone chilling. 'Who?'

'A girl.'

The silence which followed his answer was pulverizing, Sarah rising to her feet and walking to the window. Slowly she traced her finger down the glass, struggling to contain herself. So the inevitable had happened at last, she thought. Her son had got some girl pregnant. Behind her she could hear her husband sigh.

'Who is she?'

'Sally Rimmer.'

Sally Rimmer – who was that? Sarah wondered, certainly no one she knew; no one her son had brought home to introduce. She had looked forward to that day; to the time when her sons would bring home their girlfriends; when they were little she even used to fantasize about it, making the home as welcoming as she could for the visitors. Dinner could be made for them, and perhaps later they would talk . . .

It had been a romantic notion, but a comforting one. As an only child Sarah had missed close ties and longed for a time when she would have daughters-in-law, girls to talk to, listen to, share confidences with. But the time had never come, instead she was listening to her son talk about some stranger with a stranger's name.

'She's pregnant, isn't she?' Sarah asked, without looking up.

Silence.

'Tell me, Freddie.'

'Yes.'

A sudden bang made her turn, John slamming his hands down on the desk top.

'Enough! When is it ever enough?' he bellowed, rising to his feet. 'When does it stop, Frederick? How much further can you go?'

'Sssh . . .' Sarah said, walking over and pressing her hand on her husband's shoulder. Without protesting, he sat down again. 'Arguments never do any good, do they, Freddie?' she asked her son. 'Nothing ever does any good, does it? No amount of love, of money, of attention does any good.' Her voice slowed, lowered. He was unexpectedly afraid of her and startled by her calm. 'You are so stupid, so very *stupid*. You had everything. What your father and I fought for, struggled for, dreamed of, you had given to you. If you had been an only son, I would have blamed myself, believed myself at fault. But you aren't an only child, you have a brother, and he's grown up well.' Her fingers drummed on the back of her son's chair, making him tense.

'For a long time I blamed *myself*. I really believed that I was at fault. But no more. No, now I know whose fault it is – and it's yours.' Her fingers stilled, lay behind Freddie's head. He thought for a moment that she would either hit him or put her hands over his eyes and tease him, as he had teased her so many times in the past. But she did neither. 'Your life is your own responsibility – not mine, not your father's. *You* have to account for what you've done.'

'Stricken, Freddie turned.

'Mother –'

At any other time she would have softened at the tone of his voice, but not this time. He had crossed over into some wilderness she neither recognized nor wished to visit; some moral exile which was his alone.

'Freddie, you will have to sort this out for yourself.'

'But –'

'You heard your mother!' John said harshly. 'This time you are on your own.'

'She's pregnant.'

'I know,' Sarah replied, her heart banging, even though her face was impassive. For an instant she saw the child in her son's face and wanted to hold him to make everything smooth again. But she couldn't, and she wouldn't. 'You'll have to marry her.'

'Marry her!'

'What else?' Sarah asked coldly, fixing her gaze on her son and daring him to question her. 'You will marry that girl –'

'She's no account.'

'Dear God,' John said hoarsely, 'is that all you can say? That she's "no account"? You take her good name and get her pregnant and then tell us that you can't marry her because she's no account?' He shook his head disbelievingly. '*Who is this?*' he asked his wife. 'Who is this person? Who is this man? It can't be my son. He *can't* be!'

'You'll do the right thing and marry her,' Sarah said firmly. 'I don't care how rich or how poor she is, how clever or how stupid, how decent or how vulgar. But you *will* marry her.' Slowly she pulled on her gloves, pressing down each finger until the leather was smooth. 'You'll also have to get a job to support your new family –'

'A job!'

'Yes, a job, Freddie. That's something other people have

to do in order to live. That's something you never did, and now you'll have to learn.' She stared at her son and then moved to the door. 'I'm tired of you, Freddie, more tired than you could possibly imagine. I want some pleasure from you now, some good news, no more of your dirty laundry to wash. I am your mother and I demand some respect. Now might be the time to remember that.'

Stumbling to his feet, Freddie moved over to her. 'Mother, I didn't mean –'

'You never *mean* to do anything, Freddie! And that's the trouble.' Her voice rose sharply. 'Well, *I* mean everything I do, and everything I say. I mean to love your father and your brother and I mean to stop loving you so much until you've proved that you're worth it.'

Stunned, Freddie stared at his mother and then blundered past her into the corridor. A moment later his feet could be heard on the cobbles outside. Drained, Sarah sat down, staring numbly at her gloved hands. She had never felt so angry and realized that her fury was in fact disappointment. All the promise, all the intelligence and good looks that Freddie possessed had come to this: a wasted life, and marriage to a girl he did not love or even respect.

'Are you all right?' John asked, getting up and putting his arm around her.

'I love him so much,' Sarah said blindly. 'How is it possible to love someone so much when they don't love you?'

'But he does love you.'

'No,' she said simply, 'love means considering the other person's feelings, wanting their good opinion. Freddie loves Freddie.' She could feel her skin prickle, crawl with unease. 'Nothing good ever comes to people like that, John.'

For some extraordinary reason, Jim felt guilty. He hadn't been the one to get Sally Rimmer pregnant, he hadn't gambled and lied. He had been the good son. But oh, how sour it seemed. He was so predictable, so reliable, the one set to inherit, the one who deserved to. Who said? Jim wondered. Who dictated that he was worthy and Freddie wasn't? He looked at the empty place set for Freddie and the food balled up in his throat. What would it be like without his brother?

Carefully he glanced over to his mother. Sarah was staring at her food, buttering and rebuttering a slice of toast. She spread the butter to the very edge and then resmoothed it, her eyes unfocused. On his other side, his father was eating a boiled egg, the sound of the spoon on his plate unnaturally loud, the broken top of the egg discarded on one side.

Freddie's knife and fork were untouched, his cup and saucer unused. He seemed – although absent – to be more present than ever, Jim waiting for one of his flippant comments or a sudden catching of his eye. He felt disabled by the loss of his brother. His twin; his alter ego. He missed him helplessly.

'Did he say anything?'

Sarah looked over to her husband: 'Who?'

'Frederick. Did he say anything when he left?'

'Nothing.'

No, he hadn't said a word. Just packed a few belongings and left by the back door. Surprisingly he took nothing valuable: making a statement in his own way. See, I don't need you, any of you. I can manage, watch me. But would he? Jim wondered. And where was he now? Off on his travels again? Or nearer to home? He tried to imagine Freddie working, holding down a job – but he couldn't. He tried to imagine Freddie married – but that was even harder to visualize.

'Perhaps an allowance –'

Sarah stared at her husband evenly. 'No, he has to stand on his own two feet –'

'But there are others involved,' John countered. 'A woman and a child.'

'They are his responsibility,' she replied, her tone cold.

'Freddie has to look after them. He's capable and he has to grow up.'

'What if he doesn't?'

She stared at her husband for a long moment. Time stretched out like the limbs of a cat waking.

'What are you saying? That we should have behaved differently? Made it easy for him?'

'No,' John answered her. 'I'm saying that there are others involved now. It's not just our son.'

Calmly Sarah laid down her knife. The sun was trying to shine through the windows, but the day was overcast, sullen with shade.

'He has to learn,' she repeated.

'And if he doesn't?'

The question strung itself out in the quiet room, Jim glancing away and out towards the garden. In the distance he could hear a mill hooter, and he rubbed the birthmark on his temple thoughtfully. He knew where Sally Rimmer lived and wondered what she was feeling, if she was now aware of the situation or mourning Freddie's abandonment. He felt a tug of two different emotions: responsibility and resentment.

Slowly he rose to his feet. 'I've got something to do,' he said simply, kissing his mother on her cheek. 'I'll see you later.'

It took him only minutes to cross town and enter the low terrace where Sally Rimmer lived. The houses were shuttled together, cheek by jowl, each door the same, apart from the number. Here and there some tenants had tried to grow flowers in window pots, but the Oldham air had swamped the vegetation and nothing bloomed in the sooty cold. In the alley beyond, a discarded mangle lay overgrown with town weeds.

It was not his problem, Jim told himself. Better stay out of it. But somehow Freddie's problem *was* also his. He wondered why he felt responsible; a responsibility his brother would never have felt for him, but he couldn't explain or understand the emotion. It was simply there. Unasked for, yet irrefutable.

Number 17 was dark, without curtains, the windows shielded with paper blinds. On the front step there was a cat washing itself and from an upstairs window a dim light burned. Jim looked round. The street was empty of people except for one woman throwing a bowl of washing-up water onto the cobbles.

She came up behind him, her feet quick on the street. Hurried, anxious. Turning, Jim saw her smiling face and then, almost immediately, her frown. He realized at once that she had thought he was Freddie.

'Jim ... oh ...'

'Sally,' he replied, hesitating. 'How are you?'

Her hair was tied back, curls damp from the wintry air, her voice jerky.

'Is ... is Freddie with you?'

His heart sank. 'No. Haven't you seen him?'

She tried on a smile, then faltered and turned away, looking for her front door key. The cat had risen to its feet and was winding itself around her legs.

'I just wondered,' Jim began, then paused. *What* did he wonder? Dear God, what was he doing there? 'Is there anything I can do to help?'

Her eyes turned to him then she immediately glanced away, flushed with embarrassment. She was wondering how much he knew about her condition, wondering what he wanted, wondering why it was him and not his brother standing next to her.

'No,' she said solemnly. 'There's nothing you can do.'

But she didn't go in; instead she paused with her key in the lock, her head turned away.

'Is he coming to see me?'

'I don't know,' Jim answered truthfully.

From behind the door, he could hear a man's voice shouting, and remembered Sally Rimmer's brother.

'That's Frank,' she said, turning back to him. 'My brother . . .'

Jim nodded.

'He'll kill him if he finds out.' She fought to keep control. 'Where is Freddie?'

'I don't know.'

'But you came – *why*? Are you coming to tell me he's gone away? Is that it?' she asked, panic settling round the question. 'Because you should tell me – you should. Really. I might be able . . .' She trailed off, lost her verbal footing, Frank still calling out behind the three inches of wood which separated them.

'I just wanted to see that you were all right.'

She leaned against the door jamb, smiling dimly. 'I'm pregnant.'

'I know, Sally.'

Her hand was still holding the key. 'I should go in . . .'

Reluctantly Jim nodded. 'If you like.'

'They'll be wondering where I am . . . I should go in . . .'

Pity swamped him. 'Look, Sally, if you need anything –'

'I need Freddie.'

'I know, I know,' he blundered. 'But if there's anything I can do to help.'

'Make him come here,' she answered. 'He *has* to come.'

Her voice petered out; both of them knew that no one could make Freddie do anything. The air around them darkened, sour Northern rain threatened, the sound of Frank Rimmer's voice coming cold and threatening from behind the door. In that instant Jim felt such a pity for her and such an anger for his brother that he could not speak, and stared mutely at his shoes.

'Jim, thank you . . . Thanks . . . I don't suppose you would like to come in for a minute, would you?' He could sense her distress, the anguish behind the invitation. 'I mean, you don't have to, or anything. I just thought –' Frank was still shouting behind the door and she was perilously close to tears. 'I know you don't want to –'

Without another word, Jim followed her in.

Well, he'd bloody show them, wouldn't he? Think they can push him about, make him look stupid, give everything to bloody Jim! Oh well, he'd see about that. He'd do it on his own, make his own fortune . . . Angrily Freddie walked down Union Street, his case in his hand. He had packed without thinking and was only now realizing that he had put in no underwear. He hadn't really expected to go; had been expecting his mother or father to stop him at the last minute, to step in as they had done so many times before.

But this time they hadn't. His mother – his *mother*, for God's sake! – had told him to marry Sally Rimmer and get a job . . . Freddie's feet slowed as he left Queen's Road further and further behind. He couldn't get a job. What kind of job? He wasn't qualified. Besides, he didn't want to get a job to support a wife and child . . . The thought smacked into him, stunned him. A wife and child, it was too much responsibility at the age of twenty-one. Far too much. He should be enjoying himself, free, able to do as he pleased, knowing that he was going to inherit a fortune one day.

But what had happened? He, who could have had his pick of any girl in the town, had got landed with Sally Rimmer.

Freddie stared ahead, cold to the pit of his stomach and suddenly, indelibly, afraid. His support was gone; his family left behind; the future he had counted on, lost. He felt a nervous shiver start in his limbs, sweat coming sour under his arms. Oh God, he thought blindly, what am I going to do? What on God's earth am I going to do?

From her eyrie in Up Holland Hettie looked out over the town. Arnold had been and gone back to his wife, the day coming in long and empty. She was bored, tired of her lover and all too aware that she was ageing. Not that

Arnold noticed; he thought her as dazzling as he had done when they met. It was lucky that, Hettie thought, lucky that love really was blind. And stupid.

That morning he had talked. Going on and on about his grandfather, old man Cotter. It hadn't meant a thing to her; she had never liked him and had always borne a grudge for his trying to buy her off, although, to be honest, the arrangement had turned out to suit her. She smiled to herself; she had had the last laugh on the old man, Arnold providing for his mistress much better than he did for his lawful wife. Sometimes it still smarted, though. She would have liked to have been Mrs Cotter, would have liked to take possession of Marstone Hall someday. Would have liked to be respectable.

Idly she fingered the ring Arnold had given her the night before. It flashed in the daylight like a lighthouse. Again she smiled, a light to reel in her drowning lover ... then she stopped smiling and frowned, squinting to see who it was walking up her front path. Cursing, Hettie snatched up her glasses and then, with a curious expression, opened the door.

'Well, well, well,' she said simply.

Freddie regarded his aunt for a long silent moment. Hettie was still not dressed at ten thirty in the morning, although her hair was freshly washed and her make-up was immaculate.

Standing back, she bowed in mock courtesy. 'Come in.'

Sullenly Freddie obeyed, then turned. 'I wanted to come before –'

'Oh, cut it out!' Hettie replied sharply. 'We both know why you're here – Sally Rimmer.'

She had heard the gossip, the intelligence coming fast over the terraces as tittle-tattle always did. Sally Rimmer's disgrace was up for grabs, news for anyone who wanted it.

Red-faced, Freddie glanced away.

'Oh, don't go sulky on me. Put your bag down,' Hettie went on, 'and then tell me what you want.'

'I didn't come for anything –'

She laughed, slid into a chair and folded her legs under her. On the table by her arm lay her glasses, steel-rimmed, out of place.

'I was just passing.'

'Really. Going *where*?' she asked, raising her darkened eyebrows.

'I'm not sure.'

Carefully she studied her nephew. Good-looking, no mistake, and thoroughly useless if all the rumours were to be believed. He hadn't been to see her for over four years; warned off by his parents. But now, when he was in trouble – in very public trouble – he came back to her. She smiled to herself. Her father would enjoy hearing all about this later.

'So, is Sally Rimmer pregnant?'

'Well . . .'

'Well, *is* she, or *isn't* she?'

He nodded stiffly. 'Yes.'

'And what are you going to do about it?'

'My parents want me to marry her.'

Hettie's mouth slammed shut. *Marry her!* Sally Rimmer? That was a turn-up; she hadn't expected her stuck-up brother to say such a thing. But then again . . . Hettie thought back. Maybe it was *exactly* how John would react. Insist on doing right by the girl. Her thoughts raced into the future. Sally Rimmer marrying Freddie – Silly Sally Rimmer to marry into the rich Crossworth family. Dear God, she would have money, status, everything – and for what, for just lying on her back?

Hettie's jealousy filled the room. It burned against the cushions and singed the curtain drapes.

'And what are you going to do, Freddie?'

'I suppose I have to marry her.'

Hettie was sly with malice. 'A girl like *that*? Oh Freddie, think about it carefully, you could do so much better for yourself.' She leaned forward, touched his knee. 'You could marry anyone, so why tie yourself down? There are other alternatives.'

He could hardly have hoped for so much.

Evenly, Freddie looked at his aunt. 'But I don't have any money.'

'Well, that can be easily remedied,' Hettie replied, rising to her feet and walking into another room. A few minutes later she came back and handed him fifty pounds.

He counted it out incredulously. 'It won't cost this! I was told thirty-five.'

'Buy her something with the rest,' Hettie replied. 'It'll keep her sweet.'

He stood up, then kissed his aunt on her cheek.

'What would I have done without you?' he murmured, clenching the money in his fist. 'What would I have done?'

Mrs Rimmer was wearing an apron, her feet in slippers, her top teeth missing. Flustered, she saw Jim Crossworth enter with her daughter, and nearly knocked over a pan of potatoes, Frank glancing up from his chair by the fire. Above their heads a wooden clothes rack, heavy with washing, hung in the damp air, condensation running down the narrow windows.

'Oh dear,' Mrs Rimmer said blinking, her eyes red-rimmed, her embarrassment obvious as she looked at her daughter. 'You should have said you were bringing someone home.'

Sally was caught out, flustered. 'I didn't mean to, Mum. I mean . . . this is Jim Crossworth.'

Mrs Rimmer knew who it was; one of the Crossworth boys, the rich Crossworths, come courting her girl. 'Here, Frank,' she said sharply, 'give Mr Crossworth the chair.'

'I'm fine, Mrs Rimmer,' Jim said hurriedly.

'No, no you're not. FRANK!'

Angrily, her son stood up, the chair rocking backwards and then righting itself.

'I thought you were hanging around with *Freddie* Crossworth,' he said bitterly to his sister.

'That's none of your business!' his mother replied, taking off her apron and running her tongue over her toothless upper gum. 'Sally can bring home anyone she likes. She knows that. Don't you, flower?'

Jim could feel Sally wince next to him.

'Any friend of my girl's is a friend of mine,' Mrs Rimmer went on giddily. 'Tea, Mr Crossworth?'

Frank was scowling by the window; 'We've just had tea –'

'Then we'll have some more!' his mother replied shortly. 'You'll stay, Mr Crossworth, won't you? And I'll lay out the front room.'

Acutely embarrassed by the misunderstanding, Jim hesitated. Mrs Rimmer had thought he was going out with her daughter and that Sally had brought him home to meet the family. She didn't know that Sally was pregnant; that he was just offering comfort – of a sort. Mute with distress, Sally said nothing, her eyes fixed on the black kettle on the hearth.

Watching her, Jim wondered what to do for the best. 'I should be getting back –'

'Oh, not for a while,' Mrs Rimmer said helplessly. 'It'll take only a minute . . .' she went on, rushing off into the cramped front room.

The three of them stood in silence as they heard her trying to light the fire, the sound of hastily moved furniture scraping over the lino floor.

'I thought it were Freddie you were going with –'

'Shut up, Frank,' Sally said wearily.

His big face lapsed into puzzlement, then he turned belligerently to Jim. 'If you hurt my sister –'

'I have no intention of doing anything to harm her.'

Confused, Frank slumped back against the wall. 'Well . . . mind you don't.'

In the front room Mrs Rimmer was striking matches one after the other, without success.

'You could sneak out,' Sally said quietly to Jim, her voice dry with shame. 'I wouldn't mind.'

'It's OK. Honestly,' he replied, secretly wishing he were somewhere else. 'Really, it's fine.'

'We never use the front room,' Frank said suddenly, staring at the stranger, 'unless someone's special's coming.' He laughed without humour. 'Seems Mother's got her eye on you for her son-in-law –'

'*Please*, Frank,' Sally begged. 'Be quiet.'

'All ready!' Mrs Rimmer said suddenly, walking into the kitchen and smiling. Her top set of dentures was now in place. 'If you'd like to go through, Mr Crossworth, I'll bring in the tea.'

He would remember that meal for years afterwards, the shabby hopelessness of the house, the front room with its cheap table and waxed cloth, the unmatched chairs and the fire smoking intermittently from an unswept chimney. In minutes the mixture of damp and smoke had seeped into everything – his clothing, the tea, the food. His fingers were so chilled that soon he could feel nothing, the bread cold and moist against his lips, the silent presence of Sally next to him unutterably sad.

Frank left before tea. Jim wondered if that was a good thing or a bad, but couldn't decide. Mrs Rimmer chattered inanely on about her dead husband, explaining how he had originally come from something better. Then she winked, Sally flinching and staring down at her plate . . . And from time to time the smoke puffed into the room and his clothes soaked up the damp and the misery around them. Finally, an hour later, he rose to leave, Sally following him to the end of the street.

She had eaten nothing and yet her breath smelled sweetly

of cake. In that instant Jim could see what had drawn his brother to her.

'You've been very kind,' she said simply. Not Silly Sally any more, just someone desperate to say the right thing.

'Listen, if I can help you in any way, get in touch, will you?'

She looked at him, then glanced away again. 'It's not your problem.'

'I'd like to help – I'd like to be a friend to you.'

'Why?' she asked suddenly, her tone baffled.

Why? A good question, Jim admitted to himself. Because he felt sorry for her? Because he suspected that his brother would desert her? Because he wanted to say – don't expect anything, a wedding, a married life. At least, not with Freddie. But then, with whom, if it *wasn't* Freddie? Which other man in Oldham would marry Sally Rimmer now?

Jim looked into her face. She knew what he was thinking and glanced away.

'If you see Freddie –'

'I'll send him over to see you.'

'Yes . . . yes.'

He paused. Turned. Then turned back. 'Do you love him?'

He wondered for years afterwards what had prompted him to ask; what emotional curiosity had impelled him. He would never have been so inquisitive before.

'Not really,' Sally replied at last, her voice very low, 'not since he asked me to get an abortion.'

He felt as though he had lost his footing, so blunt was the admission. He had known that it was what Freddie had wanted, but had not expected his brother to have already mentioned it to Sally.

'Abortion,' Jim repeated quietly, ashamed of the word, ashamed that Sally had had to say it, let alone consider it. 'Freddie really does expect you to do that, does he?'

'He said he didn't want anything to do with a baby,'

Sally interrupted him hurriedly. 'He said if I got rid of it we could go on the way we were before.'

Timidly, she waited for his reaction.

'You don't have to tell me if you don't want to,' Jim began. His voice had hardened. 'But what did you say?'

'I didn't say anything,' she replied truthfully, 'I haven't seen Freddie for days.'

'But what *will* you say when you do?'

She put her head back suddenly, her neck exposed to the sooty air. It was, Jim thought later, a curiously vulnerable movement.

'Sally,' he repeated quietly, *'what will you say?'*

Her eyes turned on him questioningly: 'What d'you think I should say?'

Chapter Thirteen

A year later

Why should he be interested in her? Well, why *shouldn't* he? Kitty Letts wondered defiantly, sitting down in the bus. Why *not*? He may be one of the Crosworth boys, rich and eligible, but she was someone in her own right. Absently she paid the conductor and stared out of the window, looking at the Town Hall, her dark hair pinned away from her face, her yellow dress reflected in the window pane. James Crossworth, Jim Crossworth ... the name rolled on her tongue like milk, sweet and familiar. He seemed interested in her, had noticed her, talked to her, laughed with her. Seemed to think she was pretty.

But it was so hard to tell. She might only be imagining things, hoping. Her father had said as much.

We're simple people, ordinary. What would the likes of James Crossworth want with us? You're bonny enough, Kitty, he'd gone on, but you're a trainee librarian with old parents and no money ... But he's not interested in that! she had flashed back vehemently. Jim likes me for myself.

Or does he?

'Hey, luv, I was talking to you.'

Startled, Kitty turned to see a neighbour slide into the seat next to hers.

'You were miles away. What were you thinking about?' the woman asked, hot in a long-sleeved dress, her skin shiny.

'Nothing much,' Kitty lied.

'D'you hear the gossip?' the woman continued, holding tightly on to her full shopping bag as they rounded a corner. 'That Freddie Crossworth got thrown out of the Star Inn last night. Drunk as a lord.'

'That's hardly news,' Kitty said quietly.

'Drink himself to death, that one,' her companion went on, dabbing at her neck with a handkerchief. 'Hot, isn't it?'

'Very.'

'So drunk he was, they had to carry him home –'

'Isn't this your stop?' Kitty asked hopefully.

'Nah, I'm going on a bit . . . Looks dreadful too.'

'*Who* does?'

'Freddie Crossworth,' the woman replied impatiently. 'A friend of mine said she had an uncle like that – and he didn't see his fortieth.'

Determinedly, Kitty continued to stare out of the window. It seemed that every thought she had about Jim Crossworth was sabotaged by his brother's omnipresent image. Freddie Crossworth, long-haired, slightly bloated, acid-tongued, funny. Hopeless. In and out of hospital last year with some weird condition no one talked about.

'. . . brought on by the drink.'

'*What?*' Kitty asked, surprised.

'Freddie Crossworth's being ill, it's all down to drink. My first husband was killed by drink.'

'Really?'

She nodded: a fat woman in paisley. 'A milk truck hit him!'

For several seconds she laughed loudly as the bus lurched along.

The interior seemed to get hotter by the second.

'Not that anyone didn't expect it with Freddie Crossworth . . .'

Groaning inwardly, Kitty propped her elbow on the window ledge and stared ahead.

She *was* going to think about Jim Crossworth; she didn't care who interrupted her or how often Freddie staggered into every conversation or thought. Jim was different from his brother, just as she was different from her sisters, the one girl out of the three who had worked to better herself. Read every book she could lay her hands on, asked questions, won a place at the High School, and then went on to train at the library. It had seemed such an achievement – until she measured it against the power of the Crossworths.

Annoyed, Kitty kept staring out of the window. She *was* different from the other members of her family. She had proved as much and shown her determination to succeed when everyone had told her it was impossible: *Don't set your sights too high, you're riding for a fall. You should know your place* ... Oh, but she *didn't* know her place, didn't want to. She wanted her *own* place, not some little niche marked out for her. She was expecting the best for herself – and was more than ready to fight for it. So maybe, just maybe, it wasn't too much to expect that Jim Crossworth might fall in love with her? Because she was certainly in love with him.

The unexpected realization smacked into her, the bus drawing in at a stop as she hurried to her feet and squeezed past her companion.

'Hey, you don't get off here!' the woman said sharply.

'I have to go,' Kitty blustered. 'See you soon.'

The street was hot underfoot, her eyes blurring as she walked along. She loved him. *She loved Jim Crossworth.* Hurriedly Kitty crossed at the traffic lights and walked towards the park, then paused. She couldn't go there. *He* lived on the park. What if she bumped into him? Her face flushed suddenly, her daffodil-coloured skirt undulating in the soft summer air, her ears humming with the sound of the town.

She would walk up to Oldham Edge and sit, and think. No one went there in the afternoons. It would be a good place to collect her thoughts. She could settle herself down, think things through, tell herself not to get carried away. She *couldn't* be in love with Jim Crossworth. It was ridiculous.

Oh, but it was such a sweet feeling; so warm in her stomach, so gentle against her skin. The town slipped behind her, her mind racing as she drew in the clear high air on Oldham Edge. Climbing upwards she made for the top of the rise and then stood looking down over the mills and out to the Pennines beyond. The sky was blue, bluer than she had ever seen it before; and around her feet wild flowers mottled the new grass.

She would *have* to calm down. Jim Crossworth wouldn't be interested in *her*; and besides, his parents would never condone the match. After the débâcle of Freddie's wedding to Sally Rimmer – with all the attendant scandal of her pregnancy – they would want someone spectacular for their other son, someone who could more than compensate for the shame Freddie had piled on them.

The air was drowsy with insects, the mill chimneys toy buildings in amongst the toy town so far below. Slowly Kitty steadied herself, slowly she breathed, slowly she fought not to think of Jim Crossworth . . .

'Kitty.'

She jumped, almost lost her footing with surprise.

Out on Oldham Edge, where no one ever came in the afternoons, under the sweet high sun, came Jim Crossworth, waving and running towards her as though he had expected her to be there all along.

Of course someone had had to intervene after the wedding, Freddie unable to find a job, Sally ashamed and withdrawn, the cramped house at Number 17 taking in the newly married couple, Mrs Rimmer bitter with disappointment, Freddie spending his time in the pub or arguing with Frank. The atmosphere in those few damp rooms was as bitter as aloes, Freddie rising one morning and sitting on the edge of the bed in his underpants.

'Don't tell me that this is what you wanted?' he had asked Sally, lighting a cigarette.

She was lying on her back, fighting nausea. Silly Sally

Rimmer who had – for once in her life – stood her ground, and refused to have an abortion. But now she wondered why. The cigarette smoke had sickened her, her skin clammy.

'Freddie, put it out. Please.'

He had sighed and walked to the window. His back was turned to her. He never seemed to look at her at all any more.

'Perhaps if you tried looking for work again –'

'Perhaps you should.'

'Freddie, I'm due any day.'

'That's not my fault!' he'd replied, pulling on his trousers and walking over to her. 'You look a mess.'

'Freddie, don't . . . *please*.'

'You should have done it, Sally. You should have got rid of that kid and bought yourself a new dress with the money. It would all have been over then. Finished.' His voice had been weary, exasperated. 'I won't stay, you know. I won't bloody stay with you.'

But in the end he stayed long enough to see his son born and then went out and got drunk to celebrate. After all, no one could criticize a new father for wetting the baby's head, could they? But within weeks the atmosphere at Number 17 was intolerable: Mrs Rimmer sour, Sally depressed after the birth, money short. *Too* short.

'You have to work,' Sally had suggested timidly one rainy morning when the sky was like ink.

Turning quickly, Freddie had grabbed her arm: 'I don't *have* to do anything. I married you, didn't I? That's enough.'

'But my mother can't support us, and Frank won't help,' she wailed, squirming under his grip. 'You *have* to do something.'

Behind her the baby cried out fitfully from the bed. He was surrounded by well-used pillows, his nose running with a persistent cold.

'It's too damp here for the baby.'

'What am I supposed to do about that?' Freddie countered. 'He's just a mewler, like you.'

'He's a *baby*!' Sally replied, struggling against tears. 'He needs proper care.'

'So give it to him!' Freddie snapped back, letting go of her arm and walking to the door. 'I'll be back.'

'When?'

'When I like.'

For a long time afterwards Sally lay on the bed next to her son and stared at him. Nothing had worked out how she had imagined it; not the cold sheets she tried uselessly to warm; not the breast feeding which was difficult and painful. They told her to relax, but she couldn't. How could she live here with Freddie Crossworth and relax?

Silently she wiped the baby's nose and eyes, then tucked the pillows around him again. He would cry any minute, she knew he would, he always did. He would cry and she would lie down next to him and after a while his crying would hiccup into silence. But the silence never lasted. Her mind swam with confusion and exhaustion. She had never been clever, but this was too much for her, far too much.

If only there was someone who would help.

No one had hair her colour, did they? Or eyes as hazel, flecked with green. No one stood like her, talked like her, smiled like her . . . Grinning, Jim stared at Kitty and then glanced away, afraid that he might suddenly start shouting or laughing. Or he might throw himself – giddy as a hare – over the rise of Oldham Edge.

It was love: of course it was. It had to be, unless he had some kind of sickness and was mentally ill. Oh, but if he was, he wanted to *stay* ill. She was perfect; *perfect*. Her hands were exquisite, her clothes light, smelling sweetly of scent, the little scarf knotted around her neck. Her *neck* . . . Oh, her neck when she turned . . .

He was mad and he knew it. Didn't care, would gladly have shot everyone in Oldham and burned the mill to the

rested it against her hand. Reliable Jim Crossworth,
what luck to love you.
o it then.'
o you mind?'
er eyebrows rose. 'Why should I?'
ecause I want to marry you, Kitty,' he replied quietly.
ause my money will be yours and because you'll have
y in how it's spent. You might resent money going to
ddie, you might think I was a fool.' He glanced at her,
s burning. 'It's not logical, Kitty, but I'm his brother
d I feel responsible for him. I always have. Someone has
, because if he doesn't hurt himself, he'll hurt others.
nd if he did that, I couldn't live with myself if I had done
thing to prevent it.'

arah didn't know how Freddie was supporting his family,
though she knew it wasn't through working. So how
as he getting his money? Betting? She stared over to her
usband, but John was deep in thought working on the
ages for the miners. Sometimes she had wanted to inter-
ne, to call by Number 17 and see if her daughter-in-law
s coping. But something stopped her. Pride? No, more
nse of determination. If she stayed out of it maybe her
would finally change.
ut she was wrong, Freddie was the same as ever. But
he had come into money. Not that much, but enough
nt a flat for his wife and child, enough to buy a few
s of furniture. Sarah stared around her, at the lushness
ir possessions. They had been collected for her chil-
o enjoy and inherit; her sons.
nile came slowly, but stayed. Kitty Letts. At last, a
er-in-law she would know, grow to love. But the
of relief lasted only momentarily as Sarah glanced
e table to the two empty chairs. First Freddie gone,
. Her two children married. Surely it hadn't been
wo years ago that she had given birth to them?
dreaming, she *must* be. Before long she would

ground if she had asked him to. His office seemed a million
miles away, another world. His books, his ledger, his dry
accounts and listings all underwater, under earth, written
in Egyptian. All worthless, useless, stupid – because she
was all that mattered.

Suddenly Jim reached out and caught hold of her, pulling
her down on the grass, feeling the warm breath of her
laughter on his cheek. Above them the sky was open, clear,
stretching out towards other worlds, whilst on Oldham
Edge they lay together, and talked, and listened to the
crickets chatter round their heads.

So two hours later Jim was not really prepared for the
sight which greeted him outside his office. Sitting huddled
in a stiff-backed chair was Sally Rimmer.

'Sally,' he said simply, taking her arm. 'Come in.'

She shuffled next to him, and he was surprised, remembering her as taller.

'What is it?' he asked, closing the door of his office and
sitting down beside her.

'I can't manage,' she said simply. 'Can't do it.'

'Do what?'

'The baby.'

Anxiously, Jim stared at her, noticed the shadows under
the eyes and the strange white pallor around her lips. Was
she sedated? he wondered.

'Is the baby sick?'

'Cold.'

'He's got a cold?'

'The flat is cold. He has a cold.' She waved her hand
around uselessly.

'Where's Freddie?'

'Who knows?' Sally replied distantly.

'Is he working?'

She smiled, as though he had said something funny.
'Freddie *never* works.'

The heady sensation with which he had entered the mill

was now gone, and all Jim could do was to look at Sally Rimmer and remember how she had been the first time he saw her. Before Freddie.

'Sally, let me help you,' he said. 'I'll talk to my parents –'

'Freddie would kill me if he found out I'd been to see you!'

He had seen her flinch and was surprised by the extent of her anxiety. What the hell was going on?

'Believe me, Freddie won't know anything about it,' Jim assured her. 'You can trust me.'

He didn't like lying, but there was no other way. His parents had had too much of Freddie; there was no help to be forthcoming from them, so Jim didn't even dare ask. In their eyes Freddie had to work out his own salvation, just as his father had done before him.

But they didn't *really* know Freddie, Jim thought, not as he did. They believed that they could force him: shame him into working and providing for his family ... He stared down at the mill yard, a few workers idling their break in the sunshine ... But they were wrong, and only he knew it. Freddie would do nothing, *nothing* – and let his family fend for themselves. Unless someone helped.

Withdrawn and silent, Jim met Kitty later in the park. Not knowing what had occurred she was quiet, fearing rejection. Finally he looked up from the paper he was staring at.

'What should I do about Freddie?'

Freddie again.

'His wife came to see me this afternoon. She needs money.'

'What about your parents?'

'They've had enough of my brother.'

'That doesn't make it your responsibility,' she answered bluntly.

His eyes widened in surprise. 'If I go to them on Freddie's

behalf, they'll only demand that he goes to   as he
to ask for help.'   God

'So the ball is in his court,' Kitty replied.   'D

'And I do nothing?'   'D
She chewed her lip for an instant. 'Why do   H
him around?'   'T

'I don't!' he snapped hastily. 'I just think I sh   'Be
his family out.'   a s

'He wouldn't have felt the same for you.'   Fr
'And that makes it right?' Jim countered.   ey
'I didn't say that,' she responded calmly.   an

Her own parents loved her well enough, had gi   to
everything they could afford, but they had never   A
her, or her sisters. So this indulgence with Fred   n
couldn't understand. Neither could she comprehend
which bound Jim to his brother. But she was try   Sa
understand it.   a

'Why don't you go and talk to Freddie?'   w
'Sally doesn't want that,' he replied. 'I think she's   h
of him.'   w

Afraid ... Kitty shivered. She had never been a   ve
anyone and wondered what it felt like to be afra   wa
man you married.   a s

'What would Freddie do to her if he found o   sor
'I don't know,' Jim replied, 'but he'd regret i   B
it was.'   now

Her jealousy surprised her. She didn't   to r
Rimmer, didn't have any reason to think that   piece
was anything other than kindness. But his w   of th
her, and, ashamed, she leaned towards hi   dren

'If you don't go to your parents, and   A s
Freddie, what are you thinking of doing   daugh
He folded the newspaper once, twice   feeling
'Giving her some money.'   across t
'Yours?'   now Jim
'Who else's?'   twenty-t
She reached out then and touch   She was

wake up and find herself back in Birmingham in the last few days before she and John came to Oldham.

John Crossworth, *her husband*. The man of honour who had never failed anyone. The father of her children; as much the father of Freddie as of Jim ... Sarah glanced over to her husband and felt the same rush of desire she always felt, followed by a sudden, urgent thought. Does he worry? she wondered. Does he worry about what has happened? Or what will happen? Does he think – when he looks at Freddie – that it was all worthwhile? The struggling? The fight for acceptance? The success so hard won?

Or is he disappointed? The thought winded her, left her empty. Dear God, don't let him have come so far to feel that the journey was for nothing. Don't let him long for the past and worry for the future. Please don't let him grieve for having achieved his dream.

Chapter Fourteen

The Second World War – the war which was never supposed to happen – broke out in 1939, cotton demand soaring, the women working all hours in the Ash mill to meet it. The mine was active, the miners working for the war effort, Jim called up only months after war broke out. In his fifties, and already struggling with the onset of arthritis, John continued to run the mill and the pit, but began to rely more and more on Sarah. His hands were already buckled, the fingers turning inwards, the gold watch he adored now wound daily by his wife. Although in pain he never missed a day's work and felt a mixture of anguish and pride when Jim was conscripted.

He could have stayed at home, pleaded that his job was vital to the war effort; the country needed cotton and coal. But that wasn't Jim's way; he wanted to fight. By contrast, Freddie didn't. He avoided enlisting for as long as he could and pleaded sickness, citing his many periods of ill health. It cut no ice with the authorities; Frederick Crossworth's malaise was due to alcohol, nothing more. He then tried to tell them that he was involved in the war effort, that he worked in one of the vital industries. But they knew otherwise; Freddie never worked. His father did, his brother did, but the mill and the pit had been abandoned by Freddie Crossworth long ago.

Raging against his fate, Freddie was finally conscripted in the tenth month of the war, leaving on a night train without telling his wife. It was typical of him, Sally finding herself deserted with a small child, her brother also gone, her mother visiting her daily in the rented flat above the greengrocer's. Ray was by this time five years old, a dark-haired, sombre child who had learned to be quiet, to hold back. After all, any attention he drew to himself was likely to be rewarded with a threatened slap from his father.

He was silent in his movements too, slipping between the low-ceilinged rooms like a spirit without any real substance. From his earliest memories he had understood two things: that his father was easy to provoke and his mother was vulnerable. Not that he didn't love the latter; he stood beside her, walked with her, and as he grew took on a number of little jobs usually reserved for an older boy, holding his mother's stability in his child's hands.

'Do you love me, Ray?' she would ask, twice, three times a day.

He would look up at her solemnly. 'Yes, Mother.'

'For ever and ever?'

He would nod. 'Ever and ever.'

It hadn't taken Sarah long to discover who was supporting Freddie – after all, it was a small town and rumour travelled fast – but she said nothing to Jim, merely increased his salary to compensate. When he recognized what was happening, he had nearly tackled her and then resisted, keeping the knowledge as a secret. So between them they supported Freddie and his family – until Jim realized that Freddie was drinking the money and leaving little or nothing for his dependants.

So one night Jim waited on the corner until he saw Freddie leave, then knocked softly on the door of the flat.

Sally had looked frightened when she answered.

'It's only me.'

'Jim? Thank God.' She looked round anxiously. 'Come in.'

The flat was small, but clean, the window hung with some cheap floral curtains Sally had made herself. Beside a limited fire, she had pulled two chairs, a thin cat basking on one of them.

'We have to make some different arrangements,' Jim began, then realized she wasn't listening. 'What is it?'

'Are you sure Freddie's gone?' she asked timorously. 'He'd kill me if he found you here.'

'He's gone,' Jim assured her. 'Anyway he must know what's going on. Surely he must realize where the money's coming from?'

She shook her head: her hair was losing its luminous red and fading. Just as she was.

'He doesn't suspect a thing. He thinks I get it from my mother.'

'And that's all right?' Jim asked bitterly. 'To take money from your mother is all right, but he can't take money from his own family? God, I'll never understand him.'

'He hates all of you,' she said, shrinking away as though Jim might hit her for speaking out.

Over the last few years she had tried to convince her husband to seek a reconciliation with his family, but Freddie would have none of it, and threatened her if she persisted. She became so afraid of him that when she saw John Crossworth by the Town Hall one morning and timidly raised her hand in greeting, she dropped it just as suddenly and scuttled away. Baffled, John watched her go, later composing a letter to her which he never sent. If Freddie wanted to be estranged from them, it was his choice. He could always come home – when he had proved himself.

So the two families remained separate, merely catching glimpses of each other across the street, or in a shop, Jim's wedding invitation torn up and thrown into the fire at Freddie's. Hatred festered and grew in him like a nettle patch.

'Freddie's always telling me that he hates you all,' Sally stuttered on. 'I'm sorry, Jim, I'm sorry! I know I could never manage without you –'

He studied her curiously for a moment. 'Freddie doesn't hit you, does he?'

Briskly she shook her head, avoiding his eyes. What good would it do to tell him? If she did, he would have it out with his brother, and then what would happen? It wouldn't be Jim who suffered, but her and Ray. Better to keep quiet, *always* better to keep quiet.

'No, Jim, Freddie doesn't hit me.'

'And Ray?'

'He never hits the boy.'

Nodding, but not wholly satisfied, Jim returned to his previous train of thought. 'I think we should meet up each week, and I'll give you some money which you must keep for yourself.' He stared at her curiously. 'Sally, listen to me. You *must* keep this money hidden from Freddie –'

'He'll go mad if he finds out!'

'And if you don't get money, how will you cope?' Jim asked her bluntly.

He had seen his brother lurching out of the bookies' only the day before, seen him tear up his betting stubs and then meander home, passing two pubs without having the money to go in. He had imagined his temper and didn't like the thought of how he would work it off. And on whom. Sally and Ray were vulnerable and Freddie was getting out of control.

'Take the money and hide it –'

'Oh God, what if he finds out?'

'He won't,' Jim insisted, 'he won't.'

And he hadn't, or he hadn't given any thought to how Sally was still putting food on the table when he had blown the weekly allowance. He never even wondered how Mrs Rimmer could possibly *afford* to support them; he didn't want to think about it, so he didn't. But he thought about his family a good deal.

'Bloody bastards!' he roared to his wife. 'I should have had that mill, not my bloody brother. And he's got married now. I saw him and his *wife* walking round Oldham, looking like they owned the town – just like my bloody parents do. I saw my mother too, all dressed up. But I walked past without even looking in her direction. She was with Jim's piece,' he sneered, 'some gold-digging tart who used to work in the library. I bet she can't believe her bloody luck!' His mouth was slackening: it gave him a weak look. 'I suppose you're sorry you ever married me, when you could have had Jim?'

Sally hesitated beside his chair. 'I love you, Freddie,' she said woodenly.

'"I love you, Freddie,"' he mocked meanly, 'I could have had anyone, but you trapped me, you bloody trapped me . . .' he glanced over to his son, '. . . with that!' Angrily he wrenched open his shirt, his chest hairless, smooth as a child's as he rubbed it. He was, Sally realized, still beautiful. 'I could have had *anyone*! And I got you.'

She was used to him now, had grown used to the violent lovemaking when he was drunk, to the verbal abuse, and then the quick hard slap he caught her with one night when she answered him back. It wasn't the injury which shocked her so profoundly, it was the comprehension that she was suddenly in real danger. At any time her husband could injure her or her son, and he could, if he chose, kill her.

But stupidly, unfathomably, it didn't stop her wanting him. Why, she didn't fully understand, but somehow she felt *tied* to him, and never considered leaving. So to protect herself and her son she became very careful, terrified that Freddie might see her with Jim or discover that she had been going behind his back. Oldham wasn't a large town, and people talked. It was so dangerous. The wrong word in Freddie's ear might well be catastrophic. So gradually Sally became even quieter, her son following suit: both of them tiptoeing around Freddie Crossworth as though their lives depended on it.

Because they did.

Kitty was standing on a stool, reaching up for some old account books in the pit office, the sounds of the mine wheel turning outside. She liked the work, enjoyed being with her father-in-law and Sarah, who was spending more and more time working in the business. She liked being busy, because then she missed her husband less. Jim had been gone for a year, coming home on leave intermittently, handsome in his uniform. They had made love fiercely, greedy for each other and after every visit Kitty watched the calendar and hoped. But she didn't get pregnant.

Stepping down with the ledgers in her hands, Kitty walked over to the desk where John and Sarah were sitting. Outside the lights were muffled by the blackout, the curtain covering the window, the sombre sound of the mine wheel turning eerie in the dark. It was very cold.

'Here they are.'

Sarah smiled. She was so grateful to Kitty; so relieved that she finally had an ally. It was incredible to think of it, but she had been lonely for years. Even married, even devoted to John, Sarah had missed the company of another woman. Then finally Kitty arrived, married Jim and then, when the war broke out, gave up their small rented flat and moved in to live with Sarah and John at Queen's Road. Not long afterwards she had started to ask about the business, displaying what seemed to be real interest. Was it a way of getting closer to Jim? Sarah wondered. Or a means of passing time? Either way Kitty worked steadily and within months was assisting Sarah with the accounts.

Every morning they left Queen's Road together – an hour or so after John – walking, to save the petrol allowance. Sometimes they cut across the park, other times made their way through the town and paused by the shops, staring in at the limited range of clothes and furnishings, the windows plastered with War Posters – 'CARELESS TALK COSTS LIVES' and 'DIG FOR VICTORY'. Conversation was easy, uninhibited, the two women – so dissimilar in looks and background – making fast allies. In the business, they shared the same rapport, Kitty working at the pit office every day except for Thursday, when she went to the mill to do the accounts with Sarah.

It was easy to trust Kitty, Sarah thought. Easy to like her. Besides, they had shared memories now: Jim's letters from abroad, the numerous women's stories as – one by one – husbands and sons were called up from the pit to fight abroad. In time Kitty became – as had Sarah – a good listener, and had a direct, no-nonsense approach to life. What can't be cured must be endured, she said often, raising her eyes heavenwards and grimacing. Her appearance had altered too and she had developed her own style, a soft femininity which camouflaged the steel in her character. People meeting her for the first time thought her young and uncomplicated, only Sarah knowing how much her daughter-in-law worried, her anxieties controlled, mastered and shared only within the family circle. Having never fitted comfortably into her own family, Kitty had found a surrogate home – and valued it.

Slowly, Sarah's glance moved away from her daughter-in-law and rested on John. His face looked composed, but she knew instinctively that he was in pain. It was so fast, she thought helplessly, the arthritis spreading from his hands to his feet, then into his legs. It cheated him, made an old man out of him long before he was ready. Pity welled up in her, but was immediately suppressed. Pity was no good; she had to be strong to help him.

She had only realized how bad it had become when he had suddenly shouted at her; John, who had never argued with her, was suddenly hoarse with temper. Then regretful, then bewildered as he sat on the edge of the bed next to her.

'Why is it so fast?' His eyes fixed on hers, but she didn't see any fear in them, only bewilderment. 'The pain's terrible . . .'

Gently she lifted his hands and began to rub them, then laid him back against the bed and massaged his feet, working up to his knees. The room was very warm, the blackout in place, Sarah untying her hair and letting it fall over him as she leaned down. He felt suddenly transported, soothed by some touch past longing, the pain suspended between desire and the deep dark fall of her hair.

They made love carefully, timidly, Sarah moving in tune with him, ever aware of the pain he was in, aware of his knees, his hands, his feet, knowing that any carelessness on her part might sabotage the excitement and release he was feeling. Her hair swamped him, her mouth soothed him, her fingers stroking every portion of him which was not tortured and painful: and he gave himself up to her, let her take over, taking care of him as he had always taken care of her.

And when he climaxed she held him and stayed holding him until morning.

The three of them had spoken often about Freddie and his family. They had all caught sight of the silent Ray and his mother scuttling from shop to shop, always hurrying, always with their eyes averted. Once Sally had been in the same queue as Kitty, but after an initial smile of greeting she had turned away, flushing helplessly. Then shortly afterwards Sarah had seen her son walking on his own, and although she knew that he saw her, he never indicated that he had. He walked on instead. After that, she seemed to see him more often. Sometimes he was moving hurriedly – sometimes unsteadily – after a stint at the pub. The change was obvious in him: the good looks were not gone, but coarsened; he was ageing more rapidly than nature had intended, his bitterness apparent in his face and deportment. And yet – and yet – she loved him.

'Sarah?'

She looked up, startled out of her memory. 'Sorry, Kitty, what is it?'

'There's someone outside the door.'

Surprised, Sarah rose to her feet. There were footsteps outside, she could hear them.

'Sally?' she said, surprised when she opened the door. 'Come in, come in.'

'I'm so sorry, Mrs Crossworth . . . I mean, I don't want to come in. Can you come out here? . . . Can you?'

Hurriedly Sarah slid outside, pulling her jacket around her. 'What is it?'

'I had to come, I had nowhere else, not with Jim gone off to fight . . .' She paused, terrified of saying the wrong thing.

'It's all right, I know all about your arrangement,' Sarah reassured her. 'And I'm glad you've come to me now. What's the matter?'

'It's Freddie.'

It always was.

'*What* about my son?' Sarah said calmly. He was in the army, out of trouble for once.

'He went AWOL.'

She should have expected it, after all; but it was still a shock. Sarah glanced back to the slight woman standing in front of her, and it was only then that she saw the boy hovering, half hidden, beside his mother.

'Hello, Ray,' she said gently.

To have seen so little of her grandson, to have been cheated of his company because of Freddie's spite. It had been bearable – until now. Sarah looked at the child and felt her throat tightening.

'Say hello,' Sally said distantly.

''Lo,' he admitted at last.

'It's cold,' Sarah said hurriedly. 'Come in, please. We have to talk.'

Nervously Sally glanced round. 'I can't . . . I can't . . .'

'Why not? Is Freddie here?'

'No, no!' Sally replied hastily. 'They caught him, took him back to the army. They say he'll be court-martialled.'

Automatically Sarah leaned against the door, as though preventing the news from reaching her husband inside.

'Court-martialled?' she repeated hoarsely.

Sally nodded. 'So they say.'

'What about you?' Sarah said suddenly. 'Are you still getting your money?'

'Jim sorts it out . . .' Sally replied, then paused, her mind struggling to understand. Jim was away, so *how* was the money being paid into a secret Post Office account? Unless someone else was doing it. 'It's *your* money, Mrs Crossworth, isn't it?'

'That isn't important, so long as you're getting it,' Sarah replied, looking down at Ray, then extending her hand. Frightened, he shrunk back against his mother.

Sally flinched. 'He's shy.'

No, he's afraid, Sarah thought. But of what? Not his mother certainly, so who? His father? Dear God, she thought suddenly, what have you done to this child, Freddie? What have you done?

'Look, Sally, you have to come in,' Sarah repeated, but she could see that she was already eager to be gone. 'My husband would like to talk to you. You could have friends here, Sally, people who would help you. Apart from me, there's John, and Jim's wife. You know Kitty, don't you?'

But Sally wasn't listening any more; she was glancing round repeatedly, avidly. She's sick, Sarah thought with real anxiety.

'Come in, please –'

'I have to go!' Sally hissed suddenly, taking her son's hand. 'I just had to tell you what happened. I thought you should know about your son. You could help him perhaps. Could you? Maybe?' She moved away, already half in the shadows. 'And thank you, Mrs Crossworth. Thank you for the money . . .'

'Sally! SALLY!' Sarah shouted after her, but she was already gone, her footsteps – and those of her son – echoing dismally on the cobblestones.

Chapter Fifteen

Throughout the long war each of them fought their own way. For John, it was a battle against his illness and the threat of early ageing; for Kitty it was a longing for Jim, and for both of them the hope of a child; for Sally it was a daily effort to keep her grasp on reality; and for Sarah it was the struggle to keep each disparate part of her family going.

After that night she thought of Sally as part of the Crossworths, and only a day later visited the flat over the greengrocer's. She had to ring the bell six times before Sally answered, her eyes wide as she saw the redoubtable Mrs Crossworth.

'Oh, hello,' she said timidly, standing back and letting Sarah in. The room smelled of potatoes. Ray was holding the cat and rocking by a mean fire.

'I came to see if you were all right,' Sarah said. What was that smell, she wondered. Something hopeless, lost.

'We're fine,' Sally answered in the same distant tone she had used before. 'Fine . . .'

'Can I sit down?'

Sally was rigid with embarrassment. 'Of course, of course. I'll make some tea.'

'No, just sit and talk to me,' Sarah answered, trying valiantly to hold on to Sally's attention. 'We've got a letter from Jim today.'

Her eyes widened, took in some pleasure. 'Is he well?'

'He's fine. In France,' Sarah replied, glancing over to Ray and smiling. The child remained solemn, mute. 'Have you heard any more about Freddie?'

'Nothing.'

'I'm sorry about my son,' Sarah went on. 'I should have said that to you a long time ago. Will you forgive me?'

Shuffling her feet, Sally stood in front of her visitor and then finally sat down, taking Ray onto her knee. Immediately he rested his head against her shoulder.

'It's not your fault, Mrs Crossworth –'

'Sarah.'

Sally smiled oddly. 'I can't call you that.'

'Why not?'

'It just wouldn't be right . . .'

The room sighed with unease. It was cold. Too damp for a child.

'I was wondering if you would like to come and stay with us for a while,' Sarah offered cautiously. 'There's plenty of room at Queen's Road and –'

'Freddie wouldn't like that!'

'He wouldn't have to know.'

'Oh, he'd know,' Sally said hopelessly, 'he'd *know*.'

Sarah leaned forwards. 'We should be friends. I should have helped you more –'

'It's not your fault, Mrs Crossworth,' Sally said quietly. 'I wanted Freddie and I got him. I knew what I was doing.' Idly she tapped her son's hand, but the gesture was oddly stilted.

There was something wrong with Sally Rimmer.

'Will you please think about coming to stay with us?' Sarah urged her. 'Or just come to us for a meal –'

'We're OK! Ray and I are just fine.' She stared down at her son; he was watching Sarah with a wary expression. 'I have to be careful, you see.'

'Careful?' Sarah repeated. But Sally had already backed off, regretting the word.

'I talk nonsense, Mrs Crossworth. You don't want to worry about me. Silly Sally Rimmer,' she glanced overhead, as though reading something on the ceiling, 'talking nonsense, just like Freddie always says.'

'Freddie's the one who talks nonsense!' Sarah replied coldly. 'My son has no right to talk to you like that –'

'He does! He owns me,' Sally replied, shocked. 'He can say what he likes.'

'No one *owns* anyone else!' Sarah countered. 'Who told you that? And as for Freddie –'

'I don't want to talk about it,' Sally said, close to tears. 'I can't ... he'll hear me.'

A cold sensation slid over Sarah.

'Freddie isn't here, Sally. He's in the army. He's away.'

'He comes back. He *always* comes back,' Sally replied, staring past Sarah as she rocked her son. 'He said that. "I'll know what you're doing. I'll know everything you're up to whilst I'm away."' She glanced back to her visitor. 'So I have to be careful, you see, make sure I don't do anything to annoy him.'

So it had come to this, Sarah thought dismally. Her son had succeeded not only in wrecking his own life, but in crippling another's. He had terrorized his wife and turned a giddy, flighty girl into a cowering drab. She knew then what the smell was in the flat. It was fear, pungent as chlorine.

Slowly, Sarah rose to her feet and extended her arms to Ray. The child hesitated, then reluctantly allowed himself to be picked up.

'Come for dinner, Sally,' she said simply.

'I can't.'

'Come for dinner,' Sarah repeated, walking to the door and knowing that – as she was carrying her son – Sally would follow. 'Freddie's not here. You're safe.'

'I can't ... I can't ...' Sally blustered, then lost her concentration. Slowly she focused on Sarah holding Ray and then reached for his coat, listlessly putting it over her son's shoulders.

'Good. Now you put on your coat, Sally,' Sarah said patiently. 'It's cold outside.'

Drowsily she did so, then obediently followed her

mother-in-law, dropping into step with her as they reached the street.

She had thought she was pregnant; had hoped she was; had prayed that she could tell Jim the news when he came home on leave. But just the day before he was due she had started to bleed. Next time, Kitty told herself, next time. There was always a next time, it wasn't as though they were old, was it?

Splashing water on her face, she glanced out of the window and then stared at the figures coming up the path. Sarah and who else? God, was that Sally Rimmer? Kitty thought, hurrying downstairs to open the door.

'Hello,' she said, trying not to stare. 'I haven't seen you for ages, Sally. How are you?'

She smiled uncertainly in response as Sarah caught Kitty's eye. 'Sally's having dinner with us – and this is her son, Ray.'

The boy was silent, rigid against Sarah.

'Hello there,' Kitty said easily. He stood perfectly still, unmoving, and taking up as little space as he could. Anxiously, Kitty glanced over to her sister-in-law. 'Are you hungry?'

'No.'

'I bet Ray is.'

'I feed him! I do feed him, honestly I do!' Sally said apologetically, grasping her son by the shoulder of his coat. 'He's mine.'

'Of course he is,' Sarah said simply, avoiding Kitty's eye as she ushered Sally and her son into the drawing room.

A fire was burning, the blackout curtains up at the windows, a radio playing beside John, who looked up as they all came in. Without speaking, he glanced at his wife and immediately understood the situation, smiling at his daughter-in-law and extending his hand to Ray.

For a prolonged moment the child studied his misshapen fingers, stared at the warped bones and the bent nails, and then looked at his grandfather. Still silent, Ray then sat down on the floor at John's feet, the firelight playing over his unreadable face.

'You have to admit that it's fun trying,' Jim said when Kitty told him she wasn't pregnant. 'Why worry? It'll happen in time, it always does. Sometimes when you least expect it. Think of Sally.'

They both did; both seeing an image of a withdrawn woman who now visited Queen's Road daily, her son always beside her. She never spoke much, but little by little Ray began to talk to his grandfather, his mother dozing off beside him. It seemed that she slept to escape, that as soon as she knew someone was looking after her child she slid away. But how long could she carry on like this? How long before she lost concentration whilst going about her daily life. And what would happen then?

Cautiously, Sarah had mentioned that Sally might see a doctor, but the suggestion had been fiercely rebutted. Freddie would know, Sally had said hysterically. Freddie would know and then he would take her son!

'I could kill him for this,' John said one evening after Sally had left.

'You're not the only one,' Jim replied coldly. 'Has anyone heard about the court martial?'

'Nothing definite yet,' Sarah answered, turning away and putting on her reading glasses.

'I knew he was bad, but I didn't know *how* bad,' John said brusquely, staring into the fire.

Outside, the sound of a siren could be heard, then silence. Painfully, he reached out and turned on the radio. The news came on and Sarah leaned forwards to listen. But Jim wasn't paying attention, he was thinking of his brother instead; of Freddie going AWOL, being caught, then put in an army gaol. He could imagine how little it would affect him; how he would fight everyone who tried to control him. That was the only admirable quality about his brother,

Jim realized. His physical courage. He had never shirked a fight, never backed off from anyone. Except his brother. Oh, he wouldn't fight for King and Country – such loyalties didn't matter to Freddie – but for personal battles he would stand up to God himself.

You could have been someone, Jim thought, unusually depressed. You could have achieved so much. You had looks, ability, charm, courage. What happened to turn you into a vindictive, drunken bully? He wondered what Freddie was doing at that moment. He could imagine how difficult his gaolers would find him – defiant, ungovernable, inviting violence.

And inflicting it. Because Jim knew then what the others only suspected – that his brother had beaten his wife. Jim shuddered at the thought of hurting Kitty. So how did Freddie do it? And *why* did Freddie do it? Jim's memory slid over the past, coming to rest on an image of his brother banging his head against a wall. All that anger, all that fury, he thought, where did it go? Nowhere. It stayed locked inside, it festered, grew thick in its own juices and then it latched on to someone weak and drove them mad.

The newscaster on the BBC was still talking. A few streets away Sally would be in her flat. Ray where? In bed, or sitting beside his mother? She would be dozing, half asleep, half awake, listening for *what*? Footsteps on the stairs? And imagining *what*? Freddie's return? And what would she feel about that? Terror – or a sense of inevitability? Suddenly Jim loosened his tie and stood up. Only he could stop his brother now. His parents had tried to handle Freddie, but they couldn't. They didn't know how Freddie thought – only his brother, his *twin* did.

If Freddie wanted to fight, then he could. But his fight wasn't going to be with the army, or with his wife and child – his fight was going to be with his brother.

And it was long overdue.

* * *

Without actually discussing it, Kitty and Sarah took over the care of Sally and her son. Two months after Sarah had first visited her daughter-in-law, Sally came to live at Queen's Road, taking a bedroom at the top of the house with an adjoining room for her son. On the first night she walked around until the small hours; on the second, she wandered; on the third, she got up and began cooking in the kitchen, the maid waking Sarah at dawn. On the fourth night, she slept with her bed pushed against the door, Ray next to her. And on the fifth night, she woke Kitty to tell her there was someone at the door.

'Who is it?' Kitty asked, struggling to wake up.

'Freddie.'

'Freddie!' she replied, snatching up her dressing gown and looking out of the window. The moon was full, Sally's face blue in the eerie light. 'There's no one there.'

'I heard him calling me,' Sally insisted, shrinking against the wall.

'Where's Ray?' Kitty asked suddenly, surprised that he had left his mother's side.

'Safe,' Sally whispered.

'Safe where?'

Her face was white-blue. Cold. 'Very safe.'

Suddenly alarmed, Kitty ran upstairs, hurrying from room to room and calling out for Ray. But there was no reply, and only as she reached the furthest room on the top floor did she find him. He was tied to the bed leg, his hands fastened with Sally's dressing gown cord.

'Oh God,' Kitty said desperately, untying him and turning as she heard footsteps behind her. Sally was motionless, watching her. 'How could you? How *could* you?' Kitty shouted, releasing Ray and taking his hand.

The moon was full, peering in at the window and illuminating Sally's face. Her expression altered slowly – agonizingly slowly – from blankness to disbelief as she reached out for her son and then clung to him.

'Oh, what did I do? *What did I do?*' she said, over and over again. 'Oh God, what did I do?'

A week later the army authorities informed Sally by letter that the court martial was not going to take place. Instead, Freddie was to remain for a while in an army goal, his previous record having been taken into consideration.

'What previous record?' John asked bewildered, having telephoned for an explanation.

'His award.'

'His *what*?'

'His award for bravery,' the officer answered. 'Did he never mention it to you?'

'No,' John said wearily, 'he never mentioned it.'

It was the only good thing Frederick had ever done, John said later, and it was the only thing they had never heard about. It was typical, he went on bitterly, and spiteful to keep it from them.

Sarah sighed. 'So when will he be home?'

'Why?' John replied. 'Do you miss him?'

'John, John . . .' she said soothingly, 'let's not fight.'

'I don't want to, it just happens every time we talk about Freddie. I'm ashamed of him, Sarah,' he admitted, his voice low. 'I wonder why he is as he is, where he got it from.' He thought about his father, about Hettie. There wasn't that much difference between Freddie and his aunt, was there? 'When he comes home, I want to talk to him.'

Sarah glanced at her husband. His hands were folded on his lap, his legs covered by a thick blanket. He was old before his time.

'About what?'

'He's out of the will. Out of the business, the property, out of everything, Sarah.' His voice was without emotion. 'I've seen all I want to see of my son; I've seen the worst he can do for himself and for his family. I want no more of him.'

'We have to look after Sally and our grandson.'

'I know that,' John said patiently. 'They can remain with us, but Frederick, no. He has had his chance and ruined it.' His eyes moved to fix on a spot in the distance. 'No man behaves as he does, no man injures a woman so badly that he makes her mad.'

They both thought of Sally, distant, withdrawn, veering between fear and distraction.

'She'll never recover.'

'You don't know that.'

'I know it,' John replied firmly. 'I *know* it.'

Bugger them! Bugger all of them! Freddie thought, staring at the barracks as he was released from the army prison. So they weren't going to court-martial him after all – thought he was owed something for bravery. He squinted ahead against the light . . . Bravery, bet that would surprise the old man, Freddie thought, bet that would be the last thing he would expect. Smoothing his hair, Freddie moved towards the barracks, deep in thought. It was an effort for him, thinking, especially thinking ahead. Planning. But the funny thing was that since he had been holed up in prison for a while he had been forced to think – and he didn't like the route his thoughts were taking.

He had been stupid. Hell, he had been *so* stupid . . . Freddie paused in the sunlight and lit a cigarette. He had shown his hand and jeopardized everything. He should have been more careful, should have used the war to his advantage. Daily he saw men write and receive letters, letters asking for forgiveness, sending love, receiving compassion, understanding. No one – well, virtually no one – was immune to the poignancy of a letter from the Front.

His parents wouldn't be able to *resist* his plea for forgiveness. Not from their brave boy fighting for King and Country. Oh yes, Freddie thought, smiling to himself happily, he had it sorted out now. He would plead a change of heart *after all the horrors he had seen, and the miracle of the triumph of the human spirit*. He would wax lyrical, profess a spiritual awakening. And they would swallow it. It was in the mood of the times, in the very warlike air they were breathing.

He would be welcomed home. After all, the letters he had received had told him as much; odd letters from Sally, full of weird apologies and begging him to take care. She was fine, she assured him, and so was his son. His *son* . . . Freddie's mind turned over. He had nearly missed his main chance. *His son*. He was the only one with a child, the first grandson, for whom all things were possible.

Oh, Jim might be the favourite, he might be the hard-working, clean-living son who could do no wrong; might be set to run the business and live happily ever after. But he had no children. He had no heir. Freddie inhaled deeply. He had to think more clearly, plan things, not drift or he'd be out in the cold. So what if his parents couldn't stand the sight of him, they wouldn't disinherit him, not now that he had a son.

His spirits rose euphorically; he was going to be fine after all. The son he had disliked so much – the child who had trapped him into marriage – was going to turn out to be his saviour. John Crossworth might take his son to task, but he wouldn't turn on his own grandchild. Freddie smiled happily to himself. It just required a little work and a little patience, and then he would be secure.

Safe as houses.

She was having trouble writing to him; having trouble trying to make everything sound fine. Sally frowned, rubbed her chin, then scratched the end of her nose, her nails digging a little too hard into the skin. Behind her, Ray sat on the edge of the bed, watching his mother, a photograph of his father half hidden under the pillow.

She supposed that she ought to tell him she was staying at Queen's Road, but couldn't face his rage. And he would rage about it; see it as a betrayal. Tentatively she fiddled with the message in her hand. Freddie's leave had been cancelled; all his leaves had been cancelled and he was confined to barracks and given extra guard duty. At first distressed, Sally was then light-headedly relieved and slept through the night. Freddie wasn't coming home, Freddie *couldn't* come home. He couldn't watch her, or know that she was now friendly with his family. She was safe. For as long as the war lasted, she was safe.

*

Dear Mother and Father,

This is a very difficult letter to write, but I feel I have to put pen to paper. Being here has made me think, has forced me to think about my life and the way I've been behaving. I can't say that I'm proud of my past, or the way I've acted towards you both or my own family. Time to think makes you consider the past and then decide what you want to do with the future.

Have I still got a future with you? Have I still got a future with the family? Can anything I write or say amend the past? If you say no, I'll try and come to terms with your decision; but if the answer is yes, I can assure you that I will do everything to change.

Your loving and apologetic son,
Freddie.

My darling Jim,

Well, what can I say? We got a letter from Freddie the other day. Caused quite a rumpus, I can tell you. He's sorry, he said. Sorry for his past behaviour and the way he treated his family. Sorry! Can you believe it? I don't. Now I suppose I should apologize because I know that you love him. How you do – why you do, is a mystery – but you do, so that makes me think twice about judging him. If you think he has some good in him, then he can't be all bad.

I miss you. We miss you. Touch the paper when you write back to me, kiss it for me and then I can hold it against my face and pretend it's you.
Loving you,
Kitty.

Darling Kitty, darling, darling Kitty,
Food terrible, little sleep, conditions hard. No one would choose to be here. But it's for the right reasons, or so they tell us. I lost a friend the other night. A man called Bennett – only twenty-five, married with two children. Tell me that makes sense. Please tell me it makes sense because somehow – at this moment – nothing seems to.

I miss you so much that my skin burns. What are you wearing? Saying? Doing? Are you still as pretty, still happy? Tell me yes, give me something sweet to think about. Something kind, in this unkindest of times.

About Freddie – about my loving Freddie. What else would you expect? He is my brother. Now tell me that makes no sense, that people should only earn love. But they don't. They are loved because of where they are born, to whom they are born, to whom they belong. I wish him well; I wish him sincere. I wish him changed.

But then I think of Sally and wonder. I think of Ray too and wonder how my brother could treat his child that way. I wonder why he has a son. I wonder that particularly as we have no son, no child, and I envy him. But is he changed? Who really knows? I suspect him, but then I suspect everything and everyone now. War does that, it takes away sweet peace and makes a cynic out of all men.
Loving you, as always, as ever,
Jim.

The war did not end quickly. The mine was worked by the regulars until they either volunteered or were called up. Gradually other men filled their places, Bevin boys conscripted into essential industries. The mill – with its workforce of wives and daughters – continued to run as ever, now managed mostly by Sarah and Kitty, John fiercely ill with influenza, Sally incapacitated, unable to go out, Ray spending most of his time with his grandfather.

The world changed and not for the better. News of concentration camps and genocide seeped over from Europe, the BBC news huddled over in millions of homes nightly. Bombs fell, cities were devastated, the newspapers daily reiterated what everyone feared – the end of civilization. For the next three years letters were exchanged in every home; from husbands to wives, mothers to sons, and brother to brother.

Finally, peace was declared, some men returning to Oldham, others remaining buried in foreign lands. When Jim came back Kitty was at the railway station to meet him. She had taken special care with her appearance, dressing in red, her husband's favourite colour. He came down the platform – one of the last – still wearing his uniform, his head bowed. Waving, Kitty saw him, then hesitated.

Step by step she moved towards her husband.

Step by step he approached her.

She feared that he was changed, no longer pleased to see her and when she finally reached him she stopped only eighteen inches away, her arms by her sides.

'Jim,' she said nervously. 'Jim?'

His head was still down and remained down as she put her arms around him.

'Time to go home,' was all he said.

Chapter Sixteen

At the corner of the street Freddie stood looking at the greengrocer's shop and the unlit flat above. Frowning, he stared at the blank window. Where was she? It was six o'clock in the evening, she should be there. He hadn't let Sally know he was coming home, had thought it could be a surprise, but the surprise had rebounded and now he was the one left out on a limb.

Since his first letter home, Freddie had written several times, his father never responding although Sarah had answered cautiously. They would have to talk when he came home, she told him, there was a lot of bad blood between them, too much to dismiss out of hand. Her tone was cool, but not unhopeful, he thought. Gradually he wrote more, told her what he was doing, admitting mistakes and asking after Sally and his son.

But he never overplayed his hand; he was too aware of his mother's intelligence and the fact that she – and she alone – could influence his father. If he wanted to get back into the family, he had to win over his mother first.

His letters to Sally altered too. Gone was the hectoring tone, instead he was friendly, later even kind. On paper, at least. He didn't know if he could keep up the kindness in person, or whether Sally's dowdy whining would exasperate him. Still, Freddie had thought, she wasn't his first concern; she wasn't the one to court, to appease. His mother was.

Still frowning, Freddie stared up at the window. Where the hell was she? Out? Visiting? Visiting who? She had no friends and had fallen out with her own family. That's what he liked about Sally; that was what made her so manageable; she had no allies . . .

Lighting a cigarette, Freddie moved over to the greengrocer's and walked in.

'Well, if it isn't Freddie Crossworth!' the woman said, smiling at the handsome figure in front of her. 'Long time no see.'

' 'Lo, Mrs Hunt.'

She studied him avidly, looking to see if the old Freddie remained. Nearly court-martialled, she remembered, now *that* was like Freddie Crossworth, but this man? She was unexpectedly impressed by his demeanour, and besides, he was sober for once. Perhaps he had changed, had been one of the few who had had a good war.

'I was wondering where my wife was,' Freddie said casually. 'I didn't tell her when I was due back.'

Mrs Hunt glanced away, remembering all the old fights in the flat above the shop, remembering Sally white-gilled and nervous. Freddie Crossworth had made her that way, the same Freddie Crossworth who had come home. And yet he did seem different, better. Perhaps they could make a go of it after all.

'She's not here, luv.'

Freddie inhaled slowly, then exhaled, smiling. 'So where is she?'

Mrs Hunt laughed. 'You silly thing, she's where she usually is now, at Queen's Road with your parents.'

His eyes slid away from her and fixed on some vegetables, poor stuff wilting on a warped shelf. Green as bile.

'At Queen's Road?'

Mrs Hunt nodded. 'Since she was took poorly,' she said, then paused, wondering why Freddie was staring at her so oddly. Oh God, she said to her husband later, it never occurred to me that he wouldn't know.

'At Queen's Road?' Freddie repeated finally, winching a smile into place. 'Of course – I should have gone there first.'

He turned, stiff-legged, burning with anger.

'Give her my regards, luv, and the same to your people,' Mrs Hunt called out merrily. 'It's good to see you home, Freddie.'

He walked across town slowly, every inch increasing his temper, his boiling fury. She had lied to him, they had all lied to him. Whilst he was fighting for King and bloody Country his wife was in cahoots with his bloody parents. And what had they been plotting whilst he was away? He crossed over the street, and stopped dead. If his wife was with his parents they knew. They knew everything about how he had treated Sally . . . His skin flushed then drained of colour; his collar suddenly too tight. He had been writing letters home, talking about his family and saying he had changed, and all the time his wife had been there poisoning them against him.

No wonder his mother still sounded cautious, aloof. No wonder . . . Bloody woman! Freddie raged against his wife, bloody cheating, bleating, self-pitying woman, she'd ruin it for him, ruin everything. Unless . . . unless he was very careful. If he was loving, if he became the reformed character they all expected, then maybe he could still pull it off.

Slowly Freddie walked into Queen's Road, his feet turning in the direction of his parents' house. The money was still there. Even with the war the building was well tended, the garden tidy. Opposite, the park was empty of people and of noise, the greenery unchallenged. His confidence faltering, he walked up to the door and rang the bell. It sounded twice behind the thick panelling.

'Yes?' A new maid, someone older.

'I'm Freddie, Freddie Crossworth.' No response. 'Are my parents in?'

Should he have asked if his wife was there first? His son?

'Oh, come in, please.' She stood back to let him enter. 'I'll let them know –'

'No, don't bother, I'll do it,' Freddie said hurriedly, moving past her and into the drawing room. An old man was sitting by the fire, dozing. With total disbelief, Freddie realized he was looking at his father.

As though he knew he was being watched, John opened his eyes.

'Frederick,' he said simply, rousing himself and sitting upright.

'Father,' his son replied, staring down at the figure who had, for so long, occupied his thoughts.

So it had come to this: John Crossworth, respected, honourable John Crossworth was now crippled, brought low. Curiously Freddie studied his father, seeing the buckled hands, the rug over the legs. His mother had said little about his father's condition, only mentioned the arthritis in passing, as though it were unimportant.

'I didn't know you were so ill . . .'

'Arthritis,' John replied, staring upwards at the unwelcome visitor. 'It's better now. Better in the summertime.' His voice was as strong as it had ever been. 'So you're home.'

'I wanted it to be a surprise.'

'It is, Frederick.'

Discomfited, he looked away from his father. 'Where's Mother? Sally? My son?'

'Why?' John countered.

'Why?' Freddie answered him. 'Why do you think?'

John's face was expressionless; he seemed, even wrapped up and ageing, to be formidable. 'You nearly killed your wife –'

'She lied! Whatever she's been saying –'

'She doesn't say much at all,' John replied sharply. 'Sally doesn't say much about anything. She's sick.'

Shuffling his feet, Freddie hesitated. Don't antagonize the old man, he told himself. Play it cool.

'Where is she?'

'With your mother,' John replied, glancing away. 'Your mother, and your sister-in-law, look after her – and your son.' His voice was iron cold. 'You know, I've been waiting for you to come home, Freddie. Waiting to tell you what I thought of you. Waiting to let you know that whatever you do now I will never forgive you for what you have already done –'

'Father –'

'Hear me out! I read the letters, Freddie. You might fool your mother in part, and your brother, but not me. You've shamed us, and corrupted the name I protected for so long, and for that I will never forgive you.' He leaned forward in his seat, his tone deadly. 'I want you to know, Frederick – I want it to be the first thing you know on your return – I've made a will and left everything to your brother. The property, the mill and the pit. Until she dies your mother will be well provided for – as will your wife and child – but you will get nothing from me.' He stared at his son, leaving time for the words to be absorbed and do their damage. 'I want to tell you this now, Frederick, to give you a chance to leave. No one knows you're back, so if you want to leave now, you can. After all, there's no point your staying, is there?'

He had never felt abandoned before; in the past it had been he who had abandoned others. Silently Freddie stared ahead, the words reverberating in his head, shaking him, leaving him breathless, panicked as he looked at his father and knew, beyond doubt, that he would never change his mind. Jim was to inherit everything and he was to have nothing. Even his wife – even Sally Rimmer – was to be provided for, but as for him, as for the son of John Crossworth, he was cut off without a penny.

Watching him, John waited for the outburst which was sure to come, the anger, the abuse which at any moment would come from his son. Staring at him, he braced himself for the bitterness – even anticipated a physical assault.

What he hadn't prepared himself for was his son suddenly losing consciousness and falling heavily onto the carpeted floor.

Chapter Seventeen

1946

By the time his sons returned from the war, John – prematurely aged and infirm – was almost retired from the business. Kitty and her mother-in-law continued to work together as they always had, although Sarah was spending more time at home with her rapidly deteriorating husband. But John Crossworth was – as ever – up to the game. Using Jim as his eyes and ears away from Queen's Road, he bought up several more terraces and rented them out. People would always need a roof over their heads. He kept the rentals low too, and so he always had a waiting list of potential tenants, and – even crippled – still managed to steal a march on Dandry Fairclough.

But old man Cotter wasn't up to anything much any more. His health, which had been limping along for decades, was finally beyond the skill of the Manchester and London specialists and he was – up in Marstone Hall – awaiting death. Just as John Crossworth was in Queen's Road.

Up on Oldham Edge a hooter sounded high and clear below the early spring sky, the day darkening and coming down to rest. Below the lights flickered on in the terraces, the park thrown into darkness except for the three walkways lighted under the trees and the two huge bulbs at the entrance to the park gates. Turning up the collar of his coat, Ray walked along, keeping to the wall and avoiding eye contact as he moved towards his grandparents' house and let himself in.

The hall was quiet and in semidarkness, muted voices coming from the drawing room as Ray glanced up in time to see a shadow moving at the head of the stairs. The shape paused, then passed on, another following. All around the sensation of illness was palpable, deliveries of medicines on the hall table, the sound of a radio battling against the silence in a room beyond. His grandfather, his beloved grandfather, was gravely ill and this time was not expected to recover.

Somehow the whole town had heard about John Crossworth's condition, people sending notes to Sarah, the women in the mill and the men in the mine offering good wishes, a letter left on his desk for when he returned. Not that many believed he would; after all, during the war years his wife and daughter-in-law had all but run the business for him, and when Jim returned he took over. By that time Sarah had been glad to be relieved. John was ailing, his arthritis crippling him and leaving him bedridden, the most active and honourable of men reduced to a pain-riddled carapace.

His joints ached constantly, his legs unable to support him, the daily lifting from his bed to the seat by the window, agonizing. Drugs did little to alleviate the pain; only warm baths helped and Sarah's massaging. Yet he never complained, never spoke of how he felt to be tied to one room, to be parted from his beloved business and stranded in the house on the park.

The dream he had followed so assiduously as a boy – the dream of Queen's Road – had come to pass in the way he least expected and now John realized that the house was not only to be his home, but his tomb. But he never spoke of it, stared out instead towards the park and remembered the morning he left – and the day he returned.

News of life outside came to him via his visitors; many of them miners from the pit, or men like Sammy Upton and the old foreman, Graham Cox, telling their stories and sharing the old days with their sick boss. They came as a form of tribute; men who wouldn't have crossed the street to speak to old man Cotter or Dandry Fairclough, making weekly visits to the man who had stood up to the old guard and won.

But at what cost? Oh yes, John Crossworth had the house and the money, but he had also had more than his fair share of grief. Hettie, Frederick, and Sally ... there were lesser griefs too; the fact that Kitty, after ten years of marriage, had never conceived. The beloved heir, the rightful heir, Jim Crossworth, would probably have no son himself. There was Ray, of course, but there was something so distant, something so withdrawn about the boy that no one could accurately judge his future. He was not unstable like his mother, or feckless like his father, he was instead remote, unreadable, having seen too much too young and having never been able to forget.

'Remember, you don't have to do it,' Jim said to the boy a year earlier when he suggested that Ray might eventually like to work in the family business.

'I'd like to,' he had responded, dark-eyed, much better looking than any of them.

He was a stunning, dysfunctional boy with no temperament. That was what was so amazing; he never overreacted, never lost his temper, never laughed ebulliently, never mourned. He coasted – as though he were holding on to his own inner security for safety – and remained aloof from everyone. Not that he didn't love; he was fiercely protective of his mother, but to most others he was unreachable.

And yet as John grew more incapacitated, Ray was his daily visitor; his ally; his spy on the world outside. John's visitors might tell him the gossip, but only Ray could make it real. Not that he would have displayed it to anyone else, but to his grandfather he was a clever mimic, taking on the tone of voice and mannerisms of his victim with astounding accuracy. No one was safe from his scrutiny, no one escaped it – except his father.

Despite all the protestations, Sally returned to her husband. When Freddie told her he had been disinherited, he then begged for her forgiveness – not because he truly wanted it, but because he wanted the money his father had set aside for her. It did no good for anyone to try to reason with her; Freddie was her husband; what was hers, was his. John might cut off his son, but Freddie would still benefit through his wife, because John Crossworth would never disown her. It wasn't love which kept her tied to Freddie, it was something far more complicated – fear and compulsion. Fear bound her to him as affection would have bound another woman. Besides, she knew nothing else; and neither expected nor asked for more.

'Keep the money to yourself,' Jim urged her. 'Please, Sally, look after it yourself.'

She was ageing badly, timid, uncertain, but blindly loyal. Freddie had come home, Freddie had wanted to start again. It did no good to suggest that if she had had no trust fund, she would never have seen her husband again. She either didn't want to know the truth, or didn't care.

'Sally, *listen* to me. If you don't consider yourself, think of your son. Keep the money to yourself.'

He knew all along that he was wasting his breath; she might be afraid of Freddie, she might remember his previous mistreatment, but in the end all that remained was the fact that he was back. She didn't want to question why.

At first she and Ray moved back into the flat above the greengrocer's and soon Sally was jumpy, and soon the arguments were beginning again, Freddie coming in drunk late at night. The Hunts didn't live below them any more, or the family might well have been evicted, but no one heard the fights and so they were allowed to stay on, Freddie unemployed, Sally visiting the doctor regularly, Ray as quiet as no child had a right to be.

Until one day when Ray, aged eleven, arrived at the house on Queen's Road. He came in silently, asking for his grandmother, and Sarah hurried downstairs. She would always remember how he looked that afternoon, dressed in his school uniform, his cap in his pocket, his amazing face expressionless.

'Ray, are you all right?' she asked, wondering why he had come when he never visited uninvited. Was something wrong with Sally? Or was it his father? Her voice was hoarse with the threat of further anguish. 'What is it?'

He looked at her for a long moment. Whose eyes were those? she wondered and then realized that she was looking at her father, Samuel Levenson. Odd, she thought, how she had never noticed the resemblance before.

'Can I come to live here?' he asked her, self-possessed, the question obviously considered for a long time beforehand.

'You don't need to ask,' Sarah replied, although astounded. 'Is there something wrong at home?'

'No, there's nothing wrong,' Ray replied solemnly. 'I just can't live there any more.'

It was all he was going to say, she realized, and it was at the same time too much and too little.

'Ray, you know you're welcome here.'

He didn't respond, didn't show pleasure or surprise, simply nodded, like an old man.

Later that night a distraught Sally came round to talk to her son. No one knew what she said, they just heard voices through the door and refused to interfere even when a long silence developed. Then they heard crying, Sally calling Ray's name repeatedly. Finally she came out into the hall and faced Sarah. Her face, flushed with weeping, was set, her voice hard. It was the first time she had ever shown anger.

'I suppose you're satisfied now!'

'*What?*' Sarah asked, aghast.

'Now you've got my son,' Sally blurted out, her red hair faded into a dull auburn. 'Freddie always said you wanted to break up our family, and now you have.' Her nose was running, her hands clenched. 'He said you wanted Ray because Jim can't have a son of his own –'

'Ray *chose* to come to us, we didn't make him,' Sarah replied evenly.

'But you knew he would!' Sally snapped, beside herself.

Amazed, Sarah looked at the woman she had tended for years, had cared for, protected – and now she had turned on her. And all because of Freddie.

'Sally, calm down! Ray asked if he could come and stay for a while. You could stay here too if you wanted –'

She screamed sharply, out of control, then bit her lip. With horror, Sarah could see a trickle of blood run down her chin.

'Sally, calm down!'

'I don't want to live here!' she snapped back. 'I want to be with Freddie. I *have* to be with Freddie . . .' Her voice trailed off, as though she were surprised by what she had just said, then she moved unsteadily to the door. 'I'll get Ray back. I will! I'll get my son back. You'll see, all of you – you'll see!'

Unfortunately Freddie was delighted to be rid of his son, and after a week or so Sally never mentioned Ray's return. She came to see him at Queen's Road instead, subdued, aware of her outburst and guilty because of it. Relieved that Ray was out of Freddie's corrupting atmosphere, Sarah said nothing and waited daily for a distraught Sally to come back and stake her claim again.

But she never did. Instead, against all the odds, Sally became pregnant again. The news was greeted with incredulity.

'*Pregnant!* Is she mad?' John asked simply, then glanced over to his daughter-in-law.

Kitty was silent, blank-faced. She was in her thirties now, but looked younger, her manner as straightforward and honest as it had always been. Only a few fine lines around her eyes showed the passing of time, her intelligence – so valued in the business – obvious in every action and word.

For years she and Jim had tried to have a child; for years she had looked after Sally and Ray; always believing, hoping against hope that one day she would be looking after her own. And now there was an unexpected pregnancy in the family – only it wasn't hers.

Jerkily, Kitty's hand moved to her face; she was glad that Jim wasn't there.

'Are you all right?' Sarah said softly, moving over to her.

'It's not fair!' she said hotly, turning away.

The injustice choked her, made her nauseous. It was all wrong, she had done everything she could to help everyone, and now Sally was having a child which should by rights be hers. It was so stupid! They didn't even love each other the way that she loved Jim. It wasn't safe to bring another child into the world with such parents.

Angrily, she got to her feet. 'I have to go to work!'

Sarah's expression was anxious. 'Kitty, stay a while.'

'I have to work,' she said emphatically, her tone dropping. 'After all, it's the only thing I'm any good at.'

'You know that isn't true.'

But she was too clever to accept platitudes.

'I *want* to work,' she replied, pulling on her coat in the hallway as Sarah watched. 'People need me there –'

'People need you *here*,' Sarah countered. 'Without you how would I have coped, Kitty? How could I have managed during the war, and now, with John being so ill?' She leaned against the wall, a tall woman, darkly exotic. 'Don't be angry –'

'*I have a right to be angry!*' Kitty snapped. 'I have a right to say that it's not fair! I love your son. God knows, no woman could love him more, and now I wonder – is it *my* fault?' Her eyes flicked away from her mother-in-law. 'Is it *me*? If Jim had married someone else, would he be a father now?'

'He loves you, that's all that matters –'

'*How do you know that?*' Kitty replied hotly. 'Because

he doesn't say otherwise? Because he's always been kind? The good son who would never inflict injury? Jim Crossworth, loyal and considerate?' She stared hard at the floor, trying to keep the tears away. 'I've failed him –'

'How can you be so sure?' Sarah responded. 'It might be Jim's fault that you can't have children.'

'Freddie has children,' Kitty replied, her voice dry with misery, 'and so do you. There's nothing wrong with the men in the Crossworth family. So it must be me.'

There was no self-pity in the statement; it was simply the truth as Kitty saw it. She had failed and could not accept her failure because it affected not only herself, but her husband. The strength of character which made her fight her way out of the terraces, the courage which made her fall in love with, and hold on to, James Crossworth was now pushing her to make the cruellest sacrifice of all.

Steadily, Sarah looked at her. 'So what do you suggest?' she asked. 'That you separate? That he marries someone else to have a child? Would you be so cruel, Kitty? To take away the one thing he prizes above everything – his love for you?' She shook her head. 'I've lived with you and loved you for years. I've admired you too – and that's something I can't say about many people. I know it's unfair, unjust. I *know* how much you want a child, I know you feel that loss every moment – but I can't do anything about it. No one can. The *world* is unfair, Kitty, and all too often we don't get what we want, but what we need – *and Jim needs you.*'

'And what do I *need*?' she countered, walking to the door.

The light was turned off, the shadows on the ceiling indefinable, Freddie snoring beside her. He was angry about the baby at first, but now he was pleased . . . Sally smiled nervously to herself. He was looking forward to being a father again, she thought. He had proved himself a better man than his brother, after all. Her conscience pricked her, but she dodged the thought. So *what* if Jim had been good to her in the past? He could afford to be, he had the money – money which Freddie should have had. After all, he was John Crossworth's son just as much as Jim was.

Timidly, she touched her husband's shoulder and sank into a doze, Freddie feigning sleep beside her.

Another kid had not been what he wanted, but now that he had had time to think about it, it might not be so bad after all. A new son might bring in some money for him – his father would be certain to cough up, set up a trust fund as he had for the other one. And Freddie could do with some more money. He didn't like living the way he did; didn't like the way people looked at him. The useless son of John Crossworth, the son relegated to living over the Hunts' greengrocer shop, whilst his brother lorded it over the town.

Lucky Jim – but not *that* bloody lucky! Freddie thought spitefully. Not lucky enough to get his wife knocked up. He turned carefully, so as not to wake Sally. He was bored, if the truth were known; his life was aimless; he could only drink so much, and bet so much, and after that, what? A dry succession of years leading nowhere ... He could get a job, but how could Freddie Crossworth go cap in hand to anyone? They'd only wonder why he wasn't in the family business and then laugh about his father cutting him off. Either way, it was sure to lead to further humiliation.

But he had to do *something* ... Freddie rubbed his face hard. He was thirty-odd, and what the hell had he got to remember, or look forward to? Old age with Sally? The thought made him nauseous. She had lost her looks and before long she'd be the size of a brick outhouse, lumbering along with another kid in her belly.

Freddie paused. No, better not to think like that. This baby *might*, might just be the way back for him. His father would never ignore his grandchild, and if it was another boy ... Some man Jim turned out to be! Couldn't have *any* kid, let alone a boy. Unless it was his wife's fault.

Good-looking, but so bloody smug. Not so smug now, Kitty, are you? Not so smug now that my wife's knocked up and you're as dry as an old maid . . . Freddie's thoughts drifted as he pulled a blanket over his shoulder. He had to do something *now*, before it was too late. He had to work something out.

His brother was going to America soon. *Bloody America!* Typical! Jim got to go everywhere. He was off to see about cotton. *Cotton!* Freddie snorted under his breath. So Jim was running the mill while his father was buying property, cutting a swath through Oldham, and finally buying old man Cotter's place, Marstone Hall.

Freddie frowned, thinking. Cotter had taken a hell of a time to die, his bedside had been surrounded – not by family – but by his solicitor, his doctor, his accountant and his bank manager. They stayed on and off for two days, grey suited, hard eyed, hanging on every breath that old man Cotter took; hoping each would be the last. His ferret's head had been withered, his freckled hands flickering intermittently with life, his eyes opening every few hours as though to watch the professional spectres round his bed and remind them he was still in the running. If he was afraid, he didn't show it. When he finally died, his wrists were cut to make sure that he would not be buried alive. The bandages showed around the cuffs of his shroud when the body went on view.

Freddie turned over clumsily. Quite why his father had bought the old mausoleum was not understood at first. He had never visited the place, nor expressed a liking for its architecture. Yet buy it he did – the one action of his father which Freddie understood. It had been an uncharacteristic show of revenge, a way of saying to everyone, 'The old order's gone, now I have the upper hand.' Freddie snorted to himself. His father hadn't bought the house to live in, but was planning to turn it into an art gallery. Bloody art gallery! What the hell did anyone want with an art gallery? Oh, but it was obvious really – his father was ill, possibly dying, what better way to make sure that his name went on and on and on? What a respectable, honourable thing to do.

Freddie turned over in bed again. But for all his posturing, John Crossworth hadn't really got the upper hand. He was sick, everyone knew that, and Sarah was preoccupied with his nursing. The business was being run by Jim, with the help of his wife. But she wasn't the brains behind it; just the temporary guardian . . .

Freddie's eyes opened suddenly in the darkness. His parents were out of the game, Jim was going to America . . . His thoughts leap-frogged over themselves giddily. The need for fuel was as high now as it had been during the war and the Labour Government was even talking about nationalizing the pits. Freddie's eyes stared ahead. He could see it! Could see a way of finally getting his own back – *and* his revenge – at the same time.

I would never have imagined it; never, never . . . Pain comes like breathing. In and out, absorbing every thought. Speech becomes difficult. Everything – even going to the lavatory, becomes agonizing. The hobbling, the staggered effort of limbs which burn and scald.

John stared out of the window, concentrating . . . *When I was young, I dreamed of this house. I dreamed of these rooms. But I never wondered where it would lead, did I?* . . . An image of his mother came back to him; a middle-aged woman in a kitchen piled high with washing. Other people's washing and ironing, day in, day out. He had meant to come back for her – he *had* come back for her – but he had been too late.

Now she was dead, and his father was dead, estranged from his son to the end, and John couldn't even remember exactly what Howard had said that day when his son returned to Oldham.

It all comes down to nothing, John thought helplessly. Words and dreams, and ambitions, and struggle – it all comes to nothing. To an ageing man in a bathchair by a window. And who cares where the window is? In a slum or in a house on Queen's Road? What does it matter? You still feel the same pain, and die the same way . . .

John moved with difficulty, strained to settle himself.

God forgive me, but I no longer care about the business. I no longer care. I want to be comfortable, to be out of pain, to have my wife beside me. Other than that, there is nothing else of value now. My son can go to America, Jim can do what I could have done at his age. He'll look after everything and have the pride and responsibility of it. But not me. Leave me alone . . . leave me alone.

His gaze faltered, then focused again. Across the road a young couple were entering the park, deep in conversation, the man holding the woman's hand, the day breaking sweetly over them. And for an instant John felt an agony of longing, looking, as he did, at the mirror of his own past.

Chapter Eighteen

Sammy Upton was the first to hear, the news coming to him at the Star Inn. 'Never! I don't believe it.'

'I tell you, it's true,' Tim, son of George Lyman, replied. 'The pit's reopened.'

'He'd never do it,' Sammy said flatly, 'not Mr Crossworth.'

'It's 'is son –'

'Jim's in America.'

'Not Jim, Freddie.'

Sammy's eyes narrowed. 'Freddie? He's nothing to do with the business.'

'Whatever you say, 'e's reopened the mine,' Tim replied evenly. 'The men are pouring back.'

Downing his pint hurriedly, Sammy shook his head.

'I still say that the boss would never reopen that mine – and certainly never put that bloody layabout son in charge.'

'But Freddie's got a letter from 'is father to prove it.'

Sammy's eyebrows rose: 'What?'

'A letter,' Tim repeated, ''e were waving it about to show everyone. It were from Mr Crossworth all right –'

'How d'you know?'

'Had 'is name on it.'

'Hah!' Sammy responded shortly. 'Could have been a fake.'

''E said – Freddie, that is – that 'is father were real ill –'

'That's old news.'

'– and that 'e'd been asked to 'elp, seeing as 'ow 'is brother is in America. 'E said that Mr and Mrs Crossworth weren't to be bothered. Said it were 'is chance of doing summat for the family. Said they were all back together again.'

Carefully Sammy digested the news. He wasn't convinced, had never liked or trusted Freddie Crossworth. But then again, it might be true. The boss was seriously ill, so much so that Mrs Crossworth and Kitty had hardly left Queen's Road for the last three days. Frowning, Sammy stared into his pint. Maybe he *should* check it out with Mr Crossworth ... He dismissed the idea abruptly. The boss was past taking decisions, and besides, it wouldn't be right to worry his wife at such a time. She had enough on her mind, and she'd always had a soft spot for Freddie, so maybe this was her idea ... Unsettled, Sammy leaned against the bar. But how could he find out for sure? The house on Queen's Road was off limits, the windows blinded with curtains, the world outside excluded – and no one dared to intrude to bother the family at such a time. And yet it all seemed wrong. Putting Freddie in charge? Opening the old mine? Oh God, Sammy cursed, if only Jim were here ... Of course, it *could* all be above board. Perhaps the mine *had* been checked out and given the all clear, perhaps by interfering he would jeopardize a chance for the men in Oldham to do their bit towards the national productivity drive.

Apprehensively, Sammy glanced around him. 'That pit's not been used for years, since the fall.'

'I know, that's what someone else said,' Tim agreed. 'But Freddie Crossworth's been telling everyone it's all right, it's safe again. Said the pit had been made safe.'

'I wouldn't believe anything Freddie Crossworth said,' Sammy replied bluntly, moving to the door, Tim turning to watch him.

'Where are you going now?'

'The mine, where else?'

The pit wheel was turning, the vast black cage descending below ground, inching down into the earth. A wind was up, the daylight fading as another cold spring evening came into play. His head ducked down, Sammy moved across the pit yard and then ran up the steps to the mine office to find Freddie leaning against his father's desk. He looked at home, Sammy thought bitterly, taking John Crossworth's place as though the old man were already dead.

'What the hell are you doing here?'

'Piss off, Upton,' Freddie replied bluntly. 'You're not welcome.'

'This isn't your pit –'

'This pit belongs to the Crossworths, and I'm a Crossworth,' Freddie responded coolly. 'You have no right to interfere. I am in charge now.'

'Does your father know about this?' Sammy countered.

Freddie's face was bland. 'Of course he does. He approves – wants the men to work there again.'

Caught off guard, Sammy hesitated. Was it true? *Had* old man Crossworth allowed the pit to be opened again? Would he *really* make that decision after all he had said in the past? Hovering in the doorway, Sammy struggled with his thoughts. Mr Crossworth was ill, so was he able to make such a decision? But if it *was* a trick on Freddie's part, what was in it for him?

But for once, Freddie had done his work thoroughly before putting his plan into practice. He knew that certain matters had to be tackled, or questions would be asked, and he didn't want that. So when the mine was reopened the abandoned shafts were shored up and drained, the safety aspect addressed carefully. He wanted nothing to go wrong; what he wanted was to prove that he was as smart as his father and his brother. Before long everyone would see that Freddie Crossworth was also someone to be reckoned with. An also-ran no more.

So with no one to interrupt his plans – Jim away and everyone else absorbed with John's imminent death – Freddie lured back the miners by offering wages which were higher than at any other pit. For a while he would have to rely on Sally's savings for their pay, but before long he would be making big money – and a big profit for himself.

Although many were suspicious of Freddie, the Crossworth name still stood for honour and soon men were working on the reclamation of the mine, opening seams which had been blocked by the previous fall. On the promise of a cut of the profits – and an assurance that John Crossworth was overseeing the work – the miners came back, Freddie watching gleefully as his plans unfolded.

He wanted money, yes. But he wanted power too, and respect. He wanted revenge and an end of his seething jealousy – and he picked his time well.

'Are you sure the mine's safe?' Sammy persisted.

'It's been checked out and declared workable. Besides, we've reopened two shafts already and there's been no problem,' Freddie replied calmly. 'Now get out, Upton.'

'If your brother was here –'

'But he isn't, is he? And besides, I'm only doing what my father wants. Jim isn't the only son, you know. I've as much right to be involved in the business as he has.'

'Maybe so, and maybe no,' Sammy replied cautiously. 'But I might call in on your father anyway –'

'Oh, you do,' Freddie replied, his voice full of warning. 'Why not worry him about money when he's dying? Or perhaps you'd like to talk to my mother? I'm sure she has nothing else on her mind.'

Hesitating, Sammy knew he had lost. His admiration for Sarah Crossworth won the day. What right had he to intrude at such a time?

'Oh, and one more thing,' Freddie said evenly. 'I've had a belly full of you, Upton. You've always had it in for me, spying on me, reporting back to my father. Well, now I've got the upper hand and I intend to use it. Get out.'

Angrily, Sammy moved to the door, then turned.

'You're a bastard, Crossworth. You always have been

and you always will be,' he said coldly. 'You've never done anything in your life to help another person, only to help yourself. But if anything happens to anyone down in that mine, I'll come looking for you. And God help you then.'

Sarah didn't want visitors, she just wanted to sit by her husband and talk to him and share the memories that only they could recall. The world outside was blanketed off, the curtains drawn, John breathing laboriously in the high bed. Opposite her sat Ray, watchful as he held his grandfather's hand, his dark eyes fixed on the unchanging face.

If John could just pull through, Sarah thought, then hesitated, pull through for what? To struggle longer? To fight the pain and humiliation daily? To stagger from the bed to the chair at the window? It was not her decision, although she wanted it to be; wanted to challenge God and beg for a stay of execution: he's a good man, the only man I ever loved. Please let me keep him, please. Let me keep him a little longer . . .

But what right had she to beg? All they had asked for, they had been granted, the angels giving generously. So give more, she pleaded, give more. Give me my man. Give me a month, a week, a day longer with him. Give me time to say what I said too infrequently. To look after him, to touch him, to love him, to stroke his skin and burn it in my memory so that when he's gone I can remember the scent and the feel of him.

A chasm opened inside her, a loss so great that it winded her. Where is he now? she wondered. Where? Can he hear me, sense me? Or has he gone on without me? Her eyes studied her husband's face, reading it as a map of their past life. Take me with you, John, she pleaded, whenever and wherever you go, take me with you.

There was a wind up, but nothing too fierce, and no snow. Only cold, and it was always cold underground. Working steadily, the miners cleared the rubble from the blocked tunnels, the lamps on their hard hats making sweeping arcs of light as they dug.

Against his father's wishes, Tim Lyman had gone down on the late shift. He had lost his office job after the war, and had turned to the work George had always hoped he would never do. Nothing his father said could dissuade him.

'I were nearly killed in that pit. Ted Morris were killed –'

'I won't be killed.'

'You don't know that!' George replied angrily. 'I want to 'ave a word with Jim Crossworth. I don't believe 'is father would reopen the mine. I know that man, he'd never do it.'

'Jim's not there.'

George looked up, alerted. 'So who's running pit?'

'Freddie Crossworth.'

'*Freddie!*' George snapped. 'Freddie Crossworth's reopening the mine?' He rose to his feet hurriedly. 'Jesus, Tim, don't go –'

But his son had already left.

You take the steps slowly, dig a little, pull back the rubble and then work on some more. There are moods to pits, and every miner is well aware of the risks. Especially in a mine with a history. Like the one in which they now were. The usual banter between the men was absent, each concentrating on what he was doing, each anxious not to tempt fate. It was as though something was waiting for them, some force behind each blow of the pick, some spiteful spirit just waiting for its chance to do mischief.

After the fall they had got Ted Morris out, and buried him up at Leesfield, but his spirit was everywhere that night: his death, his dark demise, etched on every foot of tunnel. Steadily the miners worked on; there had been no fall during the first two shifts and they were well into the third. *Maybe* the pit was safe after all, maybe John Crossworth had been *too* careful, *too* protective in the past.

But no one said so. And no one mentioned the dying man's name or that of Ted Morris. They worked in silence instead, creeping cautiously under an earth which might – at any moment – drop its load onto their bare backs. Water dripped steadily; from either side the sleek black tunnel enclosed them; and from behind the untouched earth something shifted, altering position in the dark.

It was warm, quiet, semidark, the room housing John Crossworth and waiting for his end. As they all did. There was no world outside – and hadn't been for days – no town, no business. For a while it was all suspended, because *this* was all that mattered; the dying of a good man.

Standing by the door, Kitty watched her mother-in-law, then glanced at Ray. He should have been *her* son, she thought, she had cared for him better than his own mother, she had loved him, so why wasn't he *hers*? She studied the boy's features; the dark eyes, dark hair, he could pass for hers easily. That afternoon she had seen Sally in the town, walking up Union Street with a bag of shopping, her face blankly distant. She looked as she had looked so often in the past, detached, unfettered to the world, awaiting disaster.

Compliant ... but Kitty didn't feel compliant, she felt angry. Angry that her beloved father-in-law was dying, angry that her husband was away, and enraged, furious, blindly, hideously angry that her sister-in-law was to give birth to her second child. Her jealousy shamed her, but she couldn't control it, and realized then that there was nothing in life she *could* control.

He should marry someone else, she thought suddenly, Jim should marry again and have children. No man would be a better father ... She had watched him over the years with Ray, coaxing the child into conversation, walking with him, showing him around the mill and the terraces. He never resented the fact that Ray loved John Crossworth more; he accepted it, as Jim accepted everything. As Jim accepted that he was married to her – and that they had no children.

It didn't seem to matter to him; but she wondered. After all, if someone doesn't talk about a subject, does it mean it is unimportant to them? Jesus! she thought savagely, why don't you lose your temper, Jim? Shout at me, tell me you feel cheated, betrayed? Tell me how much it hurts? But you won't. It wouldn't be honourable to mistreat your wife; it wouldn't gel with your code of ethics. But are you happy? *Are you?* Did you want the business, the responsibility? Did you want to inherit everything? Or would you rather have been Freddie? Feckless, irresponsible Freddie?

A sound came from the bed, John murmuring in his sleep. Ray leaned towards him. Silently Kitty stared at the boy. You should have been mine, your mother doesn't care for you, and your father never gave a damn. You were a nuisance at first, then later you were his piggy bank, your trust fund raided to support him. You mean nothing to him, *nothing* ... She could feel her heart rate accelerate, her tongue moving drily over her lips. It was *me* you clung to that night when I found you tied to the bed, it was *me*. Not your mother, not Sally. But *me*. I was there for you, I saved you, helped you ...

Her hand pressed against her mouth in an effort not to cry out, and then she turned and left the sickroom, closing the door after her.

A telegram from Kitty called Jim home early. The business trip had been productive, the insight into another country stimulating – and yet he had missed home, longed for the low dark terraces, the high ridge of Oldham Edge, the bleak silhouette of the mill town – if only he'd been returning in happier circumstances.

He had missed Kitty too, worried about her as he had done constantly since they heard about Sally's pregnancy.

Of course he grieved for the family he would never have; but what good would it do to tell her that? It would only add further guilt, and to what end? He glanced out of the plane window. The novelty of flying had passed on his trip over, now he saw the clouds and wanted only to see them from the house on Queen's Road . . . He would try to talk to Kitty; try to tell her again that not having children didn't matter. *If* she would talk about it. Lately she seemed reluctant even to mention children.

Ever since Sally became pregnant. That had been the final smack to her self-esteem. Sally was older than her, and a far less capable mother, but she had conceived. With Freddie . . . the name came like a bump of turbulence. Freddie, his brother, his alter ego. Jim had dreamed about his brother the night before; he had been giving a talk and Freddie had come in drunk, lurching from table to table, insulting everyone, then he had broken down crying, his pockets full of orange peel . . .

The dream had made no sense and when Jim woke he had been tired and irritable. He didn't want to think about his brother, he had other more pressing concerns – like the fact that his father was dying. But what would that matter to his twin? Freddie would only be interested in the money the old man left . . .

Unusually irritated, Jim stood up and wandered down the aisle of the plane, walking into the toilet and bolting the door.

He was up in the clouds, but felt more bolted to the earth than ever, the worries and anxieties pressing down on him in that tiny cabin. And at the back of his mind, as always, as ever, was the shadow of his brother. What is it this time? Jim thought helplessly, why am I thinking of him now? What in God's name is he doing now?

'Sssssshhhhh!'

The miners stopped, listened.

Silence.

'Did you hear –'

'Shut up!'

Silence again.

A rumble.

Underground.

Water dropping.

'It's OK, come on.'

'I thought I heard –'

'It's OK.'

The miners all listening.

Waiting.

Then the earth shifted.

Lost its footing.

'It's a fall!'

'Shut up!'

A roar. Blackness folding in.

'Jesus! It's a bleeding fall!'

Freddie didn't hear it above, he *felt* it, a low rumble under his feet. Paralysed with disbelief, he sat at his father's desk and stared out of the window, but it was dark and all he could see was his own reflection looking back.

'Mr Crossworth! Mr Crossworth!' one of the miners shouted, running up the steps to his office. 'There's been a fall –'

Freddie was already on his feet, his eyes blank with shock. He had to get out, had to escape before anyone could blame him. Jesus, why was it always him? Why *him*? His legs felt leaden, unwilling to move as he made for the door, pushing past the miner. He had to get out.

'Where are you going?' the man asked incredulously. 'Didn't you hear what I said? There's been a fall –'

'Let me pass!'

The man lunged for him, but Freddie veered out of his way, running frantically down the steps towards the pit yard.

'Crossworth! CROSSWORTH!' the miner shouted after him. 'You bastard, get back 'ere!'

But Freddie wasn't going to stop for anyone. Instead,

his eyes fixed ahead on the pit gates, a few miners turning to watch him as he ran. His gamble had failed. Bloody failed, like everything else he did. If Jim had reopened the mine it would have been fine, there wouldn't have been a fall if his bloody brother had been in charge. But it had to happen to *him*. Running, Freddie fought for breath, the streets passing rapidly under his feet, a sudden sensation of real terror overwhelming him.

He had thought this time he would triumph. He would snatch the bloody mine out from under his family's nose, run it and prove himself – and then what? Why, then he would inherit, what else? His father couldn't leave all the Crossworth fortune to Jim, surely? He had a right to it too, Freddie thought blindly, he had a bloody right to it!

But he'd ruined his chances again. He hadn't thought the plan out properly after all, he'd rushed it, been stupid, reckless. Freddie stopped running. Jesus, he'd been a fool! He'd been blinded by revenge and envy. He'd wanted some of the power his father and brother had; wanting a piece of the business so badly that he had snatched at it too fast. And now he had blown it.

He was afraid, unbelievably afraid – both of what he had done and what would happen to him as a result. He had never been afraid before, and didn't at first recognize the devouring sensation of dread. He had gone too far; this time he had gone too far ... His legs began to feel heavy, to drag along, people turning as he passed, watching him, calling his name as he went by. There was no way he was going to get out of this; no means of escape. He was trapped by his own actions and there was no way out.

Or was there? He had to run, to hide, keep away from everyone. If they couldn't find him, he was safe until he could get away for good ... Gasping for breath, Freddie slowed and then stopped, leaning against a wall and then ducking into an alleyway.

Footsteps hurried past. Were they after him? Looking for him already? He struggled to steady his nerves ... Hold on, slow down, he told himself, they were probably people going about their usual business, or relatives who had heard about the fall at the mine. Oh God, the fall! He sunk back into the shadows. Don't let anyone be dead, Freddie thought desperately, please don't let anyone be dead. His anxiety was not for the miners, nor for their families, but for himself. If anyone had died, he was a marked man himself. He would never get away with it. But if they survived, *if* they got all the men out, his crime would seem less.

IF. IF. IF . . . the word drummed into his ears as he pressed himself further against the wall, his heart banging with fright. He would have to sneak away, not tell Sally or anyone where he was going. Thank God Jim was away. He thought of his brother and the rare terrifying anger Jim had displayed in the past, and realized that he could never explain, and that Jim would come looking for him. Shivering, Freddie leaned against the wall. The time he had spent sitting in his father's place had been sweet; he had liked the feeling of power, of prestige. It had felt good, intoxicating, to have command over people, to move them around, activate them, order them to do what he wanted.

The desk had suited him; fitted him, moulded itself around him in a way more seductive than any woman could ever have done. He was listened to, obeyed – he was respected in a way he had only ever dreamed of before. But it was over so quickly, and now he was a nobody again, and worse, he was hiding . . . Cautiously he peered around the alleyway: there was a man walking down the street, and then another. Soon there would be more and more . . . Wild-eyed, Freddie ducked back against the wall and stood there, shaking, the cold of the brickwork seeping into his flesh and chilling him to the core.

On arriving back in Oldham Jim was going to go home immediately and then changed his mind. His intuition, so finely honed, forced him away from Queen's Road, towards the outskirts of the town. He never knew why, but *something* turned the wheel of his car that night and took him to the old disused pit, the unexpected lights which surrounded it, startling him. What the hell was going on? The mine was closed, had been for years. His headlights picked out a knot of people at the entrance to the pit gates, a man he knew coming forward and knocking on the car window.

'Bill, hello –'

The man's face was hard, unwelcoming. 'There's been a fall.'

Hurriedly, Jim clambered out of the car. 'What are you talking about? The pit's closed –'

'It were reopened.'

Jim shook his head. 'No, it can't have been. My father closed it years ago. You *know* the mine was never to be used.'

'Your brother reopened it,' the man said flatly, a few women passing them and hurrying towards the pit wheel.

'*What* did you say?'

'I said your brother reopened it.'

'Oh God, no. No.' Jim turned to stare at the waiting women, then at the lighted mouth of the mine as unwelcoming as a crypt.

So Freddie had reopened the pit. He had seen his chance whilst Jim was away, and the rest of the family were preoccupied, and he had done the unthinkable ... Slowly, dangerously, Jim could feel his temper beat into life, then he moved past the miner and walked through the pit gates. The wheel rose up before him, vast in the darkness, the huddle of people turning to face him.

'Where's my brother?'

No one recognized his voice for a moment. Gone was the easy-going Jim Crossworth; this man was almost hoarse with fury.

Finally someone answered him: 'No one knows where Freddie is.'

His anger shifted inside him; bit into his gut.

'Is anyone trying to get the men out?'

'Some miners from the second shift went back down, but . . .' someone began, then glanced away.

'Well, go on!' Jim barked. 'What is it?'

'They got 'em out.'

'*But?*'

'They were too late.'

Jim stared at the man incredulously. 'Some are dead?'

'Four men.'

Four men dead, four men with four wives and four families. Dead.

'Come with me,' Jim said finally, the miner falling into step with him as he climbed the stairs to the office.

On the desk were newspapers; in a glass ashtray a couple of cigarette butts were stubbed out; and on the back of the high chair was his brother's coat. He had left in a hurry, Jim thought, made a run for it as soon as he heard about the fall. Furiously he picked up his brother's coat and flung it against the far wall, then sat down and rummaged through the desk drawers, the miner watching him in silence.

Finally he found what he wanted – the plans to the mine.

'Where were they trapped?'

The miner stared at the plans and then pointed to a section well underground.

'That was closed!' Jim said sharply. 'No one knew what it was like there, it was off limits even when the mine was in use.' Angrily he pushed aside the plans and stood up, facing the man who was watching him. 'I didn't know –'

'No one thought you did.'

'So why did the men agree to go down the pit again?'

'Money. More money than they could get anywhere else.'

Incredulous, Jim turned away. Freddie had waited for his chance, had gambled when he knew his family was at its lowest ebb; when he knew his brother was absent, because at any other time he would have been stopped. His brother had gambled – as he had so many times before – only this time he had gambled not with money, but with lives. Greed and spite had sent those men to their deaths, Jim thought bitterly, they had been killed for the sake of one man's revenge.

Without speaking, he walked down into the pit yard, past the huddle of people there, then continued quickly towards town. His feet crossed over a dozen streets, his eyes scanning every face for the one face he would recognize; the one so like his own. He was looking for his brother; the mirror reflection of himself, and he *kept* looking.

The town was stunned by the news, which had travelled quickly from the pit. Only the house on Queen's Road remained ignorant, and there a father lay dying whilst one of his sons searched for the other with murder in his heart ... Dark had come down with the cold, the streetlights wearing their auras of damp colour, the roads shiny. And *still* Jim searched. He knew every street of the town, and searched every street, turning up alleyways, walking down cobbled ginnels.

In silence, never once calling his brother's name.

Freddie had waited for almost an hour, until he felt safe enough to move. There were no footsteps, no car lights, nothing to spook him. Cautiously he peered out from his hiding place, turning up the collar of his jacket and cursing himself for not picking up his coat. It was cold, bloody cold, he thought as he stepped out into the street. He'd get a chill being out in this weather. His eyes searched ahead, but there was no one about. If he could get to the railway station he could pick up a train, get into Manchester and then catch a flight out of the country. But he had no passport, he remembered suddenly. Jesus, what a mess! Freddie's face was waxen with cold and fright. Maybe he'd just get down to London, lie low for a bit. Wait until everything blew over ... As silently as he could, he walked along. He'd head for Mumps station, pick up the connection to Manchester Piccadilly . . . He stopped, startled by a sound, but it was only a boy riding his bike and when he passed, Freddie moved on.

He'd manage somehow, he always did. Sally would miss him, but in reality he'd be glad to be away now another kid was due. He'd had enough of family life; wanted to make a new start. Just hadn't reckoned on it working out this way . . . A sound made him turn. Freddie crouched back against the wall and waited. Silence. Breathing in deeply with relief, he moved out, walked another few paces, then stopped again. More footsteps. But when he turned around there was no one there.

He was sweating now, wet under the arms, his cold face running with perspiration. Calm down, he told himself, Jim's in America, and the old man's out for the count. But he couldn't stop wondering and looking, intuition nudging him. He knew his brother was out of the country and yet, and *yet* he could sense him. He could almost feel him following . . .

Panicked, Freddie fought to control himself. Not much longer, only another five minutes and he'd be at the station. Hurriedly he felt into his pocket and drew out his money. Thank God, enough to get to Manchester and then London. After that, who knew what would happen? People would forget, Freddie reassured himself, they always did, especially if they had got the miners out safely. He might be worrying unnecessarily. The men were probably above ground now and he was in the clear. He should stop imagining the worst –

What was that?

Footsteps.

Gaining. Behind him.

Were they behind him?

Or in front?

Freddie's breathing was irregular, his chest aching. There was no one there, he told himself, no one there. Oh, but he might not see them, but he could feel them. How many? And who were they? Miners, come looking for him? Or if not them, who? His brother? Hurriedly Freddie wiped his face with the back of his sleeve. Jim was in America, in *America*.

His feet seemed suddenly to pound noisily against the pavement, giving him away. He tried to lift them higher, to soften the sound of his footsteps, but he couldn't. They were too loud, telling on him. He had to stop, wait a minute. But if he did, they would catch up with him ... Sharply, Freddie turned and ducked into an alleyway, breathing in dry gasps.

And then he felt a hand move over his mouth and the first punch land against his kidneys.

Chapter Nineteen

Unbeknown to Jim, several of the miners had followed him at a distance, sensing trouble and wondering what would happen if Jim Crossworth caught up with his brother. For miles they followed him, then held back when they saw Jim enter the alleyway. There was a long suspended moment of silence, followed by a muffled cry, then the two brothers fell out from the shadows into the street. The night was down hard, heavy with rain, the cold making itself felt. In silence the miners formed a circle around the two men, Jim's face unrecognizable with anger, Freddie's hair falling over his forehead and sticking to the blood which was coming from a cut above his eye.

It looked black in the dim light, as dark as the birthmark at Jim's temple, the knuckles of his right hand burst and bloodied. He had caught Freddie by the hair, pulling back his head and punching him viciously in the stomach, his brother doubling over and vomiting, whilst all the time trying to shake free of Jim's grasp. But Jim held on madly, his eyes blind with fury, his chest aching from where Freddie had lunged out and caught him with his left foot.

Slipping on the vomit, Freddie fell on his left knee suddenly, his brother pressing his face down into the mess.

'Look, you bastard, this is where you belong,' he shouted, 'I should make you eat it.'

But Freddie had other ideas and, twisting frantically, escaped his brother's grip and turned round, catching Jim on the back of his head. He went down heavily, his arms outstretched, a cut above his eye spewing blood. Panting and struggling to rise, Freddie kicked out at him again. One of the miners stepped forward to help – but he was immediately stopped by the other men, Jim suddenly finding his second wind and lurching towards his brother again.

They went down together, each struggling to rise, their clothes wet with rain and covered in vomit, their faces distorted and bloodied. One by one the punches landed, Jim ducking as Freddie swung out a right hook, then suddenly jerking his elbow upwards. There was an eerie crack, the bone in Freddie's nose splitting. He stopped for only an instant, his mouth hanging open as he gasped for breath, Jim sensing his advantage and ramming his head into his brother's stomach.

'For God's sake,' one of the miners said, 'we have to stop 'em or they'll kill each other.'

'Leave 'em be,' another replied. 'This is a fight that's been a long time coming.'

The rain – light before – began to fall more heavily, the streetlamps illuminating the duel as the two men fell, and rose, and staggered upright again. Physically matched, neither was stronger than the other, and neither weaker. It was, to all intents and purposes, a fight to the death.

And the miners continued to watch them; each willing Jim Crossworth on, each seeing his victory as a victory for the men who had died that night. If Jim won, justice prevailed, if Freddie won, everything they and John Crossworth stood for, was destroyed. And *still* the brothers fought; long past reason, long after they should have given way; all the time remembering why they were fighting. Jim, for the injustice, for the myriad times he had covered up for his brother, and for the disappointment he felt. Freddie for the grievances he had harboured for so long.

Almost blinded by blood in one eye, Jim tried to focus on his brother and felt – for one instant – that he was killing himself. The flesh he was hitting was *his* flesh, the body, *his*. As he weaved in and out of consciousness he was almost hallucinating. But he didn't stop, even when Freddie dug his nails into the skin of his cheek, even *then*

Jim found enough strength to push him off and land his own blow under his brother's ribs.

It was a desperate fight, the rain hardly managing to wash away the blood, the two brothers more on their knees now than upright. Some of the miners walked away, repelled and ashamed, yet unable to intervene. Others stayed in silence, watching the Crossworth dynasty destroy itself. No one knew how it would have ended if they had been left to themselves, but suddenly a figure emerged from the alleyway and walked between the two fighting men.

She stood defiantly between her two sons, then fixed her eyes on Jim.

'Get up and go home.'

He shook his head, Sarah walking over to him and repeating, 'Get up and go home. You have no place here.'

'Never!' he snapped, rising to his feet and moving over to Freddie.

But she was there before him, placing herself between her two sons.

'I've seen most things in my life, but I won't stand by and watch my children kill each other.' She stared at Jim steadily. 'You don't belong here – he *does*. I know that now.' Slowly she turned and faced Freddie. She appeared terrifying to all the men watching. 'And you – get out of this place. Get away from here and don't ever come back. Find some other sewer to live in, but not here.'

Freddie was weaving on his feet. 'But –'

'GET OUT!' Sarah snapped. 'You're no son of mine. I know that now.'

Dropping onto the street, Freddie laid his head down on his knees, his face covered.

For a long moment Sarah looked at him and then turned back to Jim. 'Come home,' she said simply, walking ahead. 'Come home, Jim. Follow me.'

He could hardly stand as he staggered to his feet, the miners moving back to let them pass, Jim's legs failing him a few yards on. Sarah heard him fall, but never even turned, simply called over her shoulder.

'Get up, you don't belong on the ground. Get up, Jim, your father would have done.'

He was almost blind, his eyes swollen. The miners followed them both in silence, Sarah pausing every time her son fell, Jim repeatedly hauling himself back to his feet. Her hair was wet with rain, her clothes darkened, her son staggering every painful foot of the way after her.

'Follow me,' she said at intervals, 'and *keep* following me.'

He moved on blindly, tracking his mother, his body aching with pain, his breathing agonizing. Street after street they went, people coming out to watch in awe. Never once did Sarah aid her son, never once did she help to lift him, or support him. She let him do it alone, as John Crossworth had done; and she let him prove his courage publicly.

At the beginning of Queen's Road Jim fell again, Sarah pausing, the followers waiting for her response. For an instant she did nothing, then she turned.

'Come home with me, Jim. I need you,' she said.

He was mute, blinded, on his knees.

'Get up. Get up! You're John Crossworth's son,' she went on determinedly. 'You have to earn the right to walk in his footsteps. You have to earn the right to be his son.' Her voice faltered just once, then strengthened. 'Get up, Jim, and walk into his house and take your rightful place there.' She was almost pleading with him. 'Please, get up in the memory of your father who died tonight.'

Jim heard the words through a humming of blood and heartbeats. He heard them and understood and somehow – no one ever knew how – Jim Crossworth stood up and walked the last yards to his father's house.

Chapter Twenty

Three years later

If she dyed it, she could get rid of the grey roots, but it didn't seem worth the bother, because who would she be doing it for? Sally stared into the mirror at her parting, then combed some hair over to cover it. Her movements were staccato, jerky, her lipstick spilling slightly over the line of her mouth.

No one could say she hadn't been a good mother. She'd tried really hard with the baby, especially after being left on her own. Well, not really on her own, the Crossworths had helped out, but then, they could afford to, couldn't they? They probably felt guilty, driving Freddie away like that. So what if he *had* made a mistake? People did. You couldn't hold it against them for life . . . That's what Hettie Crossworth had said to her only the other week. She was a nice woman really, Sally thought, despite what everyone said. Besides, no one really bothered that much about morals any more, did they? Why couldn't she see who she wanted? Hettie had been faithful to old man Cotter's grandson for years, so that was something in her favour, surely?

It all came down to taking sides, Sally decided, digging into her handbag and looking for money as her thoughts wandered. She'd go to the pictures that afternoon, take herself off and go and see something light-hearted. Funny. Hollywood must be wonderful, and a good film really took you out of yourself. She glanced over to the small bed next to hers, the little boy lying asleep and still. He'd never mind if she popped out. Not her little boy, he was as good as gold. People worried far too much, and as for that Kitty Crossworth – she sometimes behaved as though *she* were his mother.

Sally frowned. She had been like that with Ray too, but that was different. She thought of her elder son, grown into a young man of fifteen. Handsome, so handsome it made you stare. Not that he seemed to notice: deep as Methuselah, he was ... Glancing at a photograph on her dressing table, Sally felt a sudden pull of loss, mixed with relief. Where are you, Freddie? she wondered. You could have let me know where you were, I'd have gone anywhere. You know that. You and me were made for each other ... Slowly her glance moved back to Harry, still sleeping. He wouldn't annoy you a bit, Freddie, he's a happy little boy, not like Ray. He's easy, silly really.

Like me. She smiled distantly – Silly Sally Rimmer, with the best legs in Oldham – then she rose to her feet and left.

'Maybe you should hire more staff,' Kitty said over the dining table. 'You could use some more help.'

Jim shook his head. 'No, we should keep it small, I don't want to overexpand.' He glanced at his mother at the head of the table. 'Are you all right?'

Her dark eyes fixed on his. 'I thought you said that Sally was coming to eat with us tonight?'

'That's what she said yesterday.'

'So why isn't she here?'

'Maybe she changed her mind,' Jim replied evenly. 'We can't keep her on a lead.'

'That's not the point,' Sarah retorted. 'We have to think about Harry as well as her.'

'But we can't keep watch over her twenty-four hours a day,' Jim replied calmly. 'It's not possible. Besides, it implies that she doesn't know how to look after her own child.'

'She doesn't,' Kitty said suddenly.

Sighing, Jim turned to his wife. 'Listen, darling, I know how deeply you feel about this –'

'Look how she treated Ray when he was little,' Kitty replied, without letting her husband finish. 'You don't know the half of it, Jim. She wasn't fit enough to manage with him alone, that's why she came here.'

'But she *won't* come here now.'

'That's why we're worried!' Kitty snapped back heatedly.

Watching the sharp exchange between the two of them, Sarah decided for once to intervene. 'Kitty's right, Jim,' she said simply. 'Sally isn't a competent mother. We have to keep an eye out for her son.'

Shaking his head, Jim pushed away his plate. He and Kitty had never had a family and now it seemed unlikely that they ever would. Not that the gods had been unnecessarily spiteful. They might not have had their own, but they had inherited Freddie's family instead. It had seemed a strange, but good solution – for a while, at least. Kitty's maternal instincts were partially satisfied and there was an added bonus: Ray was unlike his father in every way. He neither looked like Freddie, sounded like him, nor behaved like him. There were no displays of petulance, no temper, no fecklessness. Instead Ray Crossworth was withdrawn, distant, remote.

He had always been that way, but when his grandfather died and his father left Oldham in disgrace it seemed that Ray was unable to become close to anyone. He had lost the person he truly loved, and had been deserted by his father. After that, he kept his thoughts and his feelings shielded from everyone. Not that he wasn't helpful; he was intelligent too; but the core of him was segregated from the rest of life and he was emotionally alone.

'Kitty, you *have* to stop worrying –'

'I think of Harry as one of us,' she countered, then caught the look in her husband's eye. 'No, Jim, I don't think he's *my* child, if that's what's worrying you. I think he's my nephew, and God knows, that should be enough to allow me to worry about him.'

'All right, all right,' Jim said wearily, glancing from his wife to his mother. 'You do what you think is best. I'll run the business in this family and you two run the rest.'

He hadn't been sure that she would go out, but she did most Wednesday afternoons, so he had thought it was a good idea to wait and see if she did the same today. Ray watched the window over the Hunts' greengrocer's shop and reluctantly remembered his childhood there. The damp sheets, the walls with their dark green paper, the heavy feet on the uncarpeted stairs and his father putting out his shoes on the windowsill. It wasn't anything like as bad now, although no one could ever understand why his mother insisted on staying. Come and live with us, Sarah had said to her repeatedly, Ray's already here and you could bring up the baby in comfort ... But she wouldn't hear of it, and only he really knew why – because she believed his father would return; that he would come home one day and find her waiting for him in the flat over the greengrocer's shop.

The thought saddened him; it was so silly, so patently, hideously silly. She didn't love him, but she needed him as an addict needed heroin. Addictively, blindly, compulsively. But then, that was his mother, and nothing would change her. Silly, and at times a little bit more ... But there was no reason why anyone else should know about that, Ray decided. Some things had to be kept secret, because otherwise his mother might suffer. And he didn't want that, because for all her faults she had been sweet to him in that damp flat all those years ago.

Suddenly Ray heard the door open and saw his mother step out into the street, putting up her umbrella and walking on quickly. He waited for a long moment, then let himself into the building and crept up the stairs to the flat. Just as he had anticipated, his brother was asleep, Harry lying curled up on his bed, breathing deeply. Ray looked at him and then tiptoed into the kitchen. If the past was anything to go by Harry would be hungry when he woke up.

Carefully he made some sandwiches, put on the kettle to boil, then washed up the breakfast dishes in the sink. After that, he read his mother's post and pocketed the bills to pass on to his uncle later. Finally he sat down with his own books and began to read. The time wound past slowly, Harry still sleeping, the light fading, Ray clicking on the lamp. Eventually he lit the fire and made himself some more tea, his face serious as he returned to his books.

Ten minutes later his brother woke up, Ray feeding him and telling him a story about a hermit who lived down an old mine shaft. Always cheerful, Harry listened avidly, laughing when he was supposed to and eating his sandwich voraciously. Side by side in front of the fire the fifteen-year-old boy sat with his three-year-old brother for another hour until his mother was due home.

Swearing Harry to secrecy he then left, waiting on the corner until he saw his mother go in. He knew from past experience that she wouldn't question anything; not the fire, not the tidied room, nor the food which had materialized in the cupboards. She wasn't capable of real understanding any more. Ray knew that and adapted to it – because if he didn't she would be put away. Locked up in some institution. But that, terrible as it was, wouldn't be the thing which would finally drive her mad; what would finish her for ever was the knowledge that she was away from the Hunts' greengrocer's shop – the place her husband would always come back to.

So he had to keep quiet and be very discreet to protect her, and to make sure that his brother was safe. He owed it to his mother for all the times she had protected him in the past. His grandmother and aunt and uncle were kind people, but they didn't share the history he and his mother shared and could never truly understand ... Silently Ray walked away. On Saturday he would return and re-enact the ritual. He would stand watch and protect his mother as she had done for him.

After all, it was the honourable thing to do.

Half an hour later Ray was facing his uncle in the office at the mill. Jim's desk was covered in papers, graphs and plans laying out the future of the Crossworth fortune. When the pits were nationalized, Jim decided to specialize in the things that in the post-war era would always be in demand: property and shops.

As wily as his father in business, Jim had turned from the easy-going personality of the past into an astute businessman. His fight with his brother, coming as it did at the same time as his father's death, had changed something fundamental within him. He was still kind, because kindness became him, but he was harder, more distant, and trusted few. Having been betrayed by his brother – his *twin* – he now regarded the world with a cautious eye.

The birthmark was still dark over Jim's temple, his hair carefully combed. Dressed impressively, he wore his father's old fob watch, the chain lying across his stomach, its heavy gold links catching the overhead light as he moved.

'I'm putting in a bid for Pitt Street and the shops opposite,' he told Ray, glancing up. 'There's good money in bricks and mortar, always was.' The young man made no response.

Jim knew better than to push him; Ray would clam up if he did. If there was something wrong he would tell him in his own time. Still pretending to read his papers, Jim's mind wandered. He was, if he were honest, restless. He wasn't supposed to feel that way; not *him*, not Jim Crossworth, the reliable one, the one everyone depended upon. But it was the truth nevertheless; he was restless, itchy with longing.

For *what*? For adventure? No, not that. He had more

than enough power and influence. For sex then? No, not that either. Kitty was the only woman he had ever loved, and although he might notice others, she was the only woman he had ever wanted. So why was he uneasy? Because I miss . . . miss *what*? he asked himself. My father? No, not really, he had been failing for too long, the stroke which killed him coming as a kindness in the end. So what *did* he miss?

Peace of mind? Was that it? There were too many loose ends, too many pieces of unfinished business. The night he and his brother fought was the last time he ever saw Freddie – but not the last time he ever thought of him. I should have killed you, Jim thought with unexpected vehemence, I should have ended it for ever, because now you'll come back. One day, you'll come back.

And then he realized what he missed: his brother. His other side, his sour, corrupting alter ego without whom he was never quite whole. Angered, Jim closed his eyes for a moment . . . Do you miss me, Freddie? I wonder. I wonder if there's room in your soul for anyone other than yourself.

'Jim?' Startled out of his thoughts, he looked up. 'What is it?'

'Can I give you these?' Ray asked, passing a sheaf of bills over the table to his uncle. 'They need paying.'

Without replying, Jim picked up the bills and read them. Sally had never been extravagant; these were for food, heating, and a new coat for Harry. Nothing much, nothing which would dent the Crossworth fortune.

'Is your mother all right?'

Ray's expression was shuttered, closed off. 'Fine.'

Is she? And if she wasn't would you tell me? Jim stared at the young man opposite him, then smiled, the smile returned. I like you, Jim thought warmly, and most of all I see goodness in you. If only you had been my son.

'I'll pay the bills, Ray, don't worry.' And then he broke a vow to himself, the words coming out before he could stop them. 'Has your mother heard anything from Freddie?'

They were both caught off guard.

'No.'

Jim nodded, but held on to the young man's gaze. 'Do you think about your father?' He could see his nephew mentally step back, but pushed him. '*Do* you, Ray?'

'I didn't like him.'

'That doesn't answer the question,' Jim replied evenly.

'I don't know the answer to the question.'

Pausing, Jim stared at him. 'He's your father.'

'I don't think of him in that way.'

'So how *do* you think of him?'

'As someone dangerous.'

The word sizzled like hot fat landing on snow.

'*Dangerous?*'

Ray nodded.

'Why? Did he hurt you when you were little?'

The question was intrusive, unwelcome, Ray shifting his feet automatically. He didn't want to answer his uncle, even though he had been kind, even though he was fond of him. He didn't want to answer because there were things better left unsaid, and things which still needed to be kept secret. Threatened, Ray glanced away, his eyes fixing on the mill chimney outside. When I was little in that flat over the greengrocers, sometimes – when it was summer and the air was clear – I could look out and see this same chimney. I knew my grandfather was here with you and I envied you and wanted to be with you. I kept that chimney in my sights and wondered how I could get here. I don't ever want to go back to live in that flat. I don't even want to *think* about it . . .

Watching his nephew's face, Jim could see the reluctance and felt suddenly shamed for prying.

'I'm sorry, Ray, you don't have to talk about it.'

But suddenly, inexplicably, he wanted to.

'Do you think there's real wickedness in the world? I

mean, something solid, like this desk?' Ray asked, his voice unusually animated. 'I want to know, you see. It would help.'

'Help?' Jim queried. 'How?'

'If I knew it was something real then I could imagine it. Imagine destroying it.' He paused, took a rush at the next words: 'I hope he's dead. I hope my father's dead.'

For years afterwards Jim would remember that moment and the frightening intensity of the words. He would remember it and wonder why he didn't try to protect his brother. Why he didn't – as he had done so often – make allowances for him. Instead he saw his advantage and took it.

'Ray, your father's gone,' he said quietly. 'You're safe and you have a home with us. You're like a son to me, you know that.'

There was a long pause, and then suddenly Ray moved over to his uncle and embraced him. The action was so quick that Jim had no time to respond, but for a long time afterwards he felt a pride and accomplishment beyond anything he had ever felt before.

Chapter Twenty-One

Whistling, Kitty walked down the street, smiling at a couple of people she recognized and then pausing outside a shop window. The previous night she and Jim had made love with such tenderness that she had been surprised, and in the morning they had lain in each other's arms and watched the light come up. She had felt like a girl again, the same girl who had first fallen in love with Jim Crossworth – long before the war and the disappointments of life had stolen the sweet euphoria away.

'What is it?' he had asked her when she laughed suddenly.

'Nothing. I'm just happy, that's all.'

He had touched her shoulder, her breast, her stomach, tracing a plan down her body with his index finger.

'We're lucky, you know . . .'

She murmured her acknowledgement.

'. . . *very* lucky . . .'

Her mouth found his, her tongue found his.

'. . . lucky . . .'

Still smiling, Kitty caught her reflection in the shop window and flushed. God, people would think she was crazy, she thought, acting like a kid. But when she walked on, she was *still* smiling. Jim had told her about Ray with such pleasure, his nephew's sudden and unexpected show of affection releasing something in him which had been repressed for too long.

'He hugged me, Kitty. Actually *hugged* me,' Jim had told her, then looked away: and she thought – incredulously – that there were tears in his eyes. 'He's a rare boy. A rare boy.'

She had known that all along, but she wasn't going to say so. Not that Ray had been overly affectionate with her in all the years that she and Sarah had looked after him. Appreciative, yes, but loving, not overtly. That portion of his personality had been devoted to his grandfather and when John died, it seemed that part of Ray died with him. Until now. Now their nephew had picked someone else to love – and that person was Jim.

There was no feeling of jealousy or resentment, only satisfaction. Kitty walked on happily. Her husband had a surrogate son, someone for whom he could work and to whom he could leave the business. She knew also that Sarah would be relieved.

Her mother-in-law had been unusually subdued lately, rising late and retiring early. No, she wasn't ill, Sarah assured them, simply thoughtful.

'About what?'

'The past,' she said, without sentiment. Her voice had lost none of its accent and she was still darkly handsome.

The widow of John Crossworth, visiting the mill, calling on the tenants, a part of the old world which still reminded people of past glories. Religiously she kept in touch with all her old allies; the pit foreman, Graham Cox, and Sammy Upton, now widowed, retired and living in Little Lever. Once a month she called on him, sat with him in his cramped front room with its cut out figure of a blackamoor holding an ashtray, the pile of cigarette stubs growing steadily during the hours they talked.

'He were one in a million, your husband,' Sammy said gravely. 'Best man I ever knew.'

'John was fond of you too, and he relied on you so much, especially at the end,' Sarah replied. 'He said you were his ears and eyes. Said you knew everything that went on in Oldham.'

'Remember Dandry Fairclough and old man Cotter?' Sammy asked her suddenly, glancing up.

She nodded.

'Couple of right villains, crooked as hell,' he said shortly. 'Everything were so different then, Mrs Crossworth, weren't it?'

Which was exactly what Sarah tried to explain to Kitty, but it was difficult. The older generation was beginning to die, a younger one taking its place; she could see it happening, the houses coming up for sale on Queen's Road, newcomers moving in, cars parked where the carriages used to be. Everything was so good for them, Sarah thought incredulously, so peaceful ... We never had much peace, did we, John? she thought. We always had something to achieve, something to fight for.

And then she thought of Freddie; of the son who had disgraced them, of the son she had publicly banished, exiled from her heart. Except at night, and then the young Freddie, the sweet Freddie, came visiting her dreams. He came in laughing, or putting his hands over her eyes and when she woke she would keep her eyes closed for a second to luxuriate in the sensation – before memory catapulted her back into reality.

But Kitty, much as Sarah loved and liked her, could never understand, and it would be unfair to expect her to. Some things are never meant to be shared, she thought, grateful to see the revival of closeness between her son and daughter-in-law. Besides, there were other compensations, like Ray; her grandson, the inheritor, the carrier of her husband's dream; the dark horse on whom each one of them had placed their hopes.

And as Sarah thought of Ray, so did Kitty, their thoughts in perfect synchronization, Sarah in the drawing room at Queen's Road, Kitty whistling softly under her breath at the entrance to Market Street.

He realized then that if you didn't know the North it could frighten you. The days are very short in winter, the cold intimidating. The low terraces cast long shadows and the alleyways are peopled by imagination's bogeymen. Because of the cold, the sounds vibrate and echo; each repeated dourly down the streets, lingering under lamps and chasing the cars which slow down at the Union Street lights. It's a hard place, the mill chimneys granite tors as bleak as any natural hazard; Oldham Edge wind-chased and empty, abandoned when the clocks go back for winter.

Holding Harry's hand Ray walked through the gates of Radcliffe Heights, and entered through the double doors. He walked quickly, never looking to left or right, merely following the signs, doors banging closed behind them. A concerned phone call from Kitty had set things discreetly in motion. Dr Stanley had used his 'nothing to worry about' tone. But Ray hadn't been convinced as he listened on the extension, and had decided to call to see the doctor himself. When he arrived, Dr Stanley looked surprised, a nurse taking temporary care of Harry.

'I just wanted a chat with your aunt,' Dr Stanley said, when Ray confronted him.

'What about?'

'I want to talk to her about your mother –'

'What about her?'

'She needs help.'

'She has help. *I* help her,' Ray replied coldly.

The doctor picked up his pen and doodled a kite on his blotter.

'You live on Queen's Road, don't you?'

'Yes.'

'With your aunt and uncle and Mrs Crossworth?'

'Yes.'

'Your mother used to live there too, I understand.'

Dear God, Ray thought, this man was trying to get his mother out of the flat. She'd never cope with that, *couldn't* cope with that.

'She did for a while during the war,' Ray replied cautiously. 'But afterwards she went back to live with my father.'

Dr Stanley's expression was sympathetic; his face understanding. But irritating.

'I believe your father is no longer with us.'

'He's away,' Ray said stupidly. What else could he say? He won't come back? Then his mother would have no hope at all. 'But he'll return, he always does.'

'Meanwhile your poor mother has to cope with a little boy –'

'*Harry*,' Ray said truculently. 'My brother is called Harry.'

'Yes, Harry,' Dr Stanley agreed. 'She has to look after him alone –'

'She isn't alone. I help her and so does my aunt. And my uncle pays her bills –'

'But she lives alone with Harry,' Dr Stanley insisted.

Ray could feel his colour building. Someone had been talking, spying on them!

'My mother is fine. She's perfectly all right. She's a good mother, I can vouch for that.'

'Ray, you and I both know that she leaves your brother alone sometimes –'

'He's never left! I make sure he's not –' Ray snapped, then stopped, realizing he had been trapped. 'I . . . I babysit for her.'

Dr Stanley looked at the young man in front of him and picked out his words carefully.

'Ray, I've had a report about your mother. I wanted to talk to you first and try to work out what we can do for her.'

Silence.

'She's not functioning well, is she?'

What did that mean? Ray wondered desperately.

'She's not washing, is she?'

'She's just been off colour,' Ray said fiercely. 'She felt dizzy in the bath –'

'She's not eating either, is she?'

'She eats! She eats!' Ray retorted hotly. 'Who's been

telling you lies? They all gossip round there. Always did because of my father.' His voice steadied, dropped. Suddenly he was controlled again. 'None of this is true. My mother *has* been ill, but she's fine now, and my brother is too.'

'I want to see her for myself,' Dr Stanley said impassively.

'But I don't *want* you to see her.'

'Be that as it may, I need to see her. To assess her condition.'

'She doesn't have a "condition".'

'Listen, Ray, if there *is* a problem, don't you think we should sort it out now before it gets worse?' Dr Stanley queried reasonably. 'Your mother might just need a rest, a short change. A bit of help –'

'In this place?'

'Your mother could come here for a short stay, yes.'

'She won't do that.'

'She might have to.'

'If you do that to her, she'll die.'

Dr Stanley smiled sympathetically. 'Ray, people don't die –'

'If you move her from that flat, she'll give up. And when people give up, they die.'

The doctor paused for a beat. 'Why is the flat so important to her?'

'My father always comes back there.'

'But he's been away for a long time now, Ray,' Dr Stanley said tactfully. 'Maybe your father won't return.'

'Oh, I know that, doctor,' Ray replied, his expression resigned, 'but my mother doesn't. She believes that if she stays there, he'll walk in one day. If she leaves there, he'll never come home. It's not love, you see, it's something much worse. She can't help herself, she just waits, wanting him and afraid of him at the same time.'

Dr Stanley had heard all about Freddie Crossworth over the years, and chose his next words carefully.

'Ray, your mother needs treatment –'

'Don't, Dr Stanley, please don't take her away.'

'I have to do what's best for my patient.'

'You don't know her! *I* know her. Trust me, listen to me,' Ray pleaded quietly. 'Leave my mother to me. Please.'

No one could get through to Ray the day his mother was taken away to Radcliffe Heights sanatorium. They all went with her, Kitty and Jim sitting in the car with Harry whilst Ray walked his mother to the entrance. For a long time they talked, Ray's head bent down towards his mother's, her expression tremulous. He was trying to reassure her; they knew that much, but Sally was still patently terrified. A short break, Dr Stanley had assured them. Just for a while.

'Didn't you know that Ray was covering up for his mother?' Dr Stanley had asked them earlier.

'I didn't know that, but I'd suspected something was wrong for a while,' Kitty replied as she turned to the window and looked out. The gardens of Radcliffe Heights were just as she expected; soothing, with high walls hidden by trees. Covert security.

'Sally will get out of here again, won't she?'

'No one can judge that at the moment,' Dr Stanley replied patiently. 'She's very confused and she's been neglecting Harry –'

'And Ray covered up for her,' Kitty said distantly, glancing over to Jim. 'I just wondered why he didn't come to us for help. We would have done anything.'

'Because he wanted to do it his own way,' Jim replied, remembering what the doctor had told them earlier. *Your nephew never let his brother be alone. If their mother went out, Ray sat with Harry. He took complete responsibility. He was a good and loving son.*

Sighing, Jim turned to his wife. 'I've been thinking about Freddie, thinking how dissimilar he and Ray are. My brother got Sally pregnant when he wasn't much older than Ray is, and tried his damnedest to get out of it. But his son has never let his mother down once. He took on all the responsibility of his condition for years.' She could hear the pride in his voice and watched as he turned back to the doctor. 'How d'you think he'll take it?'

'Hard,' Dr Stanley replied. 'He wanted to keep his mother in the flat at all costs – apparently she believes that her husband will come back there.'

'*If* Freddie comes back,' Jim said bitterly, 'it won't be to a few rooms over a greengrocer's shop.' He glanced down at his hands, fighting anger. 'If my brother comes back it will be for one reason, and one reason only – to brag. If he's made money, he'll be back.'

'Hey, Mum, it's fine. Everything's fine,' Ray said gently, hanging Sally's clothes in the locker of her room and putting his photograph next to Harry's by the bed. 'You'll be home soon –'

'I want you to do something for me,' she said suddenly, touching her son's arm. Her hair was deeply red; the previous day she had gone to the hairdresser's to have it coloured. To make the best of herself. It was, to Ray, almost unbearably poignant.

'Whatever you want, Mum.'

She glanced around, then dropped her voice further. As he leaned towards her he could smell peppermint.

'Will you go and live in the flat, Ray?'

He had never refused her anything, but this time, he hesitated. The flat meant cold rooms, bad memories, violence. The flat was the past he wanted to escape. Besides, no one would let a boy of his age stay there alone. But his mother didn't seem to realize this.

'Why, Mum?'

'Because your father will come back there,' she whispered. 'And you can tell him that I've just gone away for a few days.' She took her son's hand and turned it over, tracing his life line with her index finger. 'Then you can come and get me. That way I won't miss him ... He must never know about this,' she said with feeling. 'Promise me, your father will never know about my being here.'

'I promise.'

Her gaze roamed over the room fitfully. 'They think I didn't take good care of Harry, but I did.' Her voice was pleading. 'And I took good care of you, didn't I?'

'You did, Mum,' Ray said struggling to keep his voice steady. 'You looked after me better than anyone could have done.'

She smiled secretly. 'When your father gets home we'll all be a family again. You see, we'll all be together again . . .' Suddenly she lost her momentum, frowned, and then continued hesitantly. 'Tell Harry I love him, and,' she lifted her son's hand and brushed her lips against his upturned palm, 'remember, I love you always and always. You are my good angel, Ray. You are my only hope.'

He smiled, but she didn't notice he had never agreed to go back to the flat.

They stumbled through a fitful winter, Sally staying up at Radcliffe Heights, her condition deteriorating. At first she spoke longingly of her return to the flat, asking for news of Freddie, imagining – and yet dreading – their reunion, but when Christmas came and went she became more withdrawn, Kitty and Jim visiting her twice a week with Harry, Ray seeing his mother at other times. Alone.

Because lately, Sally had trouble remembering whose son Harry was.

'Hello, little one,' she said two days after Christmas. The decorations were still hanging, cheap paper trailers running from the picture rail to the overhead light. 'He's growing,' she said to Kitty, 'and he looks more like you all the time.'

Caught off balance, Kitty stared at her. 'Harry is *your* son –'

'You're very kind,' Sally said distantly, 'but my son is Ray.' Her gaze wandered, fought to settle on anything, but failed. 'Harry is very like his father.'

'Freddie.'

She smiled indulgently. 'No, Jim.'

So, after all these years, after all the longing and hoping, Kitty and Jim Crossworth finally had a son. By proxy, on loan, perhaps permanently, perhaps only until Sally's memory returned. Moved, Kitty looked at Sally and then at the small boy on her lap, her hands tightening protectively around him. Was Sally really confused, she wondered, or was she actually handing her son over? For a moment – against all reason and conscience – Kitty prayed for the latter.

After that they never took Harry to see his mother again. Instead Kitty placed a photograph of Sally by her nephew's bed and told him daily who his mother was. But he couldn't relate to a picture and gradually he transferred his affections to the people who offered him security – Kitty and Jim.

Meanwhile Ray caught the bus out to Radcliffe Heights each evening. On every visit he took his mother little offerings – perfume, food, magazines – and walked with her in the cordoned-off gardens.

'Your father was so good-looking,' she said lightly, squeezing his arm. 'Not as handsome as you, of course.'

She had lost all trace of reality; had forgotten the violence, the fear which had run through her marriage year after year. All the humiliations, the insults, the rejections were obliterated. In the end, Sally Rimmer's madness was kind to her – she now *imagined* the love she had never experienced in reality – and believed in it.

Smiling, she gave her son a sideways glance. 'You are so handsome, Ray,' her hand traced the length of his shoulder, 'and good.'

He was, as ever, touched by her affection. 'Dr Stanley said you were better.'

'Yes. I like it here.'

The statement left him winded, off centre.

'I do, Ray. *Really* I do. I feel safe here,' she went on,

looking at the gates. 'I don't want to leave – not now. Not for a while . . .'

Shaken, he stared at her. It *couldn't* be true, he thought. His mother had to believe that she would leave this place. She *had* to, or she would give up.

'Yes, I do want to stay here . . . at least until your father gets home.'

He hadn't realized that until then he had been holding his breath. With relief he exhaled, then smiled. The moment of crisis had passed. Better that his mother lived with a fool's hope, than no hope at all.

Chapter Twenty-Two

The bloody town never changes, Freddie thought disparagingly, same dirty coal hole. His gaze flicked over the town centre, resting for a moment on the Town Hall clock. Twelve thirteen. As good a time to come home as any. Hurriedly he turned the wheel of his Jaguar and headed out towards Queen's Road, then changed his mind and drove instead to the less affluent part of town. Parking, Freddie glanced at Hunts' greengrocers then looked up at the two windows above.

What a flaming hole. What a godforsaken, hideous, stinking little hole, he thought. How had he managed to stand it for so long? How *could* he have done? He thought of Sally in the cold bed, then remembered Ray lying next to her when he was a baby. Always sickly, always whey-faced. God, he was glad it was over. Glancing round anxiously, Freddie then slid out of his car and stood looking up at the windows.

His appearance was extravagant, almost flashy, his looks honed down with time and bitterness. If you had passed him on the street you would have thought him a salesman, and wondered how he got his nose broken. Coldly, Freddie thought back; remembered the night his brother and he had fought, and the way his mother had publicly banished him. His bitterness burned like acid inside his mouth. It was time to show them what he was made of; his father wasn't the only one who could go off and make a fortune. Oh no, for all they tried to make out, he was John Crossworth's son all right.

Because he had done it too. Made a pile. Heaps of bloody money, to buy cars, and women, and houses. Freddie smiled, thinking of the purchase he had made only that morning. A house on Upper Mill, six bedrooms, three bathrooms and a vast garden. Before long he'd employ staff, have a few parties, show them all how it was done. He'd made it, made good.

Well, made it anyway. If not made good. Made money ... Suddenly disturbed, Freddie turned away from the greengrocers and climbed back into his car, flicking on the windscreen wipers as a dark rainfall began. He stared at it morosely. God, he thought, even the bloody weather was the same. Nothing changes. Nothing changes at all.

Lighting up another cigarette, Sammy Upton glanced over to his visitor and wondered if he should tell her, or whether she already knew. Carefully he studied Sarah's face, the dark mass of hair greying at the front, her long back straight in the chair.

'I heard a bit of news this morning,' Sammy said evenly, 'only an hour or so ago.'

She was blandly interested. 'Oh yes, Sammy, what was it?'

'Frederick's back.'

He hadn't expected the reaction; hadn't expected any reaction at all from the redoubtable Sarah Crossworth; so when she let out a short breath and touched her stomach Sammy glanced away, embarrassed.

'Sorry, I thought ... I thought you might want to know.'

'Are you sure?' Her voice had slipped a cog lower.

'So they say. Someone saw him outside Hunts' greengrocers.'

Sarah had expected the news someday, yet now she heard it every part of her was suddenly galvanized. Her son – her *son* – was home. But what was it she was feeling? Distress? Anger? Pleasure? Excitement? Oh God, Freddie, she thought desperately, stay away. And then another thought followed on immediately: why aren't you here, John? Why aren't you with me now?

'I wouldn't have told you if I'd thought it would upset you,' Sammy said sincerely.

'I'm glad you did,' Sarah replied, glancing at the door. She should leave now, go home, act as though nothing was different. After all, he might not even come to see her. She had disowned him publicly, humiliated him, made it clear to everyone in the town what she thought of her son. His actions had killed four good men; his greed had murdered them. Frederick Crossworth was no good – even his mother said so ... But then again, she was still his mother and that could never change.

Awkwardly, Sarah rose to her feet, her usual poise diminished.

'I have to go, Sammy –'

'If you need me,' he said, standing up and facing her, 'for anything, just send for me and I'll come.'

'You don't know him as well as I do,' Ray said firmly, Kitty standing in the kitchen with the shopping still in her arms. 'Listen to me, please. I don't want him to have anything to do with Harry. We can't let him get to him.'

Immediately, Kitty flinched. She had never thought of *that* when she heard that Freddie Crossworth was back; never considered that he might want to see his son.

'He's never been interested in Harry before, so why should he be now?' she asked, feigning confidence. 'He abandoned all of you.'

'But he's back now, isn't he?' Ray countered, taking the shopping from his aunt and pulling out a chair for her to sit down. 'He's Harry's father, he has rights –'

He has rights. Suddenly Kitty was mortally frightened. Harry was her son now, thought of as belonging to her and Jim. It was the best solution; everyone agreed on that; everyone had taken it as read that Harry would stay with them and be raised by them. But Freddie could take his son away now. Freddie could take Harry away ...

'Get your uncle,' Kitty said simply, calling for Harry and

walking to the front door. 'Please, Ray, tell him to come home at once.'

They arrived at almost the same moment, Sarah walking up the front steps just as Jim's car pulled up. He got out hurriedly, Ray following.

'Have you heard?'

'Sammy Upton's just told me,' Sarah replied, unlocking the door and trying to open it as it resisted. 'What on earth?' The steel chain allowed the door to open only a few inches, Kitty only unfastening the chain when she saw who it was.

'Freddie's back.'

'We know,' Sarah replied calmly. 'Why did you put the chain on the door?'

Kitty was holding fast on to Harry's hand. 'Because he might come for his son,' she said, relocking the door hurriedly. 'Ray thinks he might come back for Harry.'

'Why? Why would he bother?' Jim replied, trying to sound confident as he turned to his nephew. 'Have you seen your father already?'

Ray's expression was unreadable. 'No. I just know how he thinks, that's all.'

'You could be wrong,' Jim countered patiently. 'There's no point in worrying your aunt unnecessarily.'

'But if I'm right, I should warn her,' he responded, his tone emphatic. 'My mother always said he would come back, and now he has. He'll try and get back what he lost. You *know* he will.'

Jim regarded his nephew thoughtfully. Ray was right – and they both knew it.

'Listen, you don't have to have anything to do with him –'

'How can you say that? You know my father could legally force you to hand over Harry – and me.'

Deep in thought, Sarah guided Kitty into the drawing room with Harry and closed the door behind them. The room was welcoming, a fire banked up just as it had always been when John was alive. For an instant she imagined her husband sitting by the fire and tried to think of the advice he would have given her. But this time nothing came through, no words to help her. This time, she was on her own.

'Kitty, calm down.'

'I *am* calm!'

'You're not, but you must be,' Sarah replied bluntly. 'We have to work this out together. *If* Freddie tries to get Harry back we'll fight him – but we shouldn't worry about it yet. After all, he might only be passing through.'

They both knew he wasn't.

'*Could* he get Harry back?'

'He left his family years ago.'

'But they're still *his*!' Kitty retorted blindly. 'Oh God, I won't let him get Harry, I swear I won't.'

Slowly Sarah pulled off her gloves and then sat down, crossing her legs and staring for a long moment into the fire.

'One of the things John always taught me was not to look for trouble – "it comes without searching for it",' she said, glancing up at her daughter-in-law. 'You've taken wonderful care of Harry, he thinks of you as his mother – and as for Jim, he's been twice the father Freddie ever could have been.'

'But would a court say that?' Kitty asked desperately. 'Would a court grant us custody if the natural father asked for the return of his son?'

'We don't know that Freddie will –'

'Ray says he will, and that's good enough for me,' Kitty replied, sitting down and drawing Harry onto her knee. The boy was tired, rubbing his eyes fitfully. 'Oh God. If I lost him, I'd go mad –'

Tightly, Sarah's hand closed over Kitty's: 'Then don't think of it. Don't even consider it. Life works out – I don't know how, or when – but everything works out in the end.' She stared away, remembering. 'John was never a religious man, never called on God, but he used to say, "I promise you this, as the moon is my witness, I promise you this..." and it would always happen.' Her fingers clutched Kitty's fiercely. 'Well, now I say this to you – as the moon is my witness, these children are *yours*. Harry and Ray are meant to be yours, and will be yours and Jim's. Not Sally's, not Freddie's, but yours. You have to remember that, and whatever happens in the weeks and months to come, you have to *keep* remembering it.'

But Freddie wasn't just passing through; they found that out only a day later, his movements relayed to them hourly. He had bought a house in Upper Mill; had furniture sent from Manchester and London; was hiring staff; was supervising work in the garden. And then, soon after his return, another piece of news broke. He had a woman with him.

Sarah's face was rigid. 'How do you know that?'

'I saw her,' Ray replied simply.

He had been to visit his mother up at Radcliffe Heights, Sally mercifully ignorant of events outside, uncommunicative, sedated heavily. She hadn't wanted to talk, had just sat in her chair wearing a cheap dress and ankle socks, her auburn tint growing out at the roots. For over an hour her son stayed with her, then Ray caught the bus to Upper Mill, looking for his father's new address and finding it just after seven.

It was a vast house, larger than the one on Queen's Road – but then it had to be, didn't it? Watching from the gate he had seen figures moving past the windows and then stepped back when a car drove past him, taking the angle of the drive too sharply and braking suddenly. He had presumed that it would be his father, but the person who got out to look at the bumper was female, slim, only in her twenties, with a tiny face, and glasses.

She had seen Ray and smiled, taking off her spectacles and grinning. 'Not much help, are they?'

Surprised, he had almost walked off, but hesitated instead. 'Do you live here?'

She was pretty, obviously so, and nodded in reply. 'Yes, since yesterday.'

'On your own?'

Her head went on one side, her smile amused. 'No. With someone.'

'What's your name?'

She came over to Ray slowly, curiously studying his face. 'You ask a lot of questions. Who are you?'

'A neighbour,' he replied calmly.

'Left or right?'

'Huh?'

She waved her glasses in her hand archly. 'Are you a neighbour on the left or on the right?'

'Right,' he lied.

Her smile was quick, small-toothed. 'I'm Lorna.'

'I'm Jim,' Ray replied, his tone even. He felt no guilt in lying, felt nothing, only curiosity. 'Do you own the house?'

'Nah, Freddie owns it,' she had replied, leaning against the car bonnet and eyeing Ray. 'Freddie Crossworth – heard of him?'

'No, should I have done?'

'He's a big man,' Lorna replied earnestly, 'made a fortune in London –'

'Doing what?'

'Minding his own business,' she answered laughing.

Ray smiled uneasily. 'Sorry, I didn't mean to pry –'

'Oh, you didn't. I'm glad to have someone to talk to –'

A shout from the house stopped her in midflow, her slight frame turning abruptly.

'Coming!' she shouted, then turned back, smiling.

But Ray had already gone.

Sarah considered the information carefully, watching her grandson. She wasn't surprised by his ingenuity; he had too much of John Crossworth in him; but she *was* surprised by the emotionless way he had described his findings.

'Does all this bother you, Ray?'

'No. I just wanted to know what was going on; whether my father was staying in Oldham or not.'

'It looks as though he is, doesn't it?'

'Maybe he'll leave us alone,' he said eagerly. 'D'you think he might? You know, just get on with his life and leave me and Harry alone? D'you think he might?'

Should she take the easy way out and lie? Sarah wondered. But to what end? If she did and she was found out, Ray would never trust her again.

'No,' she replied at last, 'I think your father came back here for a reason.'

'What?'

'Revenge.'

Ray's eyes were burning with anxiety. 'And that involves Harry and me? That involves us?'

'Revenge,' Sarah replied quietly, 'involves everyone.'

Chapter Twenty-Three

It was a matter of who had the best lawyer; and in the end, Freddie did. He was, the lawyer explained, Ray and Harry's natural father, and the law dictated that the children should be returned to him. Their mother was regrettably unable to care for them, but Freddie Crosworth was now affluent, with sufficient money to raise them in the manner to which they had become accustomed. The lawyer went on to say that Jim and Kitty Crosworth had done a remarkable job as surrogate parents, but that Freddie had worked hard to absolve his mistakes of the past and now wanted to reclaim his children and give them a stable, secure home.

'They *can't* believe that!' Kitty said, close to tears. 'No one could believe it. Freddie never gave a damn about his children. *We* brought them up.'

Beside her, Jim was bullet-faced, white with anger, staring at his brother who had never once acknowledged his family either before, or during, the hearing.

'Furthermore,' the lawyer continued, 'Mr Crosworth will take over all the finances concerning the care of his sick wife until her demise.'

'Which he will no doubt hasten,' Jim said curtly under his breath.

Mercifully Sally had heard nothing; gossip never reached Radcliffe Heights; she merely continued to talk to Ray about the day the family would be reunited. She hadn't ever considered the possibility that they were going to be reunited *without her*.

'And so,' Freddie's lawyer concluded, 'Mr Crosworth

seeks to make amends for the past by providing for his family from now on. He is a changed man.'

'Sounds as though he's trying to get him off a murder charge,' Jim said sourly, still staring at his brother. 'It's a pity he's too late; Freddie's already got away with murder.'

He had too – having been absolved of blame for the death of four men, the verdict 'accidental death'.

Sarah had seen a change in Jim ever since he heard that his twin had come back to Oldham. There was no lightness, no joy about him any more. It was as though his brother were bleeding him white, she thought, and then realized that, in a way, he was. Gradually Freddie was taking everything from Jim that he loved: Harry and Ray – Jim and Kitty's marriage was already rocking under the stress. They had been a happy couple, but now, suddenly, they were relegated back to where they had been years earlier – a childless couple, uneasy alone.

Sarah wondered if she should call to see Freddie and try to reason with him. But she dismissed the idea out of hand; she had rejected him, so he would be sure to reject her. Oh no, her son was going to bite off his revenge piece by piece, picking the Crossworth carcass clean whilst causing vicious divisions between the remaining members of the family.

'You told me I wouldn't lose Harry!' Kitty snapped at her mother-in-law after the hearing. 'You said "As the moon is my witness, this child is yours" – and I believed you. But you were wrong,' she snapped. 'Harry was supposed to be with me. He was *supposed* to be with me.'

Anxiously, Sarah reached out for her daughter-in-law, but Kitty moved away, her arms folded across her chest.

Distressed, Jim walked over to his mother's side. 'Forget what she said, she didn't mean it. She's just upset about the boys –'

'He could always do it,' Sarah said distantly.

'What?'

'Freddie – he could always divide people. That was –

and *is* – his own peculiar talent. Your father and I never quarrelled – unless it was about Freddie.' She straightened up, tired, dark shadows under her eyes and chin. 'Don't let him do it to you, Jim. Don't let him break up your marriage –'

'But he's taken the boys away.'

'I know what he's done!' Sarah replied shortly, staring at her son. 'But you must be calm, Jim. Think about your father, think what he would have done. Would he have given up? Never. No, Freddie thinks we're beaten, he thinks he's got the upper hand, but it won't last. It never does, it can't, it's not the way of things.' She stared at Kitty, standing on the pavement a little way off. 'I still say that Harry is meant to be with you – you and Kitty. I don't know how, but that child *will* come back to you.'

'And in the meantime,' Jim asked her, 'who looks after him?'

'Who else?' Sarah said, glancing behind her to where a slim figure stood motionless.

'Ray?' Jim asked, shaking his head. 'No, he'll never stay with his father, he loathes him.'

'Oh, but he will for Harry's sake,' Sarah replied. 'Remember how he watched over his brother before? And how he covered up for his mother? You know, sometimes I look at that boy and see – just for an instant – John Crossworth standing there.'

'I bet you thought you'd seen the last of me,' Freddie had said, as they drove up to the house in Upper Mill. 'I bet they forcefed you all kinds of lies about me, didn't they?'

Ray had found it difficult to speak ever since the judgment came through. He had genuinely believed that he and Harry would be allowed to remain at Queen's Road. It had never occurred to him that tonight he would be standing in his father's house, holding his brother's hand, trying uselessly to explain to Harry that they were going to have to stay here for a while.

'I don't want to!' Harry had wailed helplessly. 'I want to go home.'

'Sssh . . .' Ray had warned him as they waited in the empty hallway for their father to come in from outside. 'Remember how we used to keep secrets in the flat?' Harry nodded dumbly. 'Well, it's the same kind of thing.' He stared into his brother's four-year-old face. 'We're not staying here for long, Harry. We'll be going home soon. But you can't tell anyone. OK?' There was no response. 'OK, Harry?'

He nodded miserably. 'OK.'

'You've really grown,' Freddie said loudly as he walked into the hallway and looked at his younger son. 'And you, Ray, you're a good-looking one, I'll give you that.' He smiled awkwardly. Now he'd got his sons back he didn't really know what to do with them; his imagination had never taken him beyond the point of triumph when he was awarded custody. The reality was sobering, two solid-faced boys staring at him with ill-concealed dislike.

'I was thinking we might –'

He was distracted in midflow, Lorna appearing at the head of the stairs. She was wearing casual pants and a long jumper, her hair fastened back in a French pleat.

'So you've met our neighbour, Freddie.'

He gave her a long slow look. 'What the hell are you talking about?'

'About our neighbour,' she said cheerily. 'This is Jim from the house on the right.'

Freddie's face was a study.

'*What?*'

Her confidence lost its footing, her gaze moving from Ray to Harry. 'I thought you said you were going to bring your two boys home tonight?'

'What do these look like?' Freddie said sourly. 'Hat pegs?'

'But he's our neighbour –'

'He's Ray, my *son*!' Freddie snapped exasperated. 'And the other one's Harry.'

'So why did he say he was our neighbour?' Lorna persisted. 'That night I met him in the drive –'

'*What* night?'

'The night I came across him in the drive, just after we moved in.'

Understanding wasn't slow in coming, Freddie turning back to his elder son with a baleful look. 'Spying on me, were you? Wanting to know what I was up to?'

Instinctively Ray's grip tightened around his brother's hand. 'I'd heard rumours –'

'Why bother skulking around, Ray? Why didn't you ring the bell? Do the honourable thing?'

'I don't think you're really the one to talk about honour,' he replied coldly.

It took Freddie a moment to recover. When he did he moved towards his son quickly, his hand raised, Ray automatically pushing Harry behind him.

'*Don't you dare!*' he said darkly. 'Don't you ever dare to touch me or my brother, or I'll kill you, I swear it, I'll kill you.'

'He says they're all right,' Kitty said idly, fiddling with a pen in her hand. 'That they're doing fine.'

Concerned, Jim watched her. Since the boys had been taken away she had lost weight, her interest in the business waning. The house – she told him the night before in bed – was too quiet for comfort.

Her voice was disembodied in the dark. 'I wonder if they'll give Harry the things he likes to eat. You know he can be picky, and he won't eat vegetables.' She sat up in bed suddenly. 'He shouldn't be having too many sweet things.' Her voice was teetering on the edge of panic. 'Do you think they know about such things? Oh, Jim, do they *know*?'

'Don't worry, Ray's there.'

At the mention of his name he could feel her relax, a moment later slipping back under the covers.

'What do you think he's doing?'

'Who?'

'Ray,' she answered. 'What do you think he's doing?'

'Sleeping,' Jim lied, holding his wife against him. 'He'll be sleeping.'

Of course he could just make a run for it with his brother. It would be only too easy to pick up Harry and leave. Everyone was out, his father and Lorna having gone to Manchester. But where would they go? If he was on his own, he could manage, but with Harry it was impossible. He was only four, had to have a home, a family, otherwise people asked questions. Sliding his hands under his head, Ray stared up at the ceiling. Something bad was going to happen, he could feel it.

Oddly enough it was an improvement in his mother's condition which was making him so uneasy. Sally was slowly but certainly responding to a new drug; she was less withdrawn, more aware of her environment. Little nuances tipped him off to her improvement; she told him a joke, then another time asked after Sarah. But not her son; in her mind Harry still belonged to Kitty. For that much Ray was grateful.

But his mother never asked anything about such matters; she simply shored up her energy and climbed some little way back into life. Daily, Ray could see the progress and what would – at any other time – have been a longed-for miracle, he dreaded. Because he knew that one day she would ask him about her husband; she would ask him and her son would have to lie to her. It wasn't the lie that mattered; it was the fact that she would *know* he was lying.

And then what? The lie would be challenged; she would perhaps guess then about the flat; then he would be forced to tell her about the house in Upper Mill. *Yes, we live there now with our father* ... She would be bewildered, not

understanding ... *But I should be there* ... *You can't* ...
Why not? ... *Because there's someone else there* ... She
would know at once that it was a woman, a young woman
with *her* husband. Just as she'd know that Freddie would
never return to the flat over the greengrocer's. And then
she would realize that it was over, and in realizing that,
she would know that *she* was over too.

Turning in bed, Ray stared at the blank walls around
him. Put up some pictures, his father had said impatiently,
do something with the place! But the only thing Ray
wanted to do with the place was to leave it. And *that* he
couldn't do.

The night poured past his window, and still he didn't
sleep. Come morning he would go to the mill and see his
uncle. They would avoid eye contact, affection suspended,
Jim anticipating a rebuke, Ray an unwanted apology.

Freddie was doing his work well: inch by inch, the family
was being picked apart.

Chapter Twenty-Four

Fitful winter gave way to spring, climbed into summer, and then dipped into autumn again. The year limped past, the family separated, Ray keeping watch over Harry in the house at Upper Mill, Jim running the business, Sarah and Kitty living day to day in Queen's Road, Freddie unusually quiet. Then – one day in early December – Kitty walked into Sarah's bedroom and sat down on the bed beside her mother-in-law. It was early, yet she was fully dressed, her make-up applied carefully. She looked, Sarah thought suddenly, like someone who expected trouble and wanted to be prepared for it.

'What is it?'

'You and I have always got on, haven't we?'

Nodding, Sarah sat up in bed and pulled the blanket around her. 'Yes, always.'

'Then we have to stick together now,' Kitty went on. 'You know how much I love Jim, but he's drawn back, adjusted to the situation. He's accepted the situation.' She hesitated, unwilling to appear disloyal. 'He's given up.'

'On what?'

'On Harry,' Kitty replied. 'Jim's a good man and good men live by the law. He's accepted that the judgment went against him: he might not like it, but he's accepted it. He knows that Harry should be with us, but he feels his hands are tied. He can't play dirty.' She paused. 'Well, *I* can.'

She thought of the conversation she had had with Ray the previous night. He had called in to see her with Harry and stayed for a while, his gaze never once leaving his brother. As ever, he would tell her nothing which would worry her, but as Kitty looked at him she realized how bad the situation really was. The two boys she thought of as her own had been taken away from her; they now had the wrong father, in the wrong place, and the wrong person was taking the punishment. Ray was at an age when he should have been irresponsible, free of the burdens which were sure to come. But instead he was watching over his brother *and* his mother. It was too much; much too much.

'I won't let Ray carry on like this,' she said firmly to her mother-in-law. Her hair was newly brushed, full of body, her eyes alert. She was, Sarah realized, more animated than she had been for months. 'It's not fair – and no one's going to do anything about it – unless we do. You see, suddenly it doesn't matter to me if it's wrong; I *do* think of those children as mine.' She stared at Sarah defiantly. 'Well, why *not*? Their mother's ill, incarcerated, and their father's not fit to look after them.'

'So?' Sarah said quietly.

'If they stay at Upper Mill they'll change. They'll lose every good quality they ever learned here; Ray will become embittered and Harry – well, Harry's a young child and children copy what they see around them.' She leaned towards Sarah. 'I want to challenge the judgment. I want to appeal against it – and I need your backing.'

Sarah had also been thinking about the situation; had expected something to break long before this. But one year had played itself out and nothing had happened and now Christmas was coming round again and somehow the thought of spending the season without her grandchildren was chilling.

'We have to have valid grounds to contest the judgment,' Sarah said at last.

'So you'll help me?' Kitty asked, her expression euphoric.

'Yes, I'll help you,' Sarah replied, touching the back of her daughter-in-law's hand. 'Of course I'll help you. It always comes down to the women in the end.'

* * *

Well, Sally thought, she'd go along with it. Why not? She'd help them put up the Christmas tree and carry on passing the baubles. Her vacant eyes fixed on the golden globe in her hand although she wasn't really seeing it, her thoughts elsewhere. He was home! Freddie was home! Carefully she hid her smile. Remember, she told herself, don't give the game away, act like Silly Sally Rimmer, then no one will suspect a thing.

She had overheard the news – 'someone saw Sally Crossworth's husband yesterday' – and had been twitchy with excitement ever since. So he was back! But why hadn't Ray told her? she wondered suddenly. Maybe he didn't know himself yet. She would ask him when he came later ... The golden ball winked in her hand, her memory altered, distorted, all trace of fear obliterated. Oh, it was perfect timing, Freddie back for Christmas! She'd go back to the flat with Ray and ... Sally paused, a memory rumbling at the back of her mind. *Harry*, there was Harry, wasn't there? She had forgotten him. *Forgotten her son* ...

'Are you all right?'

Surprised, Sally turned round. 'Fine. I'm fine.'

The nurse's expression was concerned. 'Are you sure, Sally?'

Well, of course she was all right, she thought impatiently, but she wasn't going to tell them what she was thinking about. No way was she going to let them into her secret. She was going to surprise everyone instead; show them that she was perfectly all right; that she had just been biding her time here waiting until her husband came home ... the nice, kind husband she remembered of old, the make-believe Freddie Crossworth she had invented during her incarceration.

For the remainder of the afternoon Sally helped put up the Christmas decorations, then at six thirty she stood by the door waiting for her son to arrive.

'Ray,' she said simply, when she saw him. Hurriedly she

pulled him down the corridor and into her room. 'Have you heard the news?'

He was white-faced from the cold, a snowstorm making the temperature plummet.

'What news?'

His sleep had been disturbed, the tension in the house at Upper Mill escalating daily. Freddie was tired of his triumph and of his sons: he neither wanted to see them nor hear them. But he wanted to know where they were every second; wanted to be sure they weren't sneaking off to Queen's Road and his hated family. His hotel business was running itself, so time was lying heavily on his hands, and Lorna was little amusement in the daytime. He was bored – if the truth be known – and Freddie was always dangerous when he was bored.

'Have a drink with me,' he had said to Ray the previous night. 'We should talk, man to man.'

He hadn't meant it, he was spoiling for a fight, that was all.

'I don't want a drink.'

'"I don't want a drink",' Freddie parroted meanly. 'So what *do* you want, Ray? What would really please you? Like to have this house?' He waved his arm around expansively. 'Or Lorna? No?' he leaned towards his elder son. 'Let me guess what would really please you – like to see me dead?'

Exasperated, Ray turned away.

'DON'T BLOODY WALK AWAY FROM ME!' Freddie shouted hoarsely. 'You're my bloody son, you should treat me with respect.'

Inhaling deeply, Ray turned back to face his father. What would follow was always the same: Freddie would shout at him and provoke him – knowing that whatever he said Ray would never walk out and leave his brother. Yet Freddie never dared to strike his son; because if he did he knew Ray would strike back, and that was the one thing of which he was afraid.

'Well . . .' Sally said, cutting into her son's thoughts. 'Didn't you know your father was back?'

His eyes fixed blindly on the tinsel around the window, exhaustion suddenly overwhelming him. So it had happened at last, Ray thought. *She knew.* Above his head streamers of coloured ribbons hung down just as they had done a year ago when his father first came home. A year ago.

'Ray, talk to me,' Sally pleaded, taking her son's hand. 'Talk to me . . .'

Reluctantly he looked at her and wanted for one brief instant to lean his head against her shoulder. *Comfort me, love me. Make it all right for me.*

'Did you know your father was home?'

He nodded.

'Since when?' Sally asked, still excited, still hopeful.

'A while.'

It came into her eyes at that moment. He would always remember it; the first slow realization.

'*How* long?'

'Just over a year, Mum.'

She dismissed it with a short laugh. 'Never!' she said lightly, leaning towards him, her head only inches from his. 'How does the flat look?'

His eyes closed against the question.

'Get in some flowers, will you, Ray? And light the fire.' She glanced away, biting her lip. 'I need my green suit and . . . no, I think the red one. It's on the back of the bedroom door.'

It wasn't, Ray thought desperately, and it hadn't been there for years. It was packed up in a box with all his mother's other things, stored away in Queen's Road, the flat empty now.

'Will you bring it tomorrow, Ray: And some perfume,' she went on cheerfully, listing her needs, making a shopping list of items she hoped would seduce her husband and keep him home. And all the time Ray thought of the cold damp flat and the house in Upper Mill where his father was sleeping with a woman nearer his age than his mother's.

'We'll all be together for Christmas,' Sally said wistfully, squeezing his arm. 'Your father, me and you, and Harry.'

He flinched at the name. So she had remembered at last that Harry was her son. Dear God, Ray thought, his head bowing, why now? Why *now*?

'You'll make sure he looks his best, won't you?' she went on. 'And then come for me and we'll all be there ready when your father comes home.' Her hand was soft against his arm. But it felt like a tourniquet, his veins bursting, the blood roaring in his ears.

'Mum –'

'. . . We'll get some food in –'

'Mum, please listen to me –'

'. . . and something to drink for your father.' Her eyes were like a child's: unbearably poignant. Why didn't she remember the truth? Why didn't she remember the beatings, the terror, the long empty nights waiting for his father's footfall on the stairs? Why wasn't she afraid of him any more? 'Ray, do something else for me, would you?'

He was on his feet before he realized it, his voice raised, his face flushed.

'I *can't* do any more!' he snapped, Sally staring up at him as though she were looking at a stranger. 'I can't, Mum. I can't lie any more.'

Her hand went out to him, but he moved away. Tiredness and anxiety made him clumsy and he banged into the wall by the door, his shoulder aching from the blow. His eyes closed against the tears he couldn't stop; his mouth tightening. Jesus! God! he thought desperately. Let it all end. Let it all end.

'Ray?' Sally said blankly. 'Ray, what is it? What's happened? Don't you want to see your father?' Her tone was gentle. 'Because you don't have to, sweetheart, not if you don't want to. You can stay at Queen's Road for a while until things settle down. You don't have to see him if you don't want to –'

'I ALREADY LIVE WITH HIM!' Ray shouted, his mouth flecked with spittle. 'I live with him and my brother in a house in Upper Mill. We've been with my father for over a year.'

Shaking her head, Sally rose to her feet. 'Don't be silly,' she said sweetly, touching her son's face. 'You live at the flat –'

'I DON'T! I DON'T! He came back and we had to go with him –'

'With *who*?'

'My father!' Ray said, tears now pouring down his cheeks. 'My bloody father! Harry and I had to go with him. We *had* to. We had no choice –'

'Go where?'

'His house in Upper Mill.'

She was bemused, unsettled, unsteady, and yet she couldn't, wouldn't, give up.

'Then I'll come and live there.'

'You can't, Mum.'

'I can,' she persisted. 'I'm better now, I knew I would be when your father came home. I'll look after all of you, you just take me to this new house.' She reached out, stroked her son's hair away from his forehead. 'Poor Ray, I've leaned on you so much, haven't I? But I'll make it up to you, I promise –'

He cut her off. He had to. 'Mum, you can't come to the new house . . . My father's . . .' He wondered why he had to be the one to tell her; the one who delivered the blow, '. . . he's got someone else.'

She stared at him without seeing him, her head buzzing with the words. But they were no longer words, merely wicked prodding syllables evoking some terrible sensation in her. Numbness gave way to terror, then to a bloodied, gaping loss.

'No . . .' she said simply, moving away and slumping into the chair by the window.

'I *had* to tell you,' Ray said, terrified by the change in his mother. 'I had to.'

She said nothing, her eyes merely stared ahead. He thought – for one shattering instant – that she might lose consciousness.

'Mum? Mum?'

Silence.

Panicking, he kneeled beside her, touching her hands, her face, her hair. There was no response.

Chapter Twenty-Five

The night fell asleep under the snowfall, Oldham whitened, made pretty by nature. All along Queen's Road the houses slid down to rest, lamps turned off as the last residents retired. Silence settled on silence. It was bitter cold.

Sitting beside the window, Kitty stared out. She and Sarah had talked for most of the day, planning their strategy, Kitty grateful that Jim was away on one of his business trips, grateful that she wouldn't have to deceive him or excuse her actions. There was no time left; something had to be done. And it had to be done *now*.

In her own room, Sarah lay awake and listened to the quiet. She imagined that she could hear the snow landing, although she knew it was impossible, and dozing, thought for a moment that John had slid into bed beside her. The thought wasn't frightening, but comforting.

Something was in the air that night. Something dark and vengeful coming home to roost.

In the house in Upper Mill Freddie was slumped in front of the television. The programmes had long since finished, the white noise humming into the semi-darkness. Lorna was away visiting her mother in Birmingham, and above his head his sons had long since retired to bed. But although Harry slept, his brother did not. Alert and open-eyed, Ray stared out at the whitening landscape and saw over and over again his mother's face, the one word, 'No...' repeated like an echo in his head. Finally, at two thirty, he fell into an unsteady sleep.

He dreamed of his mother and his aunt, then turned over, his thoughts sliding back to his grandfather. Deeply asleep, Ray tried to concentrate on what John Crossworth was saying, but the words were jumbled and there was no sense in them. The night ground on. Then, long before light, he was woken by the sound of voices and sat up, startled. Lack of sleep and distress made him nauseous, his senses sluggish as he got out of bed, pulled on his dressing gown, and moved to the door.

Quietly he slipped out into the hallway and listened to the voices coming from below, his feet moving towards the top step then speeding up as he recognized the woman's voice. It was Sally.

'You bastard!' she was screaming. 'You hateful bastard! I want my children back! I WANT MY CHILDREN!'

Transfixed on the stairs, Ray listened. The door to the drawing room was open, a shaft of light falling across the hall floor, his father's voice coming loudly into the silence.

'For God's sake, calm down!' he shouted. 'You're not fit to look after anyone –'

'I looked after you for years!' she countered blindly. 'I looked after our children –'

'You can't look after anything,' he said dismissively. 'People look after *you*, Sally. You're in a bloody mental home, for God's sake!' He was moving away from the door, his voice becoming less distinct. 'Get the hell out of here.'

'I want my children back!' Sally shouted again. 'I won't let you have them. I WANT MY CHILDREN BACK!'

Standing on the stairs, Ray's first thought was how his mother had managed to get out of Radcliffe Heights. It wasn't even dawn; surely someone was looking for her? Besides, she had no transport, so how had she got here? Had she walked?

A sudden sound behind him made him turn, Harry appearing and rubbing his eyes.

'What is it?'

Hurriedly catching hold of his brother, Ray put his hand over Harry's mouth.

'It's a game,' he said firmly. 'We're having a game.' He could see that Harry was frightened, but continued calmly, 'Come on, we have to get dressed.' Guiding his brother back to his room, he closed the door.

'I don't want to –'

'Harry, get dressed!' Ray snapped, listening at the door as his mother's voice rose hysterically. 'Hurry up!'

Obviously terrified, Harry pulled on his clothes.

'Now put on your coat –'

'What for?'

'Do as I say!' Ray told him, taking hold of Harry's arm and then buttoning his jacket. 'Now, listen to me, we're going out –'

'But it's *cold*.'

'We're going out,' Ray repeated firmly, walking to the door and listening. 'Not a sound, Harry. We mustn't make a sound. It's a surprise, you understand? A surprise.'

The ground was hard underfoot as they reached the street, Ray hurrying his brother along and then picking Harry up and half running towards the town. The roads were empty of people, the snow fall obliterating the landmarks, Ray's breathing laboured as he struggled to carry his brother and keep his footing. Finally he reached Queen's Road and banged on the front door with his fist.

In her bedroom Sarah stirred, then woke suddenly, getting to her feet just as Kitty was running downstairs.

'What is it?'

'I don't know!' she shouted back, opening the front door and staring disbelievingly at the sight which greeted her.

'There's a fight at the house,' Ray said simply, trying to catch his breath as he handed Harry over to his aunt. 'My mother's arguing with my father.' His mouth was bloodless, his hair flecked with snow. 'I have to go back –'

'Ray, wait! You need help –'

'She needs help more than I do,' he replied, moving away and then turning. 'Look after Harry. I'll be back.'

*   *   *

Despite repeatedly gunning the engine, the car wouldn't start, Kitty swearing violently under her breath, a coat thrown over her nightdress.

'Come on, come on! Work!' she shouted.

Frowning, Sarah stood at the door with Harry in her arms. 'I'll get help –'

'*No!*' Kitty said. 'I've already wasted enough time, leave it to me. I'll go and see what's happening. Just stay here with Harry, please.' She turned on the engine again. Nothing. Her eyes closed. Time was passing quickly, too quickly. 'Oh please, *please* God, let it work,' she begged. Again she turned the ignition, there was a splutter. 'WORK, DAMN YOU! WORK!' she shouted, banging her hands on the wheel. Suddenly the engine roared into life.

Winding down the window she called out to Sarah: 'Wait there, I'll be back.' Then she drove off, turning on the windscreen wipers, and flooding the street with the headlights.

The snow was getting heavy by that time, her eyes straining to catch a glimpse of Ray although she knew that in the time she had wasted getting the car to start, her nephew was certain to have reached his father's house. Driving as fast as she dared, Kitty nearly skidded at a bend, her foot moving over the brake, her heart pulsing.

God help me! she willed silently, the icy roads passing under the car wheels, Upper Mill silent as she finally reached it. Only Freddie Crossworth's house was still lighted, the front door open. Slamming on the brakes, Kitty stopped the car and ran up the steps, then hesitated in the hall.

The silence was absolute and threatening.

No voices, no movements.

The place was – to all intents and purposes – empty.

Startled, she moved across the hall, looking into the dining room, library, and finally turning the handle of the drawing-room door. None of them moved as she walked in. Not Sally, slumped on the floor, not Freddie lying beside her, nor Ray standing motionless and expressionless with the doorstop in his hand.

'*Ray?*' Kitty said softly, moving over to her nephew.

He was rigid, unblinking, staring at his father. Slowly Kitty followed his gaze. Freddie was lying on the rug in front of the television, the humming screen sending out its high-pitched whistle, the white light dancing eerily on the bloodied face.

Slowly, she turned back, her gaze falling on the doorstop still clutched in Ray's hand.

'Give it to me.'

He didn't move, just stared at his mother, Sally sobbing quietly next to her dead husband.

'Give it to me,' Kitty repeated, putting out her hand.

He blinked suddenly, seemed to come back to life. 'What?'

'Ray, it's me,' she said calmly. 'What happened?'

'He was hitting my mother,' he replied without any emotion in his voice. 'He was always hitting my mother in the flat. *Always* hitting her . . .' He sighed, took in a breath greedily. 'He had her by the hair and punched her in the stomach.' His gaze rested for a long time on his mother, then flicked back to Kitty. 'I should have done it sooner. I should have killed him sooner.'

'Give the doorstop to me,' Kitty repeated once more, struggling to keep her voice calm. 'Come on, Ray, give it to me.'

Automatically he obeyed her, his aunt taking the bloodied doorstop from his hand. It felt heavy, cold. 'Now go upstairs. Get into bed,' she said quietly, 'and do exactly as I say –'

'I did it.'

'No, Ray, you *didn't*!' Kitty replied, staring at the boy she loved as a son. 'You've done enough over the years. *More* than enough. You're not responsible for this.'

'I can't –'

'You can do what I say!' she told him firmly. 'When the

police come I'll tell them that you came for me because your father was attacking Sally. That's the truth. Then I'll tell them that Freddie turned on me when I tried to intervene –'

'But he didn't –'

'He *did*!' she said emphatically, taking hold of her nephew's chin and tilting his head to force him to look at her. 'Ray, listen to me, I will *not* have your life ruined. You've done enough for everyone. For your mother, your brother. You've done enough and suffered enough, but you won't this time. I killed your father in self-defence. *I killed him.*'

'No –'

'Yes!' she said angrily. '*Yes! Yes! Yes!*' Her hand gripped his chin, her face moving closer to his. 'I love you, and I won't let you suffer again. I killed your father, Ray, *I* did it.' Her eyes bored into his. 'Now, go upstairs. It's over.' Gently she nudged him towards the door. 'Go upstairs, Ray. *Please*, for me. Do this for me. If you love me, do this for me.'

Chapter Twenty-Six

The murder was not just news on the front of the *Oldham Chronicle*, but on the *Mirror*, the *Express* and *The Times*, the domestic tragedy played out for millions. The interest had been expected up North – after all, the Crossworths were well known there – but no one had anticipated the nationwide coverage.

When the news reached Jim in France he returned home immediately, his mother greeting him at the airport, Sarah stiff-backed and resolute. One of her sons was dead, murdered, yet her grief was muted. Freddie, to all intents and purposes, had been dead since the night of the mining accident.

'Kitty's all right,' she said to her son. 'Believe me, she's fine.'

And she was. Since the moment she had phoned the police and called them to the house in Upper Mill, she had been in perfect control. It seemed to her then that her whole life had been in preparation for this moment; every thought, every instinct honed rapier-sharp for this second in time. When she had sent Ray back up to his bedroom she had stood for a while watching Sally, then she had helped her to a seat in the hall. She was bruised about the face and neck, but no longer crying. Instead she was silent, and would remain so for a long time to come.

The time before the police would arrive was short. In those few minutes Kitty wiped Ray's fingerprints off the doorstop and then picked it up with her own ungloved hand, so that only her prints remained. She then dropped it on the floor beside Freddie. Never once did she look at the dead man; her every thought was on detail, on hiding any clue which would prove her a liar.

Carefully she looked round and mentally rehearsed the story she had prepared for the police. Ray had woken to find his father fighting with his mother. Alarmed, he had come to Queen's Road for help, leaving Harry there before returning to Upper Mill with his aunt. On arrival Kitty had sent him to his room out of the way, before trying to protect Sally and placate a violent Freddie. But he had turned on her ... Did it sound convincing? Kitty turned to look around the room repeatedly. Well, *did* it? It might sound all right to her, but how would it sound to the police?

The television was still throwing out its static light, the high-pitched signal scratching against her nerve ends as she checked the room for the fourth time. Freddie on the floor, Sally silent in the hall outside, the doorstop apparently discarded after the struggle ... She frowned. If Freddie had turned on her, hit her, where were the marks? ... Her heart banging, Kitty moved out into the hallway and stared into the mirror.

She had only moments left. Moments during which Ray's future hung in the balance. If she could pull this off, she would protect him: if not, she would have failed him for ever, the stigma following him down the years. She could imagine only too well what everyone would say. 'Well, what d'you expect? He's his mother's son, all right, and his father's. No good, either of them ...' Silently she stared into the mirror. She didn't look as though she had intervened in a fight, in fact she looked suspiciously unmarked. Slowly Kitty drew back her hand then – closing her eyes – slapped herself as hard as she could. Her head snapped to one side. Again, she repeated the blow, wincing as she felt her teeth cut into her lip.

Then she looked back at her reflection.

Her face was swelling already; her lip bruising, blood flowing onto her chin. Almost satisfied, she then took hold of the collar of her coat and ripped it. Then, and only then, did she turn away and walk back into the drawing room to wait for the police to arrive.

The evidence was overwhelming; Kitty's story of self-defence believed. In fact her trial was brief and conclusive, and never once, in any way, did she divert from her story. As ever protective, Jim stood by her, as did Sarah, Ray even more withdrawn than usual – which people put down to the trauma of recent events. He spoke little, and when he did talk he only communicated with Kitty, the two of them developing an irrevocable bond.

Which Sarah noticed. Noticed, and wondered about as she regarded her daughter-in-law during the trial and afterwards.

'Do you see a change in her?' Jim asked his mother cautiously.

'She's been through a lot,' Sarah replied, her tone guarded. 'What do you expect? Anyone would be changed by something like this.'

'I would never have believed it possible,' Jim went on, 'I would never have thought her capable of murder.'

Turning, Sarah stared at her son. 'Do you blame her for what she did?'

'No,' he said sincerely, 'I just look at her now and wonder.'

'About what?'

'About how little we know about people,' he replied quietly.

How little we know about people – the phrase rang in Sarah's head for minutes afterwards, then repeated itself for hours into the night. Over and over she heard it, until finally she clicked on the bedside light and sat up. How much did anyone know about anyone? she wondered. Freddie had been her son, but she had never accepted his failings until she was forced to, until his actions had killed four men. Jim, also her son, and Kitty – who wasn't even a blood relative – how well did she know them?

Sarah remembered only too well that before the tragedy Kitty had asked her for help to get the boys away from Freddie. She had been determined, fiercely so. And now Freddie was dead ... The thought struck Sarah so forcibly that she put her hand to her mouth to stop herself crying out, and in the same moment she saw an image of Ray Crossworth, the boy most like John, the boy who had endured so much for so long ... She was on her feet in seconds, pacing the floor ... It was Ray who had come to the house to leave his brother with them for safe-keeping; it was Ray who had insisted on going back. Ray, who always protected his mother; Ray, who hated his father. Ray, whom Kitty loved like her own child.

Whom she would protect like her own child ... Suddenly the truth – inescapable and punishingly clear – hit Sarah. Kitty hadn't killed Freddie; Ray had. Kitty had taken the blame to cover up for her nephew, to ensure that his future would be clear of scandal, to protect him. She hadn't thought about what would happen if she was found guilty, she had thought of the boy first and last.

And in doing so she had proved herself worthy to be his mother. Never, in all the years she had been alive, had Sarah been more proud of anyone. Dear God, John, she thought, how you would have loved this woman; how you would have approved of what she's done. Everything you ever believed in, everything you ever wanted to protect – love, honour, integrity – she has protected. And she did it alone.

Or did she? Sarah wondered, thinking back to the morning Kitty had come to her. *We have to stick together now. I need your backing ... it always comes down to the women in the end*. And then Sarah remembered another conversation, a long time before. Kitty had been fighting to keep the boys, and Sarah had told her: ... *these children*

*are yours. Harry and Ray are meant to be yours, and will
be yours . . .*

She hadn't known how Kitty would take them over; only
that she would.

Walking over to the window, Sarah looked out. The
snow was melting under the soft dark night, the park gates
lighted, a couple pausing beside them for an instant to
embrace. *As we did, John,* she thought, *as we did. Under
the same night, under the same sky, with similar dreams
and ambitions. I was lucky, after all,* she concluded, staring
out. *I would change nothing, alter nothing, avoid nothing.
What was, and what is, were meant.*

*Ray must now be thought of as Jim Crossworth's son
and accepted as such. No shadow can fall over him or his
brother, nothing can be allowed to taint or touch them.*

There was a sudden soft knock on the door, Kitty walking in, and moving over to the window to look out.

'Can't you sleep?' she asked her mother-in-law.

Her face was white in the moonlight, their shared knowledge standing between them like a third, unseen, person.

'Not really. Can you?'

Kitty shook her head. 'No, but it doesn't seem to matter
any more.'

Together they looked out over the park, Sarah's thoughts
running on. *I understand you and I'll stand by you. I won't
ever ask you to tell me what happened, or betray you.
Never by a word or look will I let a hint of suspicion give
you away. We are the women of this family and, as such,
we must stay together and keep our secrets together.*

'Will everything be all right now?' Kitty asked suddenly,
her voice as low as a child's.

'Yes, everything will be fine,' Sarah answered, taking her
hand. 'It's all over, Kitty. As the moon is my witness, it's
over.'